GOTHGHUL
HOLLOW

WARHAMMER™
HORROR

WARHAMMER™
HORROR

GOTHGHUL HOLLOW

TALES OF MHURGHAST

ANNA STEPHENS

WARHAMMER HORROR
A BLACK LIBRARY IMPRINT

First published in Great Britain in 2022 by
Black Library, Games Workshop Ltd., Willow Road,
Nottingham, NG7 2WS, UK.

Represented by: Games Workshop Limited – Irish branch,
Unit 3, Lower Liffey Street, Dublin 1,
D01 K199, Ireland.

10 9 8 7 6 5 4 3 2 1

Produced by Games Workshop in Nottingham.
Cover illustration by Svetlana Kostina.

A CIP record for this book is available from the British Library.

ISBN 13: 978-1-80026-075-7

See Warhammer Horror on the internet at

blacklibrary.com

Find out more about Games Workshop
and the worlds of Warhammer at

games-workshop.com

Printed and bound by CPI Group (UK) Ltd, Croydon, CR0 4YY

For Mark and our collection of classic horror movies,
without which this book couldn't have been written.

A dark bell tolls in the abyss.

It echoes across cold and unforgiving worlds, mourning the fate of humanity. Terror has been unleashed, and every foul creature of the night haunts the shadows. There is naught but evil here. Alien monstrosities drift in tomblike vessels. Watching. Waiting. Ravenous. Baleful magicks whisper in gloom-shrouded forests, spectres scuttle across disquiet minds. From the depths of the void to the blood-soaked earth, diabolic horrors stalk the endless night to feast upon unworthy souls.

Abandon hope. Do not trust to faith. Sacrifices burn on pyres of madness, rotting corpses stir in unquiet graves. Daemonic abominations leer with rictus grins and stare into the eyes of the accursed. And the Ruinous Gods, with indifference, look on.

This is a time of reckoning, where every mortal soul is at the mercy of the things that lurk in the dark. This is the night eternal, the province of monsters and daemons. This is Warhammer Horror. None shall escape damnation.

And so, the bell tolls on.

PART ONE
THE EYES

CHAPTER ONE

'Glowing red eyes, they say, and huge. It's as big as a man, with teeth as long as your palm. It's the Curse of Null Island returned.' Oskar shivered, though his face was lit with fascinated horror as well as the weak realmlight filtering through the darkening clouds. It would rain again soon, and Gothghul Hollow's market would empty of patrons.

Pietr scoffed at his fellow trader's words and rearranged his display of protective charms into a more pleasing configuration. 'It's a mere spirit-hound, nothing more. Hunters and priests will do for it – you mark my words. And that curse is idle gossip. Now let's talk about something else before we frighten off any more customers.' He smiled for the two women approaching his stall and stepped aside so they could see the black velvet cloth and the talismans arrayed upon it. 'New protection amulets for your homes, gentlewomen, guaranteed against the loathsome undead. Hang them from the eaves and you'll be safe.'

The women seemed sceptical at the promise, but they paused

long enough to take a good look. Behind them and over the heads of the rest of the patrons, Gothghul Hollow's houses rose crooked and cramped, slate roofs shining with moisture. Talismans hung from every eave and wards were carved upon every door.

There was a dart of movement from one of the crooked alley-ways and Pietr flinched. Despite himself, the latest tales of the beast had made him jumpy. Only it wasn't the hound of the moors, but a boy who darted between their stalls like a gheist.

'Hey, you, get back here! Why, you thieving little...' Oskar's shout trailed into a grumble, but he made no effort to chase the boy, who stopped and looked back, grinning as he dangled a small amulet from his fingers. He hung it around his neck and dared a wink. Oskar shook his fist in the boy's direction, but Pietr could see the glint of amusement in his eyes.

'Do you ever make a profit, Oskar?' he asked, somewhat offended by the other trader's easy-going approach to theft. He didn't wait for an answer, knowing he wouldn't get one. Oskar usually lost a few of the smaller and weaker talismans every market day; the children knew he'd never chase them.

Pietr turned back to his customers, and a broad grin crossed his face as one of the women exclaimed over his ornamental blood-roses. 'My own design,' he murmured with a self-effacing little shrug. 'If you catch it in the light at the right angle, you will see the amber itself has been engraved with a prayer to Nagash for health and wealth.'

He gestured for one of the women to pick up the item. She tilted it into the light from the glow-lamp standing on a tall pole behind the stall. Not only was the item exquisite, the black-petalled roses suspended in clear honeyed amber, but it was also well made.

'You have a refined taste, madam,' the trader began, but then a long, ululating howl drifted towards them on the strengthening wind. It came from north of the small town. From the moors beyond the broken graveyard, out past the old gibbet where the younger children played.

Eldenor, an aged, wandering aelf who had settled in the Hollow years before and sold exotic goods, let the melancholy tune he had been playing on his bone flute screech to a halt, the last note skirling high and wild. The dozens of shoppers froze, as pale and lifeless as the gargoyles on the temple roof or the statues of the God of Death that stood sentinel at each corner of the town. There was a long, pregnant pause, and then the cramped marketplace erupted into noise and motion.

'Home, right this instant!' Oskar bellowed at the boy who'd stolen the amulet, shooing him away. The thief bolted into the crowd, his fear tracing a path like jagged lightning, arcing from one person to the next until they were all vibrating with it.

There were a few panicked screams as people fought each other to be the first into the narrow alleys and twisting streets leading away from the market. The howl came again, louder this time, closer to town.

'Pietr, come on,' Oskar shouted as he hesitated at the back of his stall.

It had taken Pietr an hour to unpack everything and lay it out just so. 'But the amber, the protection spells,' he muttered. 'My life's work. My livelihood.'

'The beast doesn't want your damn roses, Pietr. It wants *you*.' Oskar had dragged the cords of half a dozen amulets over his head and didn't wait any longer, abandoning his stall and his friend without a backward glance. Pietr tore his gaze away from his wares. He was alone, the only person left in the once crowded marketplace. The aelf had vanished as only aelves could, and even the duardin blacksmith was gone. Doors and shutters slammed in the nearest houses, and the panicked cries were abruptly cut off as the townsfolk hid their children and themselves.

'A spirit-hound at most and more likely a feral dog,' he muttered.

Yes, it had killed people, but it was just an animal. Not even one of the undead or something that had slithered across the moors from the blasted land of horrors to the east. At most a spirit-hound, and he wouldn't abandon his livelihood to it. A third howl cut through the air, seeming to shiver up from the belly of the earth itself, as long and mournful as a night-time death vigil. It came from the direction of the town gates, only a few hundred strides from the marketplace.

Pietr's nerve broke, and he snatched up the long wooden club he kept to deter thieves and backed away from his stall. His house lay in the direction of the approaching beast – *Dog, it's just a dog* – near the edge of town closest to the moors. He ran south instead, to the nearest house, and pounded on the skeleton-carved door. It didn't open, and the sick panic inside him bloomed suddenly, like blood in water, into outright fear.

He sprinted to the next house, its upper storey leaning so far out that the sky was a purple sliver between its eaves and those of the building opposite. He knocked again, crying out for aid, but there was not even a murmur from within. Pietr stumbled further down the narrow road, his shouts for help trailing off into low whimpers and then silence. Rising within that silence from not very far behind came a low, rumbling growl.

Thunder, it's just thunder.

This road led through the town and up towards Gothghul Castle on its low hill. The black stone building squatted to the west of town, towers and spires like reaching talons and crowned with a ring of gargoyles that loomed at its edges and spat rainwater onto the unwary. The moors curved around the town and then swept up to the castle like a vast ocean of gorse and heather in every shade of purple, from the most delicate lilac to the almost-black of indigo, framing it against the expanse of wild sky and lonely wind. It was the tallest thing on the horizon but for the Blood-Rock Peaks a few miles distant. It was a long way and all uphill, but it was away from the source of the howling and the Gothghuls would let him in. No one else would.

Gripping the club so tight his fingers ached, Pietr began to run, slipping on the cobbles and twisting his ankle in an unexpected wheel rut. He yelled at the flare of pain, the sound lost in a rumble that was definitely thunder and that rolled and muttered for long seconds. Using the club as a walking stick, he limped on as fast as he could. Fat, icy drops of rain fell, as if the thunder had been the clouds tearing themselves open.

The pain in his ankle faded to a steady throb and he pushed on faster, the rain increasing and the sky angry. Around him, the town was silent. The beast was silent. The road steepened and Pietr's breath grew short as he laboured upwards, the pounding rain turning the road to slick mud. The building storm roared in his ears and the wind screeched – Pietr halted and spun in a circle, bringing the club up in front of him. That wasn't the wind.

At first, he couldn't see anything as the rain drove down in thick grey curtains. Hysh's light was a distant memory, though it wasn't just its absence that made the trader shudder. He'd passed the last couple of houses and now there was nothing but glowering sky and threatening moor and the distant – too distant – promise of safety that was Gothghul Castle.

A shadow moved on the road, emerging from between the last pair of houses. Pietr stumbled backwards, blinking rain out of his eyes. 'Just a dog, just a dog, just a dog,' he panted, still stumbling up the hill. His empty hand rose to his throat, clutching at the tangle of amulets lying beneath his soaking jacket. The just-a-dog lifted its head and stared at him, and even from here he could see the red glow of its eyes. As if a low, sullen fire burnt inside it. He could see every detail of its broad head and long, pointed muzzle despite the distance and the pounding rain. He shuddered again when he realised it was as big as Oskar had said. As big as a man. Bigger, even. Black and hulking, coarse fur slicked to its body by the rain, teeth grinning silver in a flash of sheet lightning. There was a low rumble that wasn't thunder, and rainwater splashed up as it padded closer.

Pietr wanted to turn and run, but he was paralysed. He wanted to hide, but there was nowhere to go. He wanted, most of all and with an intensity he'd never experienced in the fifty-odd years of his life, to live.

The beast moved faster until it was almost flying, pounding up the road towards him, those awful glowing eyes fixed on him as if it didn't need to watch its footing. As graceful and inevitable as death, the beast closed the distance between them.

'Please,' Pietr whispered, the word lost in the rain and the thud of its paws. 'Please.' His legs took over control of his body, ignoring the terror freezing his brain, and he finally, finally, put his back to the creature and ran. The soreness of his ankle meant nothing. The slippery steepness of the road meant even less. Pietr ran faster than he'd known was possible, the club whining as it cut through the air with each pump of his arm. A thin, high sound came out of his throat with each exhalation, a cry somewhere between hysteria and terror. His legs and lungs began to burn, and then, without warning, he tripped, falling headlong into a puddle.

At first, he thought he'd stumbled into a hole or that the club itself, somehow, had tangled his foot as he ran. Soaked as he was, the puddle wasn't able to add to his misery. He registered the impact on his open palm and the knuckles of the hand holding the club, and then pain threaded like red-hot wire up the back of his leg, and he screamed.

Pietr thrashed, turning over in the road. The beast stood at his feet, its jaws bloody. More blood in the puddle, on the road, soaking out of his trousers. His blood. 'What do you want?' he screamed at the creature. It hulked over him, a thick mane of black bristles standing proud down the back of its neck. The low, rolling rumble of its growl increased in pitch as he spoke. Its breath was hot, coming in short, easy pants like steam from a kettle.

The trader scuttled backwards on hands and heels like a crab until he hit the bank at the edge of the road. A carrion crow hopped down off a nearby broken headstone – a solitary, empty tomb dug into the edge of the moor – and flapped lazily closer. The beast stalked him, the growl rising again until Pietr's muscles turned to water. 'Please,' he begged. 'Please...'

The beast paused for the barest second, head cocked to one side as if it could understand him. The rumbling growl faded away and the glow of the eyes seemed to brighten, as if someone had blown on hot coals. And then it whined, an almost questioning sound. Pietr's breath stuttered in his chest.

A loud crack rode the back of the wind from behind him. From the castle. A gunshot. The great black animal flinched and looked away, breaking eye contact, and Pietr felt the strange paralysis lift immediately, a paralysis he hadn't noticed while he'd been lost in the beast's eyes. He gasped in cold air and the rank stink of wet fur, and jerked up onto his feet. Agony lanced through his left leg and he bit down on a scream. He looked up towards Gothghul Castle and saw distant figures running towards him. Help was coming.

He looked back, eye to eye with the beast again. The scream he'd trapped in his chest broke free and soared into the storm like a wind-tossed bird, helpless to fight the tempest. He brought up the club and swung. The beast leapt to the side, dodging the strike. Its fangs flashed and it was out of range again. Pietr stared at the ragged stump of his arm, then down at his wrist and hand still holding the club that lay in the mud at his feet. Then back to his arm and its jet of arterial blood, bright against the darkness of the moors.

Back to the beast. Pietr had time for one final breath, the

deepest and last of his life. He used it all to scream as it advanced again, head lowered and ears pinned back, lips writhing from teeth as long as his palm. Another bright splash of blood arced and Pietr fell to his knees in the mud as his legs refused to hold him. A weight at the front of him, as if a heavy coin purse hung from his belt. Pink and purple ropes spilt out of a rent in his coat. Blood-warm, they steamed in the frigid air.

The last of his last breath slipped from his mouth. There was another gunshot, but it didn't matter now. Pietr looked into the beast's red eyes and calmly raised his chin, exposing his throat.

Lightning flashed, or maybe teeth. Darkness fell.

Edrea Gothghul stood aside as the body was carried in through the front door.

'Father's study, immediately,' she snapped, and the drenched figures hurried along the corridor and squeezed into the room. Her father had already cleared his desk, and Edrea's satchel of ointments and herbs was open on the windowsill next to it. She'd managed a glimpse of the man's face as he flopped, sodden and unmoving, between the carriers, and knew there was nothing that she could do for him. It didn't matter.

She pushed her way through the little crowd to the desk next to the window. 'Too many people,' she said. 'Out.'

'Grab your coats and meet me in the stables,' said Runar Skoldofr, her father's hired gunman, to the three men and one woman who'd brought in the body. They were all soaked. 'We're going straight back out. It can't have gone far.'

Edrea didn't waste time watching them go. 'More light,' she ordered. The storm, if possible, had darkened even further, and despite the wide expanse of glass in the room's tall, arched window, it was difficult to make out the victim's features or wounds. Her father, Lord Aaric Gothghul, brought another lamp without a word, standing by her side and holding it up over the body.

'By Nagash,' Edrea swore as lantern light fell across it. Aaric grabbed her shoulder, as if wanting to spin her away from the table and spare her the sight. She shrugged him off. 'Closer,' she insisted, and bent forward.

'Daughter–' Aaric began.

'He's dead, Father. He can't hurt me. Closer, I said.' Edrea could feel his frozen outrage, and the embarrassment of the room's only other occupant at her tone – Tiberius Grim, a Sigmarite priest and her father's oldest friend. Like Aaric, her Uncle Tiberius was in his sixties, but where her father was gaunt and walked with a slight stoop and occasionally an ornate, bone-headed cane, Tiberius had retained the loose gait of a much younger man. He'd strapped on his rapier when they heard the first howl, and Edrea knew he had a talent for the blade.

Grudgingly, Aaric lowered the lantern, its warmth caressing Edrea's brow as she bent almost in half and brought her face to within a hand's width of the corpse's.

'The same as all the others.'

Tiberius shifted by the fireplace. 'No blood?'

Edrea poked at the leathery skin of the face, and then pinched the flap of flesh drooping from the jagged rent in the throat and peeled it back. Her father made a tiny noise of disgust. Not at the action, she knew, but at the fact that it was her performing it. His precious *child*. She ignored him.

'No – no blood,' she said to Tiberius. 'A few smears on the throat, of course, but the way this has been torn open, the man should be coated in it, rain or not. And his skin is... wrinkled, dried. Desiccated, even. But... I think I know him. He trades down in the market, doesn't he? Look, this green coat with the blue lining. He crafts the larger talismans for warding buildings, I think. Yes, it's him – and he can't be more than fifty.'

'Then the beast has drawn the blood from the body, as it did with the others,' Tiberius said in a low voice. 'I have never heard of a creature of this nature doing such, not in all my years. It doesn't take the flesh. As if sustenance is not its goal. Aaric, this is not familiar to you?'

Edrea's father was a scholar and former Freeguild captain who had served alongside Tiberius in Lethis' Blackshore Guard. Edrea only knew him as the austere, dusty old figure in the study or the library, nose forever in a book if it wasn't raised in disapproval of her. It was easy to believe that if Aaric had seen something like this before, it would have been in a bestiary or ancient scroll, not in real life. And yet years before, he really had done all those things for which his name was still whispered among the Freeguilds and the townsfolk. He was not boastful about his exploits, nor had he invented any of them – she knew this for fact. Aaric, too, still wore a sword whenever he left the castle, and she'd spent enough childhood hours watching him prac- tise to know it was no mere affectation. And he had been the one to teach her to shoot, clean and strip a rifle – no one else.

Aaric Gothghul, hero of the Bonesplinter War and the Siege of a Thousand Nights. Defender of the innocent, devoted husband to Hephzibah. Father to a lonely child. A scholar. A wise and temperate leader of the Hollow. Scion, judge, hunter, teacher.

Edrea was struck, once again, by the juxtaposition of the man Aaric Gothghul had been and the man she knew. The man he'd become upon her mother's death.

She poked at the ragged flesh again, because it made him wince. Yes, he was all those things. But he was other things, too. A liar. A secret-keeper. A man so desperate to keep his daughter safe that he would no longer speak her mother's name for fear of invoking the same madness that had claimed her life.

'Despite all the creatures that plague us in Shyish, I have never seen nor heard its like,' Aaric said, bringing Edrea's attention back to the corpse and the room.

She straightened and flicked through the pages of the journal she was compiling that recorded what she'd learnt so far of the beast's eight victims. This was the first one she'd seen, and she could tell immediately that the information her father had allowed her to know about the others was vague and worse than useless.

She put the journal next to the trader's head and began tugging at the savaged jacket. Whatever sorcery had been performed on him had shrunk his form, and it wasn't too difficult to drag the coat down over his shoulders.

'What are you doing?' Aaric asked. The hand holding the lantern shook slightly.

Edrea gave him a cool glance. 'We need to examine the body. Someone in our midst could be engaging in the necromantic arts. I can recognise even the subtlest marks of a curse.'

'It's a sensible suggestion, and Edrea is a sensible girl,' Tiberius said mildly before her father could respond. Edrea frowned at his use of *girl*, but she wouldn't protest if he was on her side for once.

'Go to your chamber – we will conduct the inspection.'

Edrea straightened up and put her back to the table. She folded her arms and raised one eyebrow. 'No. You might be a scholar, Father, but death magic is my area of expertise. Even if he reanimates now, he is in no condition to molest me. Rest assured my honour is quite safe.' Tiberius snorted, stifling something that might have been a laugh. Aaric reddened.

'Besides, he's not the first naked man I've seen,' Edrea added, and turned back to the table. The silence was thunderous. She ignored it. The master of Gothghul Castle slammed his lantern down on top of her journal and jostled her out of the way, then wrestled the body into his arms and began removing its coat, exposing the ravaged stump of its missing right hand. The corner of Edrea's mouth twitched as she stepped back, but she let him proceed.

Tiberius caught her gaze and shook his head just a little in disapproval, but she could see the glint in his eye. She grinned, and he bit his lip and then winked before sobering again.

'Help me, man,' Aaric muttered, and Tiberius crossed to the desk and bent to the task, pulling off the corpse's boots and then trousers, while her father peeled the wet shirt off the body. He made a sound of disgust, and she pushed back alongside him and then blinked, fighting back a surge of nausea. It wasn't just his throat and arm that were ravaged – the victim had had his belly torn open as well. Only the desiccated state of him had prevented his savaged guts from stinking out the entire castle. As it was, the thin, flattened ropes of intestines were as dry as the rest of him, looping and knotting on the outside of his body.

Aaric was watching her, waiting for the first sign of weakness in order to justify sending her out of the room, but while he and Tiberius were familiar with common native curses, this particular one – if indeed it was a curse at all – was beyond their scope. But not Edrea's.

'He looks... mummified, almost,' she said. 'My notes, please, Father. And a quill.'

Still he said nothing, passing one to her and moving the lantern off her journal. Edrea took a deep breath and bent closer to the corpse, humming under her breath. 'Interesting.' She stuck her finger into his abdomen and then swiftly put it in her mouth.

'Just as I thought,' she said. 'Pure rainwater. There isn't any of his own liquid left inside his body. Nothing. If it hadn't been for the storm, he'd be as dry as a stick of firewood. The others were the same, were they?'

'They were,' Tiberius said. 'And they've already been buried by their families.'

She turned a sour glance on him. 'I know. Which is why *this* is the only specimen I have to work with.'

'Person, by Sigmar's grace,' Tiberius said mildly. 'Not specimen.'

Edrea waved her hand in acknowledgement and dismissal both. Carefully, she examined the dead man's flesh as best she could amid the ruin of his injuries. There was no curse mark she could see. Unless it had been conveniently located somewhere the aberration had attacked, her guess was there was no curse at all.

'All right, step back. Let me try something.'

'What?' Aaric asked suspiciously.

Were you like this with my mother? The words sat heavy on her tongue, a stone in her mouth begging to be spat out. She swallowed them and found others, less combative, to say instead. 'I want to see the last images of his life. It might not work, given how drained he is. Then again, it might. Either way, it won't take long, and we have nothing to lose but a few drops of blood and a couple of herbs.'

That wasn't quite true, but Aaric didn't need to know that. Edrea took her satchel and dragged out a soft leather roll that clinked as she untied it and spread it open on the deep windowsill. The lanterns and candles were behind her, and the storm was a black hand pressing against the stained glass, but the thin, tightly stoppered phials were hers, and she wouldn't have needed to read the labels even if there were any. Each one sat in its individual pocket, prepared by her own hands.

Her fingers stole over the glass phials, some containing liquids, some powders and others herbs. She selected the one that would lend her a few moments of deadsight and then took a small golden bowl and a larger stone mortar and pestle from her satchel. Half turning out of her own shadow so she could see, she unsheathed the dagger that hung at her waist and worked open a long, thin scab on the back of her right wrist. The familiar pain blistered at her, but she barely winced. The wound was clean, and she reopened it every few days for such sorcery – she was used to it.

Facing the window again, she turned her arm over and squeezed nine thick, slow beads of blood into the mortar. She caught the tenth on her fingertip before it could fall and licked it clean, then ran her tongue over the cut to help it seal. Five other lines, these ones healed, decorated her right arm so far. One for each year of her ritual craft. She wondered how many there would be before her time among Shyish's living came to its end, and then she cleared her mind, concentrated on the bright copper taste in her mouth and chanted the incantation as she tipped herbs into the blood and ground them with the pestle nine times.

Three by three. Sacred.

There was a rustle behind her. 'Deadsight? Isn't that–'

Tiberius hissed a sharp, whispered command, stilling Aaric. She ignored them both. Already Edrea felt the realm's magic rising from the mortar, and she tipped the thick mixture into the golden bowl. It smoked as it slid across the incantations engraved within it and the concoction jolted and thickened, heady now in her nostrils. Edrea turned to face the corpse, and Aaric took a long, slow breath in through flared nostrils. He also took a soft step backwards, giving her space. She rolled her head on her neck and put the bowl on the trader's chest, dipping her left forefinger into the mixture and dabbing it very gently in each corner of her eyes. Her vision pinked with blood and burnt with the herb juices; bloody tears began to leak down her cheeks.

Edrea dipped her finger again and drew the shape of an eye in the centre of her brow, and then, with one violent motion, she plunged her whole hand into the bowl, scooped up the mess of herbs and blood, and slapped it across the corpse's face. Her body convulsed, a flinch from her toes to the crown of her head. Her teeth clicked together and a low, inhuman grunt shook from her chest. Long, rasping pants clawed out of her throat as the deadsight took hold. It was weak. Too weak.

Growling, Edrea plunged her hand into the bowl again, and

this time slapped the mixture across her own face, hard enough to hurt – and to solidify the connection between herself and the corpse.

'Pietr. Crafts talismans for the priests to bless, though he sells many that have never seen the inside of a temple. Approaching fifty and unmarried. Lived in the Hollow all his life.' The words came through her, not from her. It wasn't her voice either, but one that was lower and tinged with a rage she'd never been able to identify or suppress. Her fingers dug into the desk, their short nails bending under the force. Pain blossomed at the fingertips, but Edrea ignored it.

'He heard it first, north of the town. Everyone ran and… he waited, his bravado a shiny, useless shield that broke too late into fear. He ran. He fell. The rain fell. And the creature found him.'

Edrea shook as Pietr's last moments enveloped her. She shuddered at the cold of the rain on his skin and cried out as he fell, rose, fell again. Screamed as the teeth tore out the back of her leg – they hadn't seen that injury yet – and again when she thrashed over in the rain and the creature locked its gaze with hers. Screamed, and then went silent as she tried to assess a strange new feeling.

Those ruby eyes. Those coal-bright, all-seeing, intelligent eyes. It was more than Pietr's terror or the growing toll of death magic. There was some kind of connection. *I know those eyes. I know this beast.*

You. I know you.

A faint gunshot and the burning link was severed as the creature looked away. She felt Pietr fill with desperate hope and desperate courage. He had stood again and tried to fight. The beast gutted him, and when he collapsed back into the road, Edrea clearly felt its compulsion. In time with the dying talisman-maker, on her knees in the study of Gothghul Castle, only faintly aware of Aaric's shouts, she lifted her chin and presented her throat to the beast.

The deadsight faded.

Blood and herbs had dried on her face and in her eyes, scratchy and stiff, flaking as she rubbed her cheeks and temples. Her eyes stung and a vicious headache spiked through the very centre of her brain. Aaric grabbed her shoulders, and she flinched and cried out in shock, overwhelmed by the sensation. 'Get off,' she gasped, shuddering and shrinking away. 'Too much... too much.'

He let her go as if she'd burnt him and took a pace sideways, leaving her crumpled between the window and the desk. Groaning, Edrea dragged herself up the wall until she stood, swaying slightly. Tiberius handed her a damp cloth, and she wiped her face clean, gently sponging her eyes until she could see again. 'Thank you.'

'What did you see?' Aaric asked eventually, and the impatience and worry were tightly leashed, barely audible.

'The creature did not respond to a curse placed on Pietr – nor then, I imagine, on any of the victims. It was searching for something. A person, perhaps. A way to convey...' She trailed off and coughed. Aaric handed her a glass of wine, and she took a large swallow, then nodded her thanks. 'It wants something,' she added, her voice growing less like the one that spoke through her and more like her own. 'It won't stop until it gets it. Until it gets the right person.'

'Then a curse could still be at work somehow,' Tiberius mused, pulling at his bottom lip as he stared into the fireplace without seeing. 'One imperfectly performed and thus weak. The creature knows the object of its master's ire is here, but it cannot identify who it is.'

'Then it will wreak havoc until it finds the accursed townsperson. I cannot allow that to happen.' Aaric looked back at Edrea and his hand lifted, hovered in the air as if unsure of its action, and then dropped back to his side. 'You did well, daughter. Very well. Is there anything else you can tell us?'

I know this beast. I know it.

She met her father's eyes. 'No, Father. There is nothing else.'

CHAPTER TWO

Runar had not hesitated when he'd heard the howls on the wind and spotted the small, desperate figure labouring up the hill towards the castle. He'd leapt outside and begun running, shooting when he was in range and then charging after the bullets as if he could catch up with them. Again, as always, that cursed beast had fled. And again, as always, Runar had been too late. But no more. This was the last day it haunted Gothghul Hollow.

Although it was far too late to save the man, Runar and his hunters had carried the body back to the castle and Lord Aaric for inspection before setting out again. They were on horseback this time, and they were going to track the damned beast to its lair and slaughter it.

Runar Skoldofr was a professional sharpshooter. He had fought his share of men and monsters as a gun-for-hire even before the Necroquake had driven the quiet, honoured dead into mass madness. He was used to dealing death without emotion, but this – this sparked something in him. The randomness and injustice of the attacks. More than that, its ability to elude him time after time. Runar burnt with anger and shame. This latest death was *his* fault. His failing.

The horse slithered on the slick cobbles, and he gripped its flanks a little tighter with his thighs. The five riders moved through the silent, soaking town, ducking under leaning roofs and parlour and tavern signs, their mounts snorting at the pressing closeness of the walls. If the beast came at them right now, they wouldn't even be able to turn the horses to face it.

Runar could feel people watching from inside their homes, faces pressed fearfully to the gaps in their shutters, praying he and his hunters would end the scourge. Praying they weren't torn apart in the attempt. In most of the upstairs windows, black candles burnt with purple-edged flames, begging Nagash to look kindly upon the occupants.

Runar blew rainwater off his nose and snorted. He prayed for that himself on a daily basis, to any and all gods who would listen. Mister Grim had been summoned to Gothghul Hollow two months before, when the first killing had happened. He'd examined the corpse, talked to the witnesses about what they'd heard – not seen; no one had seen anything – and immediately sent for Runar with an instruction to bring at least three others with him, all skilled in tracking. Runar had been flattered at first – not so much now. Three weeks they'd been here, and despite the beast's attacks escalating they were no closer to finding it.

He shifted in his saddle and brushed dripping brown hair out of his eyes, cursing the rain that soaked through the heavy material of his trousers to chill his flesh. They'd scoured the town as well as the low, scrubby trees dotting the hill on which the castle stood. They'd searched the moors and the Blood-Rock Peaks, that sudden outcropping of black stone hung with mist and malevolence, throttled with folklore and tales of horror. Runar had surveyed the area for half a day – aside from splintered bones long polished by the wind and rain, he'd found nothing. There were presences, of course, strong enough to sense but not quite able to overcome the power of his amulets, but no ravening beast with glowing eyes.

The creature was going to ground somewhere, but none of them could find its lair. The only thing they knew was that it came from the north, from the Peaks or nearby. And that it returned there.

There must be a lair somewhere, hidden under the heather and gorse, dug into the lee of one of those great boulders. There must be.

They were almost at the town gates when Einar, who'd ridden on ahead to a crossroads, let out a surprised yell. An instant later there was a whining crack as he fired his revolver. Swearing, Runar kicked his horse into a canter despite the treacherous footing, pulling his rifle from its holster next to his leg.

His mare put back her ears and whinnied when a savage roar sounded from the street to his left. The sharpshooter slapped her rump with the rifle, forcing her on. Einar had already disappeared down the road.

'Get back here,' Runar shouted at him, but his order was drowned out by more gunshots, by a screaming horse and flailing hooves on cobble, by shouted, incoherent threats and by a snarl that became a howl that became a snarl again.

Runar shuddered, whether from cold or fear or just the sudden spike of adrenaline in his system, he didn't know or care. Didn't have time to care; Einar was facing down that thing on his own, and Einar was young and impetuous. A talented tracker, but lacking experience in actually taking down those monsters – human or otherwise – that he tracked.

His mare reached the corner and he pulled her head around to the left. She cantered into the road and then locked all four

legs, rearing back almost onto her haunches. Lightning showed
the scene in flickering set pieces outlined in white: Einar, still
mounted, revolver spitting yellow flame as his horse whirled; the
beast, waist-high or more at the shoulder, all slick black muscle
and fur and silver-gleaming teeth, at bay against the back of a
house and yet, somehow, in control; another flash and Einar's
horse's hooves slipping; the boy on the ground, trapped beneath
the thrashing, terrified animal as the beast leapt onto it, fangs
like trapped lightning themselves.

They were in the main road, wide enough for two carts to pass
each other and more than wide enough for the beast to slip away
if they let it. Runar hurled himself out of the saddle and dropped
to one knee, pressed the rifle's stock into his shoulder and took
aim. The beast tore open the horse and blood sprayed as high
as the rooftops. The horse thrashed some more, and Einar was
screaming as its weight ground him into the cobbles. Runar took
a soft breath and gently, tenderly, pulled back on the trigger. The
rifle bucked against his shoulder, and he worked the bolt even
as he brought it back down for the next shot.

The beast howled, somewhere between rage and pain. It slithered off the horse's twitching body, using it as cover. 'No!' Runar
leapt up. It was on the same side as the trapped Einar, and the
boy was screaming louder now, not from pain but terror. Screaming and then – not. Silence, broken an instant later by a crack
of thunder and a blinding streak of lightning.

'*Einar!*' he bellowed, and fired again, not wild despite it all,
aiming down into the meat behind the beast's shoulder, into lung
and heart and death. He didn't miss this time either. Again the
creature howled and twisted in the air. The boy wasn't screaming, but he must be alive. He'd been alive when Runar took
the shot, he was convinced – just staring up at the thing drool-
ing horse blood onto his face. The beast looked right at Runar
then, red eyes gleaming through the storm. The sharpshooter

stared at it along the length of the rifle – the weapon kicked, the bullet sang, the bullet impacted; the beast roared again, staggering. Runar worked the bolt, hyper-aware of his companions dismounting behind him, coming to his sides warm and steady, armed and angry.

The creature ripped out Einar's throat.

'*No!*' Runar screamed again, and a storm of bullets flew down the road. The creature howled and fled, stumbling, but it was fast – too fast for something that should be dying. Runar himself had put three bullets in it, two of them centre mass. Its lungs should have been shredded like wet paper; it should have been a mound of bloody fur and rage dying in the road next to the horse and the boy.

The boy.

Runar sprinted through the storm and threw himself down next to Einar. He was alive, but barely – and he wasn't… drained like the others. Runar put his hands over Einar's where they sought to hold his neck together, to protect torn muscles and arteries. 'Fetch Edrea!' he yelled, and the hunter named Moll hauled herself back into her horse's saddle and vanished, hoofbeats echoing through Runar's knees as he knelt upon the slick cobbles.

'It's all right, lad, it's all right. You'll be fine, just keep breathing,' he lied. Rain fell into Einar's eyes, and Runar bent over him to shelter his face.

C-cold, the boy mouthed, but nothing came from his ruined throat except a puff of warm air against Runar's fingers – his windpipe was opened.

An older hunter, Aldo, took off his sodden coat and laid it over Einar. 'You get mud on this and I'll tan your hide,' he managed with a grin, and the corner of Einar's mouth lifted. Then he convulsed, almost gently, writhing under Runar's hands as his own lost their strength and fell away from his neck. Warm blood pooled under Runar's palms and spread across the street.

'You killed it, Einar,' he whispered to him. 'You hear me? You saved everyone in Gothghul Hollow. I saw that last bullet of yours go right through its heart. You sure you're not one of Sigmar's Chosen, lad?'

But Einar didn't smile. He was dead.

Aldo took his coat back and put it on, but Runar didn't move, and he didn't take his hands away from Einar's neck. 'Karl,' he said, addressing one of the other hunters. 'Chase after Moll. Tell her not to bother Miss Gothghul,' he said heavily. 'But if she could send someone to retrieve the body, we'd be grateful.'

Footsteps, leaving. Runar still did not move. He stared across the street at a statue of a dancing skeleton that graced the cross-roads. Its leering face, lit intermittently by the lightning, was turned to examine them. It wore a crown of wilted lotus-wort.

'Boss?' Nothing. 'Captain?'

Runar twitched. He'd never been a proper soldier, let alone an officer. Still, his hands, so slippery with blood, fell away from Einar's neck. He sat back on his heels and cupped his palms, letting the rain dilute the thick crimson until it ran through his fingers in pink streams. When they were as clean as a killer's hands could ever be, he stood. 'Fetch the horses and check your weapons. This isn't over.'

'But it's gone, captain,' Aldo said, spitting rain from his mouth.

'And we're going to track it.'

'In this?'

'Fetch the horses. We head north.'

'We've searched nor–' Aldo began, but seeing the look on Runar's face, he nodded and hurried across the street to the shivering, spooked horses.

Runar looked back down at Einar, partially crushed beneath the corpse of his horse. 'We'll get it for you, lad,' he promised in a scratchy voice. 'Sleep easy.'

* * *

Though he'd never been a pious man, Runar uttered a cry of thanks to Sigmar for his guidance when, even after the delay waiting for Karl and Moll to return, they caught a glimpse of the beast on the moors. The road out of Gothghul Hollow was lonely and wet, the wheel ruts full of puddles shattered by the horses' hooves. It cut east to west and was lined with towering bone-white trees. Above their heads, old gibbets hung from the branches, their cages holding effigies the town's children had made to play with.

To either side of the road was nothing but a stark wilderness of spiky gorse, straggling, wind-bent trees and abandoned, emptied cemeteries. There wasn't so much as a track heading north, but Runar rode slowly along the edge of the road until he found scuff marks and the remnants of a huge paw print. 'Here.' The sharpshooter clicked his tongue and turned his horse's head. It hesitated, then bunched its haunches and scrambled out of the road and up onto the edge of the moors. There were more prints here, pressed into the mud, just a few far apart, but enough for him to make out a general direction. Runar glanced that way and was unsurprised to see the Blood-Rock Peaks, crouching black against the storm that boiled and spat from one horizon to the next.

Karl muttered something under his breath, but he followed soon enough, the rest falling into line behind him.

Runar clucked at his horse again and wiped rain out of his eyes as she began to move. He caught a fleeting scent of Einar's blood on his palm and jerked it back from his face. It was clean, but he scrubbed it repeatedly against his jacket anyway, until his thumb scraped something sharp – a brooch bearing the Gothghul family crest. He ceased the repetitive motion, glanced down and straightened it. Aaric had bid him wear the brooch so that the townsfolk would know he was here by his command. In the wake of those first deaths, people were more suspicious of outsiders than usual, and there had even been rumours that Runar and his men were the cause of the blight. The brooch had done much, though not all, to dispel the gossip. Only successfully killing the beast and displaying it to the town would achieve that.

Then that's what we'll do. And not only to stop people mistrusting us.

Einar had been nineteen. They'd met on the road three years prior, when the boy was travelling to join the Freeguild. After journeying together for four days, Runar had offered him a job. A job that had killed him. Didn't matter that he'd have died in the Freeguilds, too. What mattered was that he had died – and under Runar's command. Even without the contract to kill the beast, that would be enough for the sharpshooter to track it to its lair.

Close to the road, the gorse wasn't too thick, and they made decent progress. Soon, though, it tightened up and his mare began to shy – the spines on the plants were long and barbed, made for hooking into flesh and holding it tight until the gorse-rats that lived among the roots could bite the animal to death and feed the gorse with blood and scraps of flesh. They'd come this way a week before, but the passage they'd forced then, with the horses' flanks and chests protected by thick wool, had vanished as the springy shrubs closed back in. Runar's legs above his boots were already scratched and bleeding, his mount's too, and the gorse-rats were chittering. White bone gleamed among the dark peat and tangled, stained roots. He reined in his mare and stood in the stirrups, searching for a clear path through.

'We're losing time,' Aldo said from the rear. 'Beast's fur looked thick enough that this gorse won't hinder it.'

Runar grunted and swung out of the saddle. 'We go on foot.'

'What?' Karl demanded, his voice hollow with disbelief. 'We bloody won't. I won't.'

'You bloody will,' Runar grated, 'because you're being paid to follow my orders. Dismount, grab weapons, bullets – anything else you need from your saddlebags. We run.'

Karl and Moll exchanged looks of disgust, but they dropped out of their saddles and smacked their horses' rumps, sending them back to the tree-lined road lest there be nothing left of them but bloody tack and bones.

'Want me to kiss that better?' Aldo asked, puckering his lips as Karl cursed loudly and sucked at a cut from a gorse spine on the back of his hand. He laughed at the poisonous look the other man shot him. They were both taller than Runar, with blond hair darkened to brown by the fading light and the rain, but otherwise unalike, with Aldo's easy-going banter making up for his partner's short temper. Runar still hadn't worked out what they saw in each other.

'Enough,' he snapped. 'We have work to do.' He gave the three a cursory glance and received grim-faced nods in return. He led the way, weaving through the thickets until he could break into a run. The squelch of feet on sodden earth echoed behind him, and soon enough his world contracted to glancing ahead towards the Peaks for the telltale gleam of red eyes and dropping his gaze back down to search out his path. His breath whistled but moved easily through his lungs, and his rifle was a comforting, familiar weight in his hand.

Wet clothes hung heavy from his shoulders and chafed at the backs of his arms and fronts of his thighs as he ran – but running was something else that Runar was good at, and not, despite Tiberius' oft-stated conviction, because it was how he'd survived most of the battles he'd found himself in when attached to the Blackshore Guard as a tracker.

There were more dangers than just gorse-rats on the moors, as Moll discovered when she fell into a smashed-open tomb. Aldo and Karl were covering the entrance with their weapons before her shout had stopped echoing, but whatever had been laid to rest there had since escaped, and she was scraped and shaken but otherwise unhurt.

They had to move slower after that, despite the urgency flickering like dark fire beneath Runar's skin. He wouldn't risk his squad. The bulk of the storm passed by as they ran and the thunder muttered far to the east, but the wind was strong and icy, and cut through them like knives.

The Blood-Rock Peaks grew in his vision, and they were halfway there when a mournful howl drifted to them on the wind. The quartet skidded to a halt and listened. It came again and was answered from the west. 'Wolves,' Aldo panted. 'Not our quarry. Too thin, too high.'

Runar grunted agreement, spat, then checked their faces. They were mud-spattered and bleeding from the gorse spikes, but disciplined too, eager to avenge Einar and get back to the castle, and safety. He nodded once and they nodded back. It was enough. Sucking in a deep breath, he took off again with the same tireless, ground-eating stride.

The rain had eased by the time they were running over the stone and boulders beginning to push up through the skin of the moor. The gorse thinned and was replaced with tall amethyst grass, lilac ferns and patches of brittle heather. The landscape held all the colours of a bruise, one that reached deep into the bone.

Runar finally slowed to a walk as they neared the Peaks, taking deep breaths to bring down his heart rate. It would spike again soon enough when they confronted the beast. He waited for the sighs of relief or the complaints about the weather or the speed they'd moved, and felt a bloom of satisfaction when they didn't come. All of them were focused on the hunt now. They understood what they were up against, and Runar knew they had his back.

'There,' Aldo said quietly, and the sharpshooter looked to where he pointed. It was faint and nearly washed away, but he could just make out half a muddy paw print on the side of a boulder.

'That's recent,' Runar agreed, and without discussing it, they came to a halt. 'Check your weapons. I don't know how we missed it last time, but its lair has got to be somewhere in those rocks. This time we're going to find it, even if we have to lift up every single pebble and splinter of bone. We're not leaving until we've flushed it out and put all the bullets we have in its flea-bitten hide, and then arrows and knives and every other weapon we've got. I want to be able to use its skin as a sieve when we're done, you understand?'

They all nodded, their hands checking belts and pouches, the breeches and chambers of guns, patting at sheathed knives. Moll took a bowstring from a waterproof pouch and strung her longbow. She'd never liked firearms, and Runar had seen her take down a plagued bear with only three arrows. This time she had forty in two quivers and two long, curved knives sheathed at the small of her back.

'That said, don't be fools. Stay in each other's eyelines, and when you make contact *do not* try and take it alone. We've seen what it can do when it has time with its victims, and we saw what it did to Einar and his horse in only seconds. I don't expect you want either fate to be yours, do you?'

This time his squad shook their heads.

'No, boss,' Karl said, and Aldo slapped his arm.

'The question was rhetorical, idiot.'

'Rhe–what, now?' Karl asked, winking. Runar couldn't really blame him for wanting to dispel the burgeoning tension, but he couldn't have anyone losing focus. When Aldo had finished glaring at his partner, the sharpshooter fixed him with a look of his own. Karl licked his bottom lip and nodded, his eyes sharpening.

'We searching the ground around the Peaks first, boss?' Moll asked as she turned from scouting their backtrail. 'We didn't spot it in the rocks last time – maybe that's because its den is somewhere else. Past the Peaks, even. Keep going north. It moves faster than the wind – it could cover a bigger distance than we anticipate.'

'My gut tells me the Peaks, despite our failure last time, but I agree,' Runar said. 'We need to exhaust all possibilities. The Peaks give it a height advantage and plenty of cover, but whatever this thing is, maybe it doesn't think the way an ordinary animal would. It could be dug in under the gorse. Aldo and Moll, head east around the rocks. Karl and I will go west, and we'll meet at the back. Stay near each other and raise your damn voices if you need us. Do not be heroes.'

'See you soon, captain, and preferably in one piece,' Aldo said. As always, Runar frowned at the title but didn't correct him. Aldo had earned the right to call him what he wanted; they'd fought together for years.

He took a step sideways, giving him and Karl the illusion of privacy for their goodbye, then looked at them all a final time. 'Eyes open, weapons up,' he murmured, and the hunters nodded and sank into their focus. Aldo led Moll east, and Runar sucked in a deep, cold breath and stepped out. His rifle was loose against his shoulder, finger lying along the barrel above the trigger. An errant trickle of rainwater ran out of his hair and down his brow, onto his nose. He ignored it, his focus moving outwards from his body, alert to every shiver of foliage or scrape of noise above and below the soft keen of the wind through the Blood-Rock Peaks.

Karl was a silent shadow a pace behind and to his left, covering his flank. He made eye contact, pointed at himself and then the ground, at Karl and then the Peaks. The other man nodded, training his attention upwards in case the beast was there and leaving the scanning of terrain to Runar. They skirted wide around the Peaks, wide enough that if it leapt at them from on high it couldn't – he hoped – land directly on top of them. He squinted into the shadows at the base of the rocks, looking for scat or prints or disturbed earth where it might have dug a den.

I shot it at least twice in the chest. Tore its lung even if I missed its heart. How can it have run this far? How can it still be living? That shot would've put down one of the undead... He shivered and told himself it was the wind in his wet clothes.

This thing was a creature of Chaos – it had to be. Some foul new breed conjured by one of the Dark Gods' cultists, impervious to ammunition, perhaps to everything save sorcery. Ordinarily, he'd have wished for Tiberius to be there to aid them; the warrior priest's abilities had saved Runar more than once. Now, though, after three weeks of living in the same castle as Lady Edrea Gothghul – and no doubt very firmly against her father's wishes – he would have given up one of his guns to have her stalking the moor at his side.

He hadn't seen her perform much more than a few cantrips, but he'd observed her austere, unflustered focus as she opened her veins to add her own life essence to herbs and potions he couldn't name. He'd seen a window's glass tremble in its frame as the realm's magic gathered within her and flexed beneath her skin. The rawness of her connection to this power disconcerted him, not least because he suspected not even she knew how much of it she could handle.

Lord Aaric's protectiveness over his daughter was legendary, though Runar had known it only second-hand through Tiberius before he'd arrived in the Hollow and witnessed their curious bond for himself. Now that he had, though, it didn't seem strange that Lady Edrea seemed more at home on the moors and in the forests. And like her preference for the wild places, her connection to Shyish's magic appeared to him just as untamed and powerful. But such a gift could be as perilous as it was useful.

Runar pushed thoughts of Edrea and her talents from his mind.

She wasn't here, and neither was the priest. He had Karl, Aldo and Moll, and a truly impressive number of weapons. It would be enough. It had to be enough.

They began to follow the curves of the huge outcrop of boulders sitting isolated and leagues from any mountain range that might have deposited them here in millennia past. Runar picked his way past a neat pyramid of animal skulls that sat on a low, flat boulder, trusting Karl to have the heights covered. The peat softened, the tough tussocks of grass springy, slick, until it was easier to slip into the ankle-deep water and then high-step through the puddles to minimise noise. Their pace slowed further, and despite the chill in the air, sweat slid along Runar's ribs to mingle with the rainwater beading on his skin.

There was movement ahead, and the rifle tucked into his shoulder as easy as blinking, the barrel swinging swift and silent towards the target even as he dropped to one knee in the freezing water.

There was no cover here. The rocks were thirty paces through bog and water to their left, but they could shoot and move if – when – they needed to. The slide of movement came again, low and furtive, and Runar eased back on the bolt, checking there was a bullet in the chamber. He took a long, slow breath in through his nose, not directly looking at the spot where he'd seen movement, letting his peripheral vision pick up the details. And then he breathed out, faster, sharper, and let out a low whistle before he stood up.

Aldo cursed and straightened, the barrel of his own rifle tilting up and away from Runar. So the beast was not around the base of the rocks after all. The four hunters eyed each other and their surroundings before turning, again, to the Blood-Rock Peaks.

Runar tilted his head in that direction, then made a series of gestures that asked Aldo if there was a route up from his side. The other man nodded. They already knew there was a way up on the south side; if there was another to the east, they could come at the beast – supposing it was there – from two directions.

But it splits us up.

Runar spared a swift look at Karl. The man was still scanning the rocks above, covering them. He touched his arm, then pointed back the way they'd come and indicated Aldo and Moll would take the eastern route. Karl blinked his understanding, nodded once towards the others and focused again on the rocks.

The sharpshooter gave the signs for slow and stealthy, waited for Aldo's acknowledgement and then turned away, following Karl back through the terrain they'd so painstakingly traversed. They couldn't coordinate their push up the rocks, and there was a possibility one pair would ascend faster than the other and confront the beast without backup, but the risk was worth it if they could seal off its avenue of escape and corner it at the top of the Peaks – the plateau upon which Hollow legend claimed blood rituals had once been performed.

He pushed that bit of knowledge away. Whether they were confronted with the beast itself or some depraved disciple of Chaos or Nagash caught in the act of summoning it, Runar planned on ending the threat with extreme prejudice and not a little spilling of blood.

Adrenaline sang in his veins until his vision was crystal clear and his hearing rivalled that of the fox or the owl. The slide of grass and fern against Karl's boot, the soft squelch of mud and bog, and the high, distant call of a lark looping through the last of the afternoon all came to him, distinct, present.

They reached the gap in the rocks they'd used the last time. The path was narrow, winding, full of blind curves and outcrops behind which all manner of enemies could crouch. Karl paused until he had Runar's attention and flicked his trigger finger up and left – the side of the path he'd cover. Runar nodded, and they stepped off mud and vegetation onto the thin, winding trail that began between two upright boulders that loomed above their heads, leaning close at their tops like old men imparting secrets to each other.

Like a gateway. Or a portal.

Runar blinked sweat from his eyes and winced as gravel crunched under his boot, scanning the rocks and trail to his right in steady arcs. Karl was a solid bulk in the corner of his vision, quiet, stealthy and remorseless as he stepped upwards. The trail closed around them and the wind lessened, dropping from freezing gusts to chill, playful fingers that swirled around the Peaks and raced up the path from behind to shove at them. More than once, Runar spun to walk backwards, but if there were any moor-gheists nearby, they did not deign to show themselves. Gods, but he hated spirits. Something he could fight, something that could bleed and die, no matter how lethal, was always preferable to the hidden malevolence of a gheist.

He sweated some more, though his fingertips were cold against the metal of the rifle. Only years of practice kept his breathing soft and even, which in turn calmed his heart and steadied his hands. Only years of practice kept the rifle sweeping in regular arcs, kept his feet stepping gently, weight on the balls and the toes, kept his shoulders relaxed. Because there was something here, a sense of something, a *presence*, and he didn't need Edrea's witchsight to point it out to him.

Karl felt it too. He could tell by the hunter's slowed steps and the tiny rasp in the base of his throat as he breathed. Runar closed the gap between them and pushed his shoulder against the man's back, a gentle brush of contact, no more, but enough. *I've got your flank. Keep going.*

They made it another dozen or so feet before coming to the blind right-hand turn Runar remembered from their last ascent. Karl stopped and gestured – he'd go high and Runar low. The sharpshooter patted his arm in acknowledgement, paused to check behind them and then gave another, single, hard pat, this time to his shoulder.

Karl stepped around the bend and Runar moved with him, a long, low lunge so that he rounded the corner on one knee, sighting along the bottom of the path while the other hunter covered the rocks to either side. Nothing.

Runar's breath hitched in relief just before there was a sharp cry from ahead. He didn't need to say anything – Karl raced forward, barely slowing at the bends in the trail, forcing Runar to cover him.

The twang of Moll's bowstring, another yell – this time of rage – and an explosion of barking too big and too deep to be a dog's or a wolf's. The distinctive roar of Aldo's rifle, and 'On me!' the man yelled, and Karl put on a burst of desperate, panicked speed.

Runar's heart told him there was only one beast and it was ahead on the plateau – told him to just put down his head and sprint to the aid of his squad, but his training wouldn't let him. He ran, but softly, slightly hunched, gun leading around the bends past which Karl had vanished seconds before. No such concerns from him when Aldo was in danger. *One of us needs to keep our head.*

And, a part of him reasoned, *faced with three armed opponents, the beast might not notice me. Clean shot to the skull. End this mess.*

It was the right approach – the sensible, trained approach – but as a screamed denial, a screamed plea, broke the dank air and shivered across the moors, Runar found that right and sensible faded and the need to sacrifice stealth for speed took over.

The wind picked up, blowing straight down the path at him, cold and whining – he was coming to the open space in the centre of the rocks, shaped like a bowl or a cupped palm surrounded by several colossal, stiff fingers of stone. One side, left of his position, was open to the moors, a sheer drop of at least thirty feet. On his right, tightly packed and clawing rock reached for the sky and cut off any escape.

More gunshots and a howl so close and loud that it bypassed Runar's lifetime of training and self-control and lit up the fear centres of his brain. He stumbled, slowed and then forced himself forward, his breath shrill and cold sweat slicking his back and his palms. He loosened his grip on the rifle, moved his trigger finger back to the barrel – hadn't even realised he'd slipped it through the guard – and counted the gunshots.

Two weapons. Aldo and Karl were still up and firing. Still alive. Still fighting. So the scream had been Moll's? An image of her angular face, either smiling or scowling – her only two expressions, it often seemed – flitted before Runar's eyes, there and gone, and then he was out of the claustrophobic closeness of the path and into a scene painted black and grey, and red.

So much red.

Moll was down. Moll was… in pieces. The beast – the *thing* – was atop one of the fingers of rock to his right, so high Runar had no idea how it had got up there, and although it appeared to be at bay, one look at Aldo and Karl told him that the situation was very firmly out of their control.

'Fire in turn and shout when you're reloading,' he bellowed, and then dropped to one knee and took aim. The bullet flew true, straight for the beast's skull – and yet, somehow, it missed. As if those blazing, magnetic eyes had diverted it. Red eyes, gleaming in the gloom, that were fixed on the sharpshooter to the exclusion of all else. It ignored Aldo and Karl, ignored the bullets kicking up stone chips or ripping into its flesh as if it couldn't even feel them.

'We need to bring it down here and surround it,' he shouted.

'Are you kidding? *Look at Moll!*' Karl screamed. Despite his experience, there was an edge of hysteria in his voice. 'It won't die!'

'Stay calm,' Runar ordered. 'We've handled worse than this before.' They hadn't, of course. They'd never faced anything that could shrug off rifle bullets the way this beast was able to, but what else could he say?

He saw the beast's haunches bunch, but it was so far away. Surely too far. It wouldn't... It leapt, from fifteen feet up and at least thirty feet away. Straight at him. He jumped up and instinctively sideways, slamming his elbow into the rock and spoiling his aim, but Aldo's next shot took it in the shoulder and it stumbled, a snarl ricocheting around the plateau until it seemed as if there were a dozen massive, hulking, shaggy-haired abominations about to pounce on them all. Blood was matting great swathes of its fur into gleaming plates. It spun faster than was possible and crossed the ground in a heartbeat, this time aiming for Aldo.

Three rifles kicked in succession, but although it squealed, it didn't slow. Aldo had his back to the precipice, and Runar heard the sound of the hammer falling on an empty chamber. He didn't have time to reload. Karl threw himself at Aldo and knocked him from the beast's path with a wordless cry.

The beast didn't slow, merely exchanging one target for another, and Aldo, face down and dazed on the stone, didn't see the spray of blood arc high and perfect against the sky, nor his partner vanish over the edge of the cliff. But Runar did. He saw Karl's eyes widen and his mouth stretch in the beginning of a scream before he vanished below the lip of rock. The scream itself was barely born before it was cut off with the thud of impact.

'*No!*' Runar roared, and fired again, three shots before his rifle emptied, every one of them hitting the abomination that was tearing them and Gothghul Hollow apart, one life at a time. He pulled his revolver and kept on firing, sprinting to Aldo's side as the beast leapt impossibly back up onto another of the rock fingers.

Aldo had managed to roll onto his back and was blinking

vacant eyes up at the lowering clouds, barely conscious. Runar shoved his rifle into the man's hand, got his fist in his jacket collar and started dragging him backwards towards the trailhead. They could get some partial cover there, especially if they could worm under the slight overhang. Take a second just to breathe, to reassess and formulate a plan that would see them live, even if it didn't see the beast die.

Aldo was a dead weight, doing little other than scrabble his left foot against the stone in a pathetic attempt to push himself along. Blood was sheeting down his face.

'Karl?' he managed, his voice groggy. Runar gritted his teeth and kept pulling. 'Captain? Where's Karl? *Where is he?*'

The beast cocked its head to one side, drool slavering from ivory teeth.

Runar was silent as he dragged the other man backwards, the revolver steady as he pointed it at the beast's snarling face. Aldo's senses were returning now, and he started looking left and right, shouting for Karl.

Red eyes studied them, redder than the blood slicking it almost from muzzle to tail – redder than Moll's, which pooled and glistened and splashed, or the single, elegant spray by the cliff edge that had been Karl's. A low, constant rumble rolled from its throat. Hackles raised, it leapt back onto the plateau and stalked them across the bloody stone, the tick of claws on rock clear, regular counterpoints to its growl.

'Reload the rifles,' Runar shouted, sweat stinging his eyes. 'Aldo! Reload the damn guns now!'

Aldo choked back a sob, but then tucked both weapons in his armpit to fumble at the ammunition pouches slung on bandoliers across his chest. He'd got one, maybe two in the breech before the beast's stalk became a silent, purposeful rush, low to the ground, its dark hide rippling like living shadow dragged behind its red eyes, gleaming teeth and pink, gaping maw.

Runar stopped pulling and straightened up, emptying the last two bullets in his revolver into the oncoming monstrosity. It stumbled and slowed, snarls ratcheting up into something half scream, half howl. It gave Aldo enough time to load another bullet, and Runar snatched his own rifle from the man's grip and slammed a single cartridge in the breech, then hauled Aldo up. He shrieked in sudden pain, his weight shifting off his right foot as he hopped backwards, trusting Runar to hold him steady.

He did, bracing to take the man's weight. 'Shoot!' he yelled. Aldo exhaled, low and controlled, and Runar knew from experience that any pain he might be feeling was lost in the wash of concentration and bright rush of adrenaline. Still... *'Shoot!'*

Still Aldo held, and Runar was swinging up his own weapon with its solitary bullet when the beast bunched and leapt, arcing into the air in a long, graceful leap, so high it blotted out the clouds. For the barest instant its chest was exposed between its stretching forepaws and Aldo's first, second and third bullets all ripped deep through its ribs. The creature twisted in on itself in mid-air, its stretching limbs suddenly contracting and blood spraying from its throat as it howled. Hot blood on hot breath, so close it coated them both in a fine coppery mist. Its leap fell short – instead of bearing them both to the ground, it slammed to the stone barely a foot in front of them and skidded into Aldo's legs hard enough to take his feet from under him.

They both fell, and white light, brighter than lightning, burst in Runar's vision as his head slammed into the stone, a scattering of stars released from deep inside his brain. He heard a yell – it might have been his own – and flailed with thick, clumsy hands to try and shove Aldo off him. *Gun. Where's the gun?*

Aldo's weight disappeared. There one instant, gone the next, too fast, just the echo of a surprised gasp brushing past Runar's ears.

He breathed through the pain and tried to focus, tried to

understand what it was he was hearing. Laughter. Maddened, hysterical laughter edged with desperation.

Runar rolled his head to his left and there was Aldo, sitting back on his heels and staring up into the beast's face. Into its gleaming red eyes barely three feet from his own. And he was laughing. His hands were still gripping the rifle, but it lay across his knees and he made no effort to reload it. He just looked into the foaming jaws and bloody eyes and laughed. Runar wondered if his wits had snapped. Karl's death, his head injury... but Aldo wasn't like that. He was a soldier and a hunter – a killer. Losing Karl would only make him cold. Lethal.

'Aldo...' Runar's voice was a choked croak and ended with a groan as he shifted and the pain in his head flashed anew. 'Aldo, what are you doing?' Neither man nor beast paid him any attention, seemingly lost in their perusal of each other. Runar patted the stone next to him with his right hand, blindly scrabbling for revolver or rifle. Nothing. He dared to look away, scanning the ground. There. Out of reach, but there.

The sharpshooter began to inch sideways. As soon as he moved, the beast growled a warning, one that cut off Aldo's mindless laughter and froze Runar to the spot. There was an imperative in that growl, a *command* for stillness. It spoke without words, having no need to paint the image of what it would do to Runar if he disobeyed. The evidence was all around them: Moll's torn corpse and the bright, obscene sweeps of blood tossed so lavishly across the plateau; Karl's missing body; the spent cartridges and heavy, cloying tang of cordite misting the air in the bowl of rock. And it was Aldo's mindless, broken laughter. *Move and you're next. Move and die – slowly.*

The beast had seemed set on slaughter; now that they were unarmed and bloody, it was toying with them. Anger was a warm flood in Runar's chest, swamping the chill of fear. He fixed his eyes on the beast and held up his empty left hand, part acknowledgement, part supplication. 'Aldo, I know you can hear me,' he said, keeping his voice soft. 'I need you now, Aldo. Karl needs you.'

The faintest twitch at that, a hitch in the man's breathing. Shame twisted in Runar, but he ignored it. 'He fell over the side, but he might have made it,' he continued. 'Landed on an outcrop, maybe, or only broken a leg. I need you to think about that, Aldo. I need you to stand up and move away and reload. Can you do that for me? Aldo?'

Runar didn't know whether it was the repetition of Aldo's name or the lies that tumbled so easily from his scratchy throat, but the hunter's chest shuddered as he exhaled and looked away from the beast. Awareness seemed to return to him, and his face suddenly drained of colour. 'Captain?'

'I'm here. Can you stand?'

'I-I don't know, captain. My leg...' He sucked in a breath and his voice firmed. 'Yes. Yes, I can move. You got a plan?'

'Back to the trailhead. There's an overhang we can get under to protect our backs. You'll need to be fast.'

Aldo slid a cartridge out of his ammunition pouch and raised the rifle to load it. The beast's snarl went up in volume and intensity, and it coiled as if to spring. Very carefully, he lowered the weapon again. 'I've got a knife. Can you cover me?'

Runar felt a laugh of his own bubble up. He'd shot this thing in the heart, the lungs and the head, and it had shaken off the injuries as if they were insect bites. 'I've got one bullet in the breech and then I need to reload.' He didn't need to say any more, Aldo understood.

'On my mark. Three. Two. One. *Go!*'

Runar didn't see what Aldo attempted because he was rolling to his right and snatching up his rifle. An explosion of snarls and curses and then an echoing chaos of barking. Something black in the corner of his vision as he made it to one knee and fired,

and then fumbled cartridges into his hand and into the breech –
two, three, four – even as he began scrambling backwards.

Aldo, knife in one hand and swinging the rifle like a club in the
other. He was backing towards the precipice, and Runar realised
his mistake. Aldo wasn't going for cover. He was going for Karl.

'*Get back here,*' he shouted, but his second in command ignored
him. Runar blinked against the unsteadiness of his vision and
centred on the beast, then changed his aim. Nothing had worked.
Nothing had so much as slowed it. The rifle kicked, the shot so
loud in his abused head that he winced. The bullet tore into the
creature's left forepaw and there was a puff of blood mingled
with stone dust as it went through its foot into the rock beneath.

The beast howled, curling the paw up to its chest.

'Aldo, get away from there!' he shouted as the creature gave
Runar its undivided attention. Even on three legs, it was fright-
eningly fast. He aimed at its right forepaw this time, and, as if
it knew what he was planning, it snarled and leapt sideways –
straight at Aldo. Runar's shot missed and the other man went
down under the beast's weight, his cry ratcheting up into a
scream. Flash of a knife blade, silver and then red, a twisting
maelstrom of black fur and more blood fountaining from the
thrashing form on the stone.

'*Aldo!*' Runar's third shot blasted into the creature's jaw and
he saw a tooth shatter. The beast shook its head – and then put
its injured paw on Aldo's face.

It cocked its head to one side, looking straight at Runar. Its
tongue came out in a canine grin and slowly, deliberately, it
shifted its weight and pressed down. As the pressure on Aldo's
skull increased he let out a thin, high whine, and Runar caught
a glimpse of his eyes, glassy but pleading.

It was a test, a deliberate provocation from a beast that had
far more intelligence than they had realised. It knew what it
was doing. It had chosen this fight as surely as Runar had, and

now it showed the sharpshooter the consequences of his decisions. Clear across the plateau, Runar heard the crack of bones as Aldo's face broke beneath the beast's weight.

'*Bastard!*' he screamed, and fired the last bullet in his rifle.

The beast swiped away the corpse and hurled through the space towards him. The bullet hit – somewhere – and Runar flipped the rifle, holding it by the barrel in his left hand and drawing his knife with his right. It was long and slightly curved, its single edge wickedly sharp. He'd driven it through the ribs of countless creatures in his time.

He wasn't coming down from these peaks, that much was clear. But if his last act in Shyish was to gut this thing like a fish as it tore out his throat, it would be worth it. For Karl and Moll and Aldo and Einar. For Gothghul Hollow and Mister Grim and Lord Aaric.

For Edrea.

The beast leapt, claws and teeth and blazing red eyes. Runar swung the rifle stock into the side of its head and its teeth just missed him, snapping together by his ear, and then they were down in a tangle of limbs and hot breath and soaking, bloody fur. Runar drove his knife up and into the soft underbelly. The beast screamed and twisted, its hindquarters slipping sideways, and he lost his grip. It snapped at his head, but he shoved his rifle between the creature's jaws. The sharpshooter let out a manic laugh as he strained to push it away. 'Finest duardin sunsteel,' he shouted at it. 'Strongest metal in–'

The barrel crumpled in its jaws, squealing and grinding against its teeth as it warped, and Runar's taunt cut off in a yelp of surprise. 'No,' he groaned. 'No.' But the creature was implacable and its strength was far greater than his. With everything he had left in him, Runar flung himself into a final surge, twisting the warping rifle over and up. The beast staggered to his left, off balance just enough that he chanced a flailing, desperate grab for the knife still embedded in its belly. His fingers brushed the hilt as it tore the ruined rifle from his grasp, and with a toss of its head, cast it far across the plateau.

'Come on then,' Runar breathed, knife slashing wildly at the thick fur and thicker muscle. 'Come on!' he screamed – and it did, its long, shining canine carving a bloody trench from the corner of his eye down to his jaw. He roared at the pain of it and the beast roared back, and then paws bigger than his hands thumped down on either side of his head and it pushed its muzzle into his face.

Runar rolled to his right and slammed the blade down on the paw, severing a claw and the toe it was attached to. The beast *squealed*, and then its teeth were in the side of his neck, in his shoulder, dragging at him. Pain lanced through Runar, but not as much as he was expecting, as it dragged him up off the stone. Its teeth had tangled in the heavy leather bandolier. It had scored his flesh and the pressure of its jaws might crack his bones, but it hadn't quite set its fangs in him.

Runar slid his elbow through the bandolier pulled tight under his arm and wriggled out of it. His back thumped down onto stone and he lunged straight back up, the knife in both hands, driving for the underside of the beast's throat. Bullets and arrows hadn't worked, no matter how deep each small, individual missile had penetrated, but surely not even this supernatural abomination could combat a slit throat?

The beast caught his hands in its jaws, and although the tip of the knife scored through its muzzle, it didn't even flinch. Runar tried to pull free and the pressure increased, skin parting under sharp teeth. He tried to angle the knife towards an eye and the pressure increased even more until he was gasping with pain. The beast's breath blew past his hands and arms to roast his chest and belly. Thin ribbons of blood streaked down his wrists, and those fiery eyes were intent, sharp with an unholy intelligence that made Runar's spine shudder. He followed the beast's ruby gaze – to the Gothghul family crest pinned to his jacket. Its ears were pricked and the bones of his hands shook as it growled, only there was a... *question* in that growl. An interrogation.

'Gothghul,' Runar whispered, and the growl spiked into warning, but then the beast's eyes fixed upon his. He remembered Aldo's weird behaviour when he'd stared into its eyes, and Einar's too. Einar had just lain there, looking up at his impending death. 'Gothghul,' he whispered again. 'I work for Aaric Gothghul.'

It let him go. Runar readied the knife again, but the beast didn't tear his face free of his skull, nor crack it like an egg in its jaws. It cocked its head and watched him. Perhaps waiting. Perhaps contemplating how best to kill him. Then, it huffed into his face and padded away.

Runar watched in silent bewilderment as it stalked towards Aldo's corpse, circling it until they were both within his view. He saw the body shrink and wither as its essence was drawn into the beast. Drained. *Like the others*, Runar thought, but it was getting harder to focus and his eyes were blurring. Exhaustion and injury built like a storm, like a tidal wave hovering over his head.

Had the Gothghul name protected him, or had the beast decided he was no longer a threat and was merely planning to kill him at its leisure? Runar clenched a bleeding fist and focused on the spike of pain to keep him awake. He couldn't see much past the toes of his boots where he lay, sprawled upon the stone. There was a smear of movement. A flow of something lithe and loose-limbed up onto the fingers of stone surmounting the Blood-Rock Peaks – and then, nothing. It had moved like liquid.

Like shadow.

The air in Runar's lungs was heavy with peat and blood and cordite, with the aftermath of lightning and rain. Beneath him, the stone was softer than feathers, and the pain in his hands, in his head, in the other wounds he'd sustained without even noticing, was distant. He stared towards the place where the beast had vanished, until the black spots in his vision joined up and stole his sight.

CHAPTER THREE

They'd been gone for so long. Hours.

Edrea knelt on the chaise longue beneath the lead-paned window of her room and stared down at the dark smudge of the town. The storm had passed a few hours before and they still hadn't returned. Glow-lamps were being lit and people were milling about again. Wherever the beast – and the hunters tracking it – was, it wasn't near Gothghul Hollow.

She'd concluded her examination of Einar's body, noting differences between it and the others to her father and Uncle Tiberius that she couldn't really explain until the hunters returned to tell her what they'd witnessed. The young man's throat had been torn open, a messy, ragged gouge that was both like and unlike the wounds on Pietr. The biggest, most obvious difference was that Einar's corpse was still… fresh. His body had been leaking blood when the castle guardsmen found him. Aaric and Tiberius had gone too. But, as always, Edrea had been ordered to stay behind.

Her mouth twisted at the memory, but she moved purposefully

back to her workbench beneath the far window overlooking the castle grounds. She could have set up her crafts in one of the many empty rooms in the castle, but Aaric had a tendency to pry, and her bedchamber was the only place he wouldn't enter without invitation.

It meant the room was cramped, the bulky, solid oak four-poster bed and wardrobe huddled together on its far side, the wall between the door and the windows lined with shelves surrounding a portrait of her mother. But it guaranteed her privacy.

The ingredients she'd combined and set in a glass alembic had turned a deep lilac and begun to foam. She took a cautious sniff and immediately began coughing.

'That's... not good,' she spluttered, and then the alembic cracked. 'Oh.' Edrea ran to the adjoining bath chamber and lugged back a bucket full of water. Holding her breath and using a long bone wand, a few precious motes of grave sand embedded in its ornate hilt, she poked the alembic off the bench and into the bucket. A splash, a hiss, and a cloud of violet smoke rolled up, and Edrea coughed some more, putting her arm over her face as her eyes began to sting and then to burn. She leant over the bench and flung open the window, leaning out to suck in deep, cool draughts of untainted air.

Turning back to the room, she noted a pale haze of noxious vapours and tied a scarf over her nose and mouth, then pulled a pair of duardin-made leather-and-glass goggles over her eyes. Her chest was tight, but she opened the second window and got a decent breeze circulating.

She pushed the bucket under the workbench and picked up the thick, hide-covered compendium she'd been using to produce a rather complex remedy. Or *not* produce it, so far. The script was faded, barely legible towards the end, where the final ingredient and its amount was written in cramped, tiny lettering against the very edge of the page.

'Well then, it's definitely not shadeleaf. Shadewort, perhaps? No, that wouldn't work.' She tapped a slender finger against the page, frustrated at both her inability to make the remedy work and the hunters' long, increasingly worrying absence. She needed to get the recipe right, and quickly, in case they were injured.

'Come on,' she muttered as she measured out the ingredients she could read again and tipped them carefully into a new alembic, making a mental note to order more from the glassblower. She stared at the small heap of herbs, leaves and powders. 'Tell me what you need. What you want. Two base aims – to heal wounds and relieve pain. Healing we can do, and the shadeleaf is a painkiller. Why doesn't the shadeleaf work?'

Edrea straightened up and slapped her palm against her brow, almost knocking askew her goggles. 'Because shadeleaf becomes toxic when mixed with dire-moss, of course. Edrea, you fool, you nearly killed yourself.'

Guiltily, she wafted a hand in front of her face and took a couple more breaths of clean air at the window, using it as an excuse to peer towards the town again for horses, riders. Runar.

A small smile crossed her face. 'Well, I haven't made a remedy, but we now have a rather potent poison. If I could stabilise the compounds, maybe I could sell it. No doubt Runar consorts with assassins.'

She paused suddenly, eyes fixed unseeing on the wall opposite. Something teased at her mind, the tantalising breath of an idea. A connection. 'Assassins. Thieves… shade-*thief!* It has to be. It even grows around dire-moss.'

Edrea snatched up the compendium and pressed it close to the lamp, squinting at the tiny writing. 'That's it. Shade-thief.' Her excitement burst like a bubble on a stream. 'But do I have any?'

Tossing the book onto the chaise longue, she hurried to the wall of shelves, stacked precariously high. One half was her personal library; the other was what Aaric liked to call her apothecary.

Hundreds of bottles, carefully labelled in her neat, precise hand, and some others, sealed so many years ago and the labels written by her mother. Edrea had opened one, once, and caught the faintest hint of a scent: dew-kissed grass and clean earth. She hadn't opened any of the others, reluctant to waste the essences Hephzibah had so lovingly collected.

She bypassed that shelf now and quickly found the bottle she needed. Shade-thief, harvested four months before. Its potency might only be half what it had been, and there wasn't much, but she could perhaps supplement it with chamomile. 'Besides, even half potency is better than nothing if they've been injured by something supernatural.'

She took the small bottle back to her workbench and took a deep breath. She'd begun the process of translating the remedy as a way to distract herself from the passing hours and the hunters' absence, but now it was imperative that she get it right. Her witchsight was stirring. After the Necroquake, when the quiet dead became violent, Edrea had been convinced the madness that had taken her mother's life would claim hers as well. Her attunement with the land had increased tenfold, a hundredfold, until she couldn't blot it out, until it roared and laughed and gibbered in her head like a thousand gheists. It had taken months of research, meditation and spellcraft, performed long into the nights, before she could control herself. For her vision to be pulsing now could only prophesy calamity.

Carefully, Edrea brought her mind into the still centre of her power. 'Fire and water,' she muttered, and carefully poured twelve drops of distilled water into the alembic before taking up a taper and snapping her fingers. The end burst into flame and she counted to twelve again and then blew it out. She broke off the charred end and dropped it in.

'Now, shade-thief – and intent.' She closed her eyes for a long moment, breathing deep through her nose, centring her spirit and her energy, calling upon the strength of her blood and the magic infused into the very bones of Shyish.

'In the town or on the heath, heal my pain with this shade-thief. Night and day, stay awhile, mend my wounds with chamomile. If bones are broken or blood is lost, renew, replenish, dire-moss. Plants and herbs, hear my plea, grant me thy sweet remedy.'

There was a pop and a hiss, and Edrea felt a curse lift to her tongue at another failure, another set of wasted ingredients, but then the mixture sank back in on itself. It wasn't lilac now, but a rich, vibrant purple. It didn't bubble and, most importantly, its scent was clean and fragrant even through her scarf.

Edrea took a breath and felt the burgeoning headache at her temples fade away. She nodded, satisfied, and quickly trans-ferred the medicine to a copper jar to preserve both the magic and the herbs' potency. Then, very carefully, she transcribed the ingredients and accompanying ritual out of the compen-dium and into her own herbology. Her father didn't know she'd taken this book from a section of the library he'd forbidden her to access, and would likely have an apoplectic fit if he found out. The forbidden shelves were full of her mother's books of local lore and ritual, both those she'd procured and others she'd written herself.

It had taken Edrea four long, torturous years to undo the prayer-binding Tiberius had invoked upon the shelves to pre-vent her accessing them. Four years of cautious experimentation and repeated failure, and three separate occasions when she'd quite literally blown herself across the library from the rebound of a failed incantation.

Four years, and every one of them worth it to have her mother's knowledge at her fingertips. Still, she could borrow each book only for short periods of time – her father passed those shelves every day during his scholarly pursuits, and his sharp gaze would notice any missing books instantly. She'd only been able to risk it today because of the talisman-seller's death and then Einar's. Even Aaric had more on his mind than spell books.

Which proves how very narrow that mind has become over the years, despite his deep studies. Despite his long evening debates with Uncle Tiberius. Despite everything I've tried to talk to him about.

The bitterness that she felt growing each day in her core stung at her throat, but she pushed it away and picked up the book, and then slipped from her room on the castle's third floor, rubbing the hand of the statue of the robed warrior as she passed, a habit so old she didn't know when she'd started doing it. The polish on the black marble it was carved from had worn thin, giving the hand an aged, skeletal appearance. She took the servants' stairs down, as the route would force her to pass Aaric's study. As long as he was in there, she could safely return the book to the library without discovery.

Edrea emerged onto the ground floor of the castle and headed towards the family wing. Narrow stairs and stone walls became wide, wood-panelled corridors along which hung thick tapestries and portraits of Gothghul ancestors, alternated with moody landscapes and scenes of ritual. At the far end of the hall, a grandfather clock stood near the front entrance, its regular hollow tick echoing in the chilly space.

As expected, she could hear her father and Uncle Tiberius in his study, engaged in a low-voiced, intense conversation.

'...clearly her writing, Aaric.'

Edrea paused in the shadows. The door was open a crack, unusual in itself. Aaric didn't like interruptions or distractions caused by people passing as he worked.

'Impossible. Hephzibah was never plagued with... *this.*'

Edrea's breath stopped in her throat. Her mother? She heard the rustle of paper and then a thump, as of a book being placed firmly onto a desk.

'"Bloody-eyed hound of portent", Aaric,' Tiberius said. 'Right there. Written during the very midst of her madness, only days before she... before Edrea was born. It cannot be coincidence.'

'What exactly are you saying?' her father demanded, his tone low and full of warning. Edrea ghosted closer. She could see neither of them through the crack in the door, but she didn't need to. Aaric would be seated behind his huge mahogany desk and Tiberius would either be in the chair facing him or, more likely, would have rounded the desk to stand at his side, one gnarled finger poking down at the relevant page. It was a scene she'd witnessed so often it was engraved upon her mind's eye.

'I'm saying that this... *apparition* might be the same one that haunted Lady Hephzibah during the last weeks of her life. That it has returned because of...' His voice lowered until she could barely hear it, but Edrea thought he said her name.

Me? It's returned because of me?

She remembered the strange conviction she'd had when examining Pietr's corpse with deadsight. That she knew the beast somehow. That they were linked. If what Tiberius was saying was right, then it had been responsible for her mother's death just moments after Edrea was born. And now it was back, to what? Finish the job? Kill her too? But why?

But none of that makes sense. No one ever spoke of a beast, or any sort of apparition at all, at my birth. Then again, no one speaks of it at all. This could well just be the latest in a lifetime of lies and obfuscations surrounding Mother's death.

'Zib didn't once speak of a hound or a beast,' Aaric said, confirming Edrea's own line of thinking. 'Her madness was far more mundane. It was an imbalance caused by her pregnancy, by fear for her unborn child and her obsessive research. It was–'

'It was supernatural, Aaric. Why else would you have summoned me to watch over her? Pray over her? Why else did you hide her journals and all they contained from Edrea? Lady Hephzibah was haunted by something neither of us could explain then or since, and even I could not exorcise it. Now, twenty-five years later, another curse. A beast bearing the same description your wife wrote over and over in her journals. If it truly is a "bloody-eyed hound of portent", we need to know exactly what it portends. Why it's here, why it has returned to this place – or to this family – for a second time.'

'You are grasping for meaning, Tiberius,' Aaric snapped, but his voice was weak. Lacking conviction. 'This is not the Curse of Null Island. Runar and the others will destroy the rabid beast, and our torment will be over.'

'In the current situation, Aaric, I am examining every possibility, as it is my duty to do. You sent for me precisely because you know in your heart these events are linked. You heard that first rumour of a beast with glowing eyes and *you knew*, as I did. As for Runar and his hunters, they've been gone far too long. I fear they are lost.'

Lost? They were late, yes, but surely not lost. Not dead? Edrea's hand darted to her belt and the many pouches it contained, but she'd left the remedy in her chamber. As much as she wished to stay and hear more, there was no time. She hurried on, silent as a shadow, and slipped into the library. Astonishingly, the forbidden shelves were unlocked. Perhaps in his haste to show her father what he had discovered, Tiberius had forgotten to reseal them. It mattered not. She stuffed the compendium back into its proper place and left, taking the main stairs two at a time, her skirts bunched in her fists.

As for Tiberius' assertion that the beast might be here for her, she did not know what to think, but the idea of it gnawed at her. Panting, she reached her chamber, snatched up the remedy and put it in one of her belt pouches, then cursed and changed her skirt for a pair of heavy riding trousers, though she wouldn't be mounted. She had a faster method than horseback

Edrea hung her ritual blade back at her waist, its weight intimately familiar and the knife itself never out of reach. The scar on her wrist was already itching as she began to draw on the magic of Shyish. She crept back down the stairs and out of the front door, closing it behind her with a soft click, and then hurried across the castle grounds north, bypassing the main road leading down to the Hollow. As soon as she was on the moor and out of sight behind the tombs containing the remains of her ancestors – she could hear scratching from one of them and would have to come back later with offerings and prayers to soothe its occupant – she unsheathed her blade and drew it through the cut on her arm. Deeper than normal, needing a stronger connection between her body and the death magic. A sharp cry broke from her and tears stung at her eyes, but she breathed through the flare of pain and focused her will and intent on the spellcraft.

The words she spoke were ancient, a dead language long forgotten by most, and the voice – as ever – was low and angry and needy. Hungry. Magic blossomed inside her, warming and urgent, and she let it spread through her limbs, focusing on her desire. Speed. A twitch in the muscles of her legs and she looked down to see the cut had dried, though fresh blood dripped down to her fingers. Shyish had accepted the offering.

Edrea sheathed the knife, took in a deep breath and squinted through the approaching dusk towards the Blood-Rock Peaks. 'Runar Skoldofr, I'm coming to find you,' she murmured. She began to walk, and then to run, and then to sprint, her body flying at her command, spotting the clearest path through the heavy gorse without hesitation, faster and faster until the landscape blurred around her and only the spellcraft prevented her bones and muscles from tearing apart under the immense strain of her speed. Spines ripped at her hands and arms and legs, and gorse-rats were crushed beneath her boots, their dying squeaks lost in the wind howling past her ears.

The miles to the Blood-Rock Peaks melted away in moments under her tireless feet, and when she came to a halt a few hundred yards away, her breathing was calm and even, though mud reached to her thighs. She studied the Peaks and the ground around them, looking for signs of violence. There was a faint track visible in the last of the light, and Edrea pulled a short, dry stick from one of her pouches, concentrated on it and snapped her fingers. The tip burst into flame, brighter and hotter than it had any right to be, and slow burning.

Although this spellcraft was small and basic, added to the use of deadsight, the creation of the medicinal remedy and the speed she'd used to reach the rocks, it would be another hurt when it came time to repay the debt. Her blood could only cover so much – after that, the magic required its due.

As long as I can put it off until I find them, it doesn't matter.

But she didn't find the hunters. Edrea found the beast.

The howl was faint on the wind, as if distant.

Edrea's head snapped up from her perusal of the mud and scrub around the base of the Peaks. The wind was strengthening again, as if the storm earlier had been but a precursor to something bigger, nastier and full of teeth. The magical fire whipped sideways, close to her face but not making contact. The flames *bent* at the last second, entirely against the force of the wind, to protect her skin.

The howl came again, and it was closer this time. And it was... calling her. A summoning that something deep in her chest felt and responded to, stretching towards that voice on the wind. Without thinking, she answered, stepping forward and into the shadow pooled at the base of the rocks. Out of the blackness, a black shape emerged, its raised head almost level with her own.

The bloody-eyed hound of portent. Tiberius' warning rang again in her ears, but it rested in the scales against her vague conviction that she had some sort of kinship with the beast. That conviction was not enough to prevent a surge of fear at its appearance, and there was a long, frozen moment where Edrea was sure she was staring at the manner of her own death.

What in Sigmar's name am I doing? she asked herself, but by then it was too late. She could smell it – blood and wet fur and rage – though it bore no visible wounds. *So whose blood am I smelling?*

The magic still rushed beneath her skin, her connection to Shyish steady, and Edrea was confident she could outrun this creature if she needed to. It padded closer, silent on the thick black dire-moss, a living shadow with ruby eyes and a long, low snarl that made the hairs on her arms stand up. Her fingers twitched towards her blade and the snarl rose in volume, as if it recognised the weapon and the damage it might do. Very carefully, the sorceress put her hands behind her back. The snarl lowered back to its previous rumble.

Interesting.

'My name is Edrea Gothghul,' she said. The beast's growl spiked again and then faded. Its ears pricked forward. 'This is Gothghul Hollow, my ancestral home. Are you... Were you born here? There are a hundred legends surrounding the Blood-Rock Peaks – perhaps this is where you died?'

The beast whined in its throat, the sound somehow frustrated. Edrea shared its sentiment. She knew this creature, she could feel that they were linked, but even if it understood her words, she could not interpret the noises it made. Unless... The idea was staggering in its scope and audacity. She knew the words and the offering needed but had never cast this particular spell. Yet if it was successful, she might be able to end the beast's reign of terror here and now. The risk was worth it.

'I have... I don't know if this will work, but I have a spell that might let us understand each other?' She paused again, her fingertips tingling with the urge to reach out and touch it. 'It's me, isn't it?' she whispered. 'It's me you've been looking for in the town. There's... something in your voice that resonates within me, the way magic does. I can't explain it, but you're in my bones somehow. As if we know each other.'

The beast took another step forward. Edrea could see it clearly now despite the advancing evening, and her conviction that it was here for her was growing. Still, she kept her movements slow and smiled with her lips firmly over her teeth.

'I need to access the realm's magic,' she said calmly as nerves fluttered through her stomach. 'And to do that I need to access my blood. I won't hurt you.'

Edrea took three careful steps backwards and then eased onto her knees. She lifted her chin, baring her throat in submission. The beast's ears flattened and then pricked again. It didn't move. Edrea planted the flame-stick in the peat and then drew her knife. A snarl spiked through the gusting wind, and she lifted her chin a little more and then lowered her eyes and slashed through the cut on her arm. Too much – too many cuts today. The pain was deep and intense, stealing her breath, and the blood was sluggish, reluctant. Her body understood what this would do to her, but she was relentless. Death magic surged in the air, its scent mingling with blood and peat.

The beast cocked its head, and as she put the knife away, it padded towards her. Curious. Edrea focused her will and intent, focused it through her blood and offered it to the realm.

'Though our worlds are different and we share no land, by magic's grace, may we understand. Though our paths do not cross, we have words to send, within this spell, may we comprehend.' A bubble of silence grew around them, the wind stirring the amethyst grass but everything between sorceress and beast still and breathless.

'As above, so below, be it fire or be it snow. Within this circle, which price I pay, may our minds absorb what we both say.' A sphere of faint iridescence limned the tips of the beast's fur and added a second, paler glow to the scarlet of its eyes. It lowered its head and huffed out a breath. Edrea felt curiosity and wariness steal over her. The beast's emotions? Her heart jumped with excitement and she strove to contain it. If she could read the beast, then the beast could read her. She needed to be calm and in control.

'Do you understand me?' Edrea asked carefully. It took effort to maintain the sphere, but she feared to hurry the contact. Her conviction that the beast was here for her notwithstanding, she would have no defence if she startled it into attacking. She was burning through her reserves too fast. She didn't have her speed any more. Nothing but a ritual blade and a head full of spells, useless with a body that couldn't be the conduit for any more magic.

A blast of chaotic emotion assailed her: hate and anger and a deep, wrenching dislocation – a loss – of self and sanity and awareness of anything but the need to search. To find.

Edrea rocked on her knees. 'So much,' she choked. 'It's so much, what you feel. How can you stand it?' Her hand rose of its own accord and the growl came back, sharper. A forbiddance that seared through her. *Do not touch me.* She did not.

'Can you... show me why you are here? Show me what it is I must know, or must do?'

More emotions battered at her, more hate and desperation and a dark place, full of howling and absence. *Trapped. Alone. Afraid. Angry.*

Edrea caught her breath. The sphere was weakening, but she could come back when she'd recovered. She'd come back and try again. Learn more. But first...

'You must stop killing,' she said, more loudly than she intended, and the beast snarled in clear warning. The sorceress looked

down and bared her throat again in apology, and the snarl cut
off. Edrea could hear the wind again – she was at the limit of
her ability to direct the magic and the spell was fading. She had
so many questions, including whether Tiberius' theory that this
beast had killed her mother was true, but before she could think
of a way to ask, she was startled by a touch as of fingers caressing her cheek She flinched and looked up into ruby eyes, clever
and malevolent and, perhaps, desperate.

Edrea raised her hand again and leant forward, wanting, *needing*, to make contact, to learn the truth of whether this thing she
felt such odd and undeniable kinship with had slaughtered her
mother even as she birthed Edrea to the world.

Again it snarled and flattened its ears, and then the sphere
burst and sound rushed back in, including the echo of a gunshot.

The beast leapt sideways and Edrea saw blood puff from its
flank Snarling, hackles raised and stiff-legged with threat, it
advanced on her, but she was leaping to her feet and scanning
the dark moor to the south As expected, Aaric and Tiberius. Her
father was in the lead, his horse in a full gallop as he steered
with his knees, rifle in his shoulder.

'Father, no!' Edrea screamed, putting her body between him
and the beast. He jerked his second shot wide to miss her, shouting something over the wind that she couldn't hear.

The beast was already fleeing, racing up the narrow, barely
visible track into the Peaks. Cursing her father and the onrushing
wave of her own magic-debt, Edrea picked up her flame-stick
and ran after it.

'I'm sorry,' she called ahead into the darkness as she scrambled
and slipped higher. 'I'm sorry, please come back I won't let
them hurt you.' Her foot skidded on loose scree and her knee
slammed into the stone. She yelped at the pain The magic-debt
was coming fast now, hard enough to blur her sight and shiver
her lungs and tighten her throat until she was dizzy. Still, Edrea

laboured up through the rocks. She could hear her father shouting over the wind, but nothing mattered other than finding the
beast and protecting it.

The trail finally opened up into a plateau surrounded on three
sides by taller rocks. The uneven stone beneath her feet was
puddled with blood and strewn with corpses, as if all the town
legends and stories about the summoning of spirits and monsters,
devils and even gods, had been brought to horrible life and agon-
ising death right here.

The sorceress came to a horrified stop, the back of one hand
pressed to her lips. 'What have you done?' she murmured, though
the beast itself was nowhere to be seen.

Three bodies lay scattered across the stone. Moll had been torn
apart, great sweeps of blood pooling beneath the various pieces of
her corpse. Edrea had to pick her way through to reach the body
near the edge. She thought it was Aldo, but it had been withered
in the same way as Pietr and the other eight dead townsfolk.

She turned to the final corpse, her heart in her throat. 'Oh,
Runar,' she murmured. The body twitched and a faint moan rose
from its lips. '*Runar?*'

Edrea forced her heavy legs across the stone as fast as she
could and threw herself onto her knees by his side. Runar
moaned again. She didn't even think about it, just dragged her
fingernail through the cut on her arm, just enough for a few
drops of blood, and fed the magic into the flame so that it
roared high and bright. Under its radiance, she examined him
with feverish eyes.

She dragged the copper jar from her belt pouch and uncorked it,
whispered a brief incantation to activate the potion and then lifted
his head, his hair sticky with blood, and helped him to swallow.

Gently, she laid him back down. Then she stopped and went
very still. She bent closer, looking not at the man but at the stone
on which he lay – at the bloody shapes imprinted either side of

his head, one displaying five fingers, the other only four. *Hand-prints.* But they weren't hers and were too small to be Runar's. The man mumbled again, and she pushed away the mystery to concentrate on him.

'Edrea!' Aaric bellowed, the thread of panic in his voice reaching her.

'Over here. Mister Skoldofr is hurt.'

Aaric and Tiberius hurried up the path. Her father ran to her side while Tiberius prowled the rest of the plateau, checking the bodies and looking for danger.

'What do you think you're playing at?' Aaric demanded, grabbing her shoulder in a bruising grip. She glared up at him and he blanched. 'My gods, how much magic have you used? You need to rest. Tiberius!'

Edrea shook him off. 'Runar is wounded. His hands and wrists, he's got a head wound, his face and who knows what else. Tend him, not me.'

The sharpshooter's eyes opened, hazed at first and then sharpening with awareness and fear. 'Load... load my revolver. Please. If it comes back.'

'It won't,' Edrea said without looking at Aaric. 'It knows you three want to kill it, and it no longer trusts me.'

Runar's face twisted in incomprehension. 'Trust?'

Edrea sighed, shakes beginning in her hands and nausea starting to burn at the base of her throat. Tiberius appeared with a satchel and began examining Runar, and Aaric drew his daughter to her feet and a few steps away.

He grabbed her shoulders again, and this time she let him, unsure whether her legs would hold her for long. 'Just what exactly did you think you were doing? This is not some game, Edrea. This is life and death.'

Anger flared hot enough to firm her spine and knees, and again she shrugged out of his grip. 'Just who exactly do you think you're talking to?' she demanded, skating the very edge of collapse and made reckless with it.

'You are my daughter!'

'I am also Hephzibah's daughter, and she was a sorceress without equal – you told me that yourself. Do you have even the faintest idea of how many of her instincts I have inherited, of how I have trained and cultivated my power or the size and scale of the spellcraft I can perform? Do you have even the slightest clue, Father? I found the beast and I was *communicating with it*, discovering that it is so much more than a mindless killer, when you shot it! When you undid all the hard work, all the strength and will and ritual I had employed. When you *shattered* that, as if it was nothing.'

Aaric stared at her, angry and surprised. 'I didn't know.'

'No, Father, you didn't know because you never think – you just presume I need your protection and you smother me, imprison me. You do not trust me and I think you do not even love me, not as anything other than a possession or a… a pale imitation of my mother. And I am not her, though her strength is in my blood. And do you know something else?' she added before he could reply. She grabbed his hand and dragged him back over to Runar and Tiberius.

Runar's eyes were open again, but Edrea ignored him and pointed to the bloody prints either side of his head.

Aaric stared at them, confused. 'What?'

Edrea knelt down and put her hand next to one. 'They aren't mine, and they're certainly not yours or Runar's. No one else is up here. So who do these belong to?' She glared up at him. 'What is this beast that it leaves human handprints behind? And why is it… known to me? In here?' She rubbed her chest and then swayed suddenly, and Runar reached up, alarmed, and then winced. Edrea gently placed his hand back on his chest. 'I am all right,' she murmured, but her voice was more air than sound.

'The beast's paws were there,' Runar said, groggy but adamant. 'It stood right over me, paws either side of my head. But they were *paws*.'

'We need Hephzibah's books,' Tiberius said in a quiet voice. 'We need to know whether we're dealing with the same entity as the one that led to her death. And this time, we need to stop it.'

Edrea looked at him. 'Finally,' she muttered, and let the magic-debt take her.

PART TWO
THE VOICE

CHAPTER FOUR

It was the deepest part of the night when Runar awoke, startled and then racked with pain as he shot up in bed, hand grasping for the gun under his pillow and coming up empty.

'Who's there?'

His voice, too, was no threat – as hollow as the curl of his fingers around air. He squinted in the dying red glow of the fire, the familiar furniture of wardrobe, table and chairs humped and brooding in the gloom. Misshapen and monstrous. The room was draped in shadows deep enough to contain spirit, risen corpse or the beast itself. As Runar pulled his hand from beneath the pillow, a fingertip scraped against something hard and curved. He clutched it on reflex. It ended in fur and soft, sticky meat, and Runar shuddered, but he kept hold of it for now. The claw he'd severed from the beast's paw. He must have been delirious to have shoved it under there in the first place, but he knew first-hand how much damage it could do, and it was better than nothing.

'I'm warning you,' he said as he slid from beneath the blankets. The respective pains in the back of his head and his cut face had joined into a single monstrous note that throbbed like a temple bell in the centre of his skull. His hands were swollen and hard to close, pulling at the stitches in the worst of the bite marks, and the multitude of bruises and abrasions and tweaked muscles only added to his misery.

Yet none of it showed on his face as he put his feet down on the freezing flagstones and straightened. He didn't remember reaching his room or his bed, and clearly whoever had put him here hadn't done more than remove his boots and shirt. The air prickled against his chest and back, a sudden wash of ice from the nape of his neck down his ribs. Runar shuddered again and turned. The room behind him was empty; the window was firmly latched.

'...nar.'

Runar spun again, the claw held up in front of him. 'Who is it?' he demanded, sharper now, a trickle of fear dripping its slow poison into his stomach. Was that his spare rifle propped by the door? Tiberius would have known to leave him a weapon. He took a step in that direction, though his mind screamed at him to run to the fire and throw wood on it, that he needed light.

No. My eyes are adapted to the dark. And they're telling me this room is empty.

He went for the gun anyway.

'Edrea.'

It was clear this time. A voice. Ethereal and impossibly distant, broken with desperation and sweet like honeyed poison. Its edges curled with malice. The air shivered behind him, and something brushed the bare skin of his back.

Runar leapt at the doorway and snatched up the rifle, checking the breech – someone had loaded it before they left and he breathed a swift thank you at them – before wrenching open the door and sprinting out and towards the long, sweeping staircase leading up to the Gothghul family's private floor. The five hunters had been housed on the servants' level, something he hadn't cared about before, but now he needed to run up to the guest level and then up again, find Edrea's room and confront whatever might be threatening her in there. There was still a cold line on his skin from where the invisible speaker had touched him, and he shuddered once more as he ran.

The sharpshooter's bare feet slapped stone and rug and stone and then wood as he pounded up the first flight of stairs, every muscle and wound protesting. He ignored them all. There was no time, no time to slow or breathe or plan. Edrea was in danger.

The staircase came out on the middle of the guest level and continued straight up, but Runar skidded to a halt as he saw a figure disappearing into the darkness, the sweep of pale skirts and long, fluttering dark hair just glimpsed in the moonlight coming through the high glass dome that sat in the centre of the castle's roof.

'Lady Gothghul?' he called. There was no response, and he put his hand on the banister before he heard a light laugh. 'Edrea?' he asked, uncertain, and turned to follow her. 'Is everything all right? Do you need anything?'

She flitted on ahead of him and Runar hurried to follow, holding the rifle loose now.

The figure paused at the end of the corridor and looked back, slight and almost invisible except for the paleness of her clothes. '...nar,' she called again, barely audible. Unwilling to wake up her father, no doubt. Despite its low volume, her voice was laced with desperation.

'Edrea?'

She vanished through a door and Runar broke into a run. What was she doing? Where was she leading him? Had the beast returned? He'd heard something in his delirium at the Blood-Rock

Peaks about her communicating with it. Did she want him there now as protection?

He moved with quiet focus until he reached the end of the corridor and the room into which she'd vanished only a few seconds before. It was – impossibly – empty.

The room was small and densely packed with furniture: a large four-poster bed with hangings and a pool of inky shadow beneath; a huge wardrobe with carved panels on the doors; a heavy dresser littered with fetishes and a cracked crystal bowl in which a dark residue had long since dried; and a deep window seat nestled between rich, dark drapes. Edrea was nowhere to be seen.

'Lady Gothghul?' He wondered, for just an instant, if it was some sort of game, though why she'd play a trick on a wounded man in the middle of the night he didn't know. It didn't fit with what he'd learnt of her over the last few weeks.

A sudden shattering of rain against the window drew his attention, and then the clouds parted just long enough for a sliver of bone-white moon to light up the room. Runar's gaze was caught by marks scratched into the stone walls. Runes or symbols, he couldn't tell before the gloom fell again like an executioner's blade.

The bedroom door slammed shut behind him.

Runar spun to face the entrance, rifle at the ready. The room was still empty, but the sound of the lock turning was clearly audible.

Runar wrenched on the handle, to no avail. He pounded on it with his fist. 'Edrea,' he roared, 'what game is this?' There was no answer other than the wind whining around the eaves and a hint, perhaps, of laughter, but it was so faint he could have imagined it. Still, the hairs on his arms stood up, and he'd long been accustomed to listening to his body when it sang of danger.

He wished desperately for his revolver instead of the rifle. Long guns were harder to manoeuvre in close confines. *Good for shoving between a beast's teeth, though.* Runar dismissed the thought as soon as he had it. It would never fit beneath the bed, and there were no other hiding places to accommodate a creature so large. Whatever was in the room with him – and something was, his every sense told him so – it wasn't that. The notion was less comforting than he'd expected.

Moving slower than ice forming, he crept to the bed, keeping his naked back to the wall. His skin scraped stone, smearing sweat. There was nothing on the bed, nothing behind the hangings. Taking in a slow breath – it shuddered, just a little; the room was cold – he dropped to one knee and let the rifle lead him down to peer underneath. If there was something there, it was too dark for him to make out. He held his breath to listen, but the room was silent.

He stood again and edged back to the door, tried the handle without looking, just in case. Still locked. He slid towards the window facing the bed, braced, and poked the gun barrel into the closest drape. Nothing, no explosion of movement or sound. The seat itself was empty, and there was nothing behind the second curtain either. That left the dresser and the wardrobe, but before checking either of them he returned to the window. Stepping onto the deep seat with the rifle facing into the room, he fumbled backwards, blindly, for the latch. When he found it, his fingertips buzzed at contact with magic – the window was enchanted. Magically locked. No way out.

A gust of icy air brushed against the side of his face and then something dug into his chest, scratching, clawing downwards. A low, barely heard chanting teased at him, dark and smoky and cruel, and Runar jerked backwards from the invisible talons, almost squeezing off a shot. Blood welled on his chest and the breeze came again, across the nape of his neck. Like something breathing.

Runar threw himself away from the window and then lunged past the dresser, covering the hidden space on the far side – nothing – and over to the wardrobe. Not daring to lose his momentum, he grabbed the handle, angled the barrel at the gap and pulled.

The wardrobe door squeaked and the sharpshooter was enveloped in a puff of dust and the scent of faded perfume sachets. A few garments hung from pegs and he used the gun to poke at them. Nothing attacked him.

Runar was wound so tight he was almost disappointed. His eyes fell again on the bed and, more specifically, the looming blackness beneath it. He'd checked once, but it was so dark he might have missed something.

He thought about shouting for help, but his tongue was stuck to the roof of his mouth, and even if anyone heard him, whatever gheist or other undead was in here might do its best to kill him before aid arrived. So far, it hadn't been hostile. Runar wanted to keep it that way.

His fingers found the familiar roughness of a fire-striker among the scattered objects on the dresser. There was a stub of candle in a small holder next to it. The sweat was running freely now, and Runar had to bite his lip against the stab of pain in his hand as he squeezed the halves of the fire-striker together. The spark was blinding, but for a blessing, the wick caught first time and the flame licked up with a tiny crackle.

He let it settle while he quartered the room once more, feeling as if he knew its every crevice and shadow now – or had, until the dancing flame threw everything into ambiguity again. The markings he'd seen on the wall reappeared and then vanished, taunting him. They made no more sense now than they had before. He couldn't read whatever language they were written in. Distantly, he wondered whether the enchantment on the window was to keep the spell dormant here in this room. Perhaps that accounted for the door locking itself, though not for how Edrea had walked into this room and then disappeared. Runar put the candleholder on the floor and slid it towards the bed with the end of the rifle. He didn't like how low to the ground he had to be – it made him too vulnerable. A sudden glint beneath the hanging blankets froze the breath in his chest, but it was dull and flush with the floorboards, and he relaxed the pressure on the trigger. Aside from dust and the glint, there was nothing there.

Runar exhaled, the breath long and shaky. He took in another and used all of it to voice a long, inventive string of curses. He slumped back onto his heels and stared at the room, at the bed, and then again at the glinting object.

With a grunt, he wriggled forward, closed his fingers around it and dragged it out. It was a locket. Gold, heavy, old. As he examined it, someone laughed in his ear, low and unkind, and he scrambled for his rifle.

The door unlocked, then slowly creaked open.

Locket dangling from the fingers supporting the barrel, Runar approached the door and stepped to the hinge side, flattening himself against the wall. He reached for the handle and wrenched it towards him. Nothing. No one leapt into the room.

He tried to peer through the gap between door and frame, but the darkness was thick and clinging. He edged out from behind the door, took a breath and stepped quickly across the opening to the other wall, glancing swiftly. There was no attack, no gunshot or arrow or snarling mass of black fur, white teeth and red eyes responding to his movement. Just the laughter again, and the cold, dead breath on the back of his neck.

'Shit,' he whispered, and slid through the door in a low crouch. The corridor was empty. Wait. No – it wasn't. At the far end, back by the main staircase, he spied a pale dress and long, flowing hair once more.

Caution vied with fury and lost. 'Stop,' he called, loud and commanding. 'Turn around.'

The figure obeyed neither order, instead flitting up the stairs and out of sight.

'Runar.' Her voice floated back to him, teasing and beckoning, and confusion swamped him again. *What game is this?*

Runar sprinted back down the length of the corridor and practically flew up the stairs in her wake, fully prepared to strangle the mistress of Gothghul Castle to get some answers. The faintest billow of her skirt caught the corner of his eye, and he turned just in time to see into which room she vanished.

He ran after her, slowed to a stop just before the door, then dragged on the handle and spun in, leading with the rifle.

The fire here hadn't burnt so low, and the last flickers of light showed him a large bedroom lined with shelves of bottles, a heavy worktable under one window, a chaise longue under a second, and a figure sitting upright in the bed, a wickedly curved knife in one hand. His finger tightened on the trigger and he swung to face them.

'What are you doing?' he shouted.

'What's going on?' Edrea yelled at the same time.

Less than a breath later, a cold circle was pressed against the back of Runar's neck. 'What are *you* doing half naked in my daughter's bedchamber in the middle of the night?' Aaric demanded, his voice so soft that gooseflesh prickled on Runar's arms. That was a voice that promised death.

The sharpshooter very carefully removed his finger from the trigger and held both hands up. The rifle was snatched from his grasp and the gun on his neck jabbed hard enough that he sank to his knees and laced his fingers behind his head.

'Lord Gothghul,' he said, wincing as the barrel prodded harder at the words. 'Lord Gothghul, please, there's something in here, a gheist or something. Please search the room. I won't move, I swear.'

Aaric and Edrea both began asking questions, ignoring his request. Over the babble, he heard another set of footsteps and tensed despite the gun at his neck. Was it coming back?

'What is all this shouting? Edrea? *Runar?*'

Runar recognised Tiberius' voice, and he thanked Sigmar under his breath.

'That is precisely what I would like to know,' Aaric replied.

'Mister Grim?' said Runar quietly. 'Would you search the room, please? There's something inhuman in here. Please.'

Aaric was still scoffing, but Tiberius slipped past him into the chamber, bringing a lit candelabra and an unsheathed rapier. He asked no questions as he put down the candelabra and took a powerful warding talisman he kept hanging from his belt, holding it aloft. The sight of it brought an abrupt silence to father and daughter.

'What exactly am I looking for?'

'Most likely a gheist, but its behaviour was unusual and its ability to manipulate objects extremely strong,' Runar said. 'Lady Gothghul?' Aaric jabbed him with the gun in warning, and the sharpshooter fervently hoped his finger wasn't on the trigger. 'If you could stand by your father?'

Edrea's gaze flicked between him and Tiberius, who began reciting a prayer in the centre of the room. She nodded and climbed out of the bed, and Runar looked hastily away from the short, nebulous slip she was wearing. The candlelight outlined her through the wispiness of her nightwear as she slipped out of the blankets and onto the rug. She pulled a robe from the end of the bed and shrugged it on, then moved next to Aaric.

Silently, they watched the priest as he called upon Sigmar to quiet any entities that had invaded the castle. He was almost at the end of the prayer when an icy, foul-smelling wind tore through the cluttered chamber, overturning a few small bottles and ruffling curtains and blankets and hair. The candelabra was snuffed, but the coals in the grate flared bright for a few seconds.

Edrea muttered something and then snapped her fingers; the candles flared back into life.

'It's gone,' Tiberius said after an endless, tightly wound pause.

'All right, Father, let him up.' Edrea said immediately. 'You've got his rifle and it's extremely clear Mister Skoldofr wasn't lying about his reasons for coming in here.'

Aaric didn't move; neither did Runar.

'Just to be clear, it wasn't you I saw down on the guest level, was it, Ed– Lady Gothghul?'

'No,' Edrea said, confusion limning her voice. She knelt opposite him, ignoring her father's huff of disapproval. 'Well, if you won't let him up, I can hardly speak to him any other way, can I?' she said evenly. 'Unless you'd prefer him to look up my skirt? Didn't think so. Tell me what happened, Mister Skoldofr.'

Before Runar could speak, Aaric moved the gun and ordered him to stand. Evidently, the spectacle of his daughter kneeling on the rug in her nightclothes was too much for his dignity to bear.

The sharpshooter managed to suppress his hiss of pain as he stood. Now that the imminent danger appeared to be over, his exhaustion and hurts had caught up with him once more. Aaric's comment on the state of his undress was also belatedly making its presence known, and he reddened. He took his hands from the back of his head and felt a sharp tug on his hair as the locket's chain, still looped around his fingers, snagged and then pulled free.

'Turn around. Edrea, next to me.' Aaric's voice brooked no dissent, and his daughter merely rolled her eyes as she rose to her feet and stepped away from Runar. He turned and then backed off two paces, so the men with weapons would feel safer, and kept his hands where they could see them.

'Someone was in my room,' he said without preamble.

'Did they burst in with a gun, threatening you as you did my daughter?' Aaric demanded.

'Father!'

'It called my name. When I left my room, I saw the figure of a woman – dark hair, long pale dress. She – it – led me up to the guest level and into a room. When I went in, she wasn't there, but the door locked behind me. I thought it was Lady Gothghul, that she was either playing some random trick or... or that the beast had mesmerised her as it did Einar and Aldo...' His voice cracked, and he had to pause to clear his throat.

Edrea's face twisted with sympathy, and even Tiberius looked reflective, but Aaric continued to glare.

'I swept the room, but it was empty. Then, for no reason I can understand, the door unlocked. I came back out into the corridor, and there she – you – it – was again, heading up here. I followed it to your door. I didn't know whose room this was, but I couldn't risk that your daughter might have been coerced into hurting you, my lord, so I... made a tactical entry.'

There was a snort of what might have been muffled laughter from Edrea, and Aaric's formidable eyebrows drew even tighter together. Runar was vividly reminded that this man had a fearsome and well-deserved reputation among the Freeguild companies of Shyish.

'I was asleep until then, Mister Skoldofr,' Edrea confirmed. 'It was the cold air as you opened the door that woke me.'

Runar twitched. 'Cold air? Please, Miss Gothghul, think back. Did you feel cold as I came in, or before? You were already sitting up when I entered, and you'd retrieved your knife. I've seen the speed of your reactions, but even so.'

'What are you saying?' Aaric demanded.

'I felt a coldness too, in my room, and in the room on the guest level. And there are these...' He touched the scratches on his chest as he trailed off. 'It clawed at me.'

Tiberius snatched up the candelabra and held it up to illuminate Runar. He poked at the claw marks with his forefinger. 'Hmm, I don't think... Edrea?'

Runar had to force himself not to back away as Edrea leant so close he could feel her breath on his skin. She chewed her bottom lip and then ghosted her fingertips over the scratches, eyes closed. Finally, she stood up, and he let out his held breath. 'No, there's no curse. You're lucky.'

'Thank you, my lady.'

Edrea rolled her eyes. 'Please, there was only one lady of Gothghul Castle, and she died twenty-five years ago. Edrea, or "miss" if you must.'

'And this presence that you followed?' Tiberius said before Aaric could object. He reached out and gently lowered the man's gun hand.

'It won't be local. The graveyards are all blessed and the offerings made on time. Our dead sleep, or at the least they are quiescent.' This from Aaric, who exchanged a long, complicated look with Tiberius that Runar couldn't interpret. He got the sense there was more going on here than he was privy to. 'Which guest room were you led to?' he asked heavily.

'Last door on the left,' Runar replied.

Both men twitched, and then Tiberius strode forward and snatched at the sharpshooter's hand. 'What's this?'

'What? Oh, yes. I found it under the bed in that room, just before the door unlocked.' He passed over the locket, and Tiberius hurried to examine it. He swore, very quietly.

'Aaric. This... It's hers.'

'Whose?' Edrea asked sharply, crowding past her father, who put out his arm to hold her back. 'My mother's? It's Hephzibah's? Let me see it!'

Runar didn't miss the flash of pain on Aaric's face as he took the locket and squeezed it in his fist until his knuckles yellowed.

Edrea was prising at his fingers, trying to make him relinquish the necklace, until Tiberius pulled her away.

'Give him a moment, girl. That locket's been missing for a long time. Since your birth.'

Runar frowned. Missing? But the room hadn't been particularly dusty; servants cleaned it regularly. How could it have lain hidden – very poorly hidden – beneath a bed for twenty-five years without being discovered?

He hadn't really taken the time to examine it and watched with curiosity as Aaric finally loosened his grip enough to show the locket sitting on his palm. A heavy gold oval, lavishly decorated. Aaric clicked it open with fingers that shook, and Runar had a glimpse of miniatures inside, portraits – of Lord and Lady Gothghul, presumably – and then Edrea's back blocked his view.

Tiberius came to his side, giving the pair a semblance of privacy. 'You found it just lying under the bed?' he murmured, and Runar was glad that his suspicions were shared by another. Though he should have guessed the old priest wouldn't have just accepted it – in their long association, he'd come to have a great deal of respect for Tiberius' quick mind.

He grunted affirmatively.

'And the door unlocked the moment you found it?'

Runar thought back. 'Yes. Almost immediately.'

'So the gheist led you to Hephzibah's locket.' Tiberius hummed beneath his breath, then returned to Aaric's side and asked him a quiet question. Reluctantly, he handed over the locket.

The three of them faced Runar, and he felt a sudden twist of tension.

'You said you thought the person you saw was Edrea,' Tiberius said, and though he spoke softly, there was a thread of steel command wound through his voice that Runar's body reacted to. He stood at attention.

'Yes. Tall and slender, with dark hair and the same... the same easy grace of movement,' he said, and then cleared his throat, flushing slightly. He refused to look at Edrea, though he couldn't help but notice from the corner of his eye the way her lips parted at his words and then curved into a small, secret smile. He wanted, very badly, to fold his arms across his naked chest. He wanted to put on a shirt even more – the bandages around the bites in his shoulder and the side of his neck were entirely too small to relieve even the slightest bit of his embarrassment.

'And she knew my name, came to my room. But then, later, as I was following her, she said "Edrea",' he remembered. 'I wondered why she'd call her own name, but thought I'd mistaken it. Her voice was very, very quiet. And when she disappeared and the door locked, I thought the beast had returned and was controlling her somehow. That she'd led me there to my death.'

The others nodded. He'd managed to relate the full story of their chase of the beast and the attack in the Blood-Rock Peaks between bouts of unconsciousness. Edrea had been fascinated by the idea it had been able to manipulate Aldo's mind even in the extremity of his fear and grief. Or perhaps because of it, because the walls of his mind had crumbled with Karl's death. She'd told him of her use of deadsight and that Pietr had also appeared paralysed in the seconds before he died. 'What was she wearing?' Aaric asked, his voice hoarse.

'The… spirit? A long pale skirt, perhaps white or cream or even a pale blue. Shirt a few shades darker, with billowing sleeves. Her hair stirred too,' he added, 'as if she was in a perpetual breeze, but I only ever felt her – or something's – cold breath on the back of my neck.'

'And did you look in the locket?'

'Mister Grim, I was chasing down what I thought was Miss Gothghul under the beast's control coming to kill her father. There wasn't really the time for stopping to admire jewellery.'

Edrea was staring at him with something that was almost hunger, and Aaric's face was dark with old pain. Tiberius stepped forward and held out the locket. Runar hesitated and then squinted down at it. Then he recoiled.

A young, handsome Aaric Gothghul smiled out from one miniature. The other... 'That's her. That's who I saw,' Runar said, reeling back as if the portrait might reach out and grab him by the throat. His gaze rose first to Tiberius and then inexorably to Edrea, who looked so very much like her mother.

'Impossible,' Aaric said. 'Impossible.'

CHAPTER FIVE

Edrea felt as if her skin was too tight, her scalp prickling and a strange buzzing in the tips of her fingers. She rubbed them together absently. The effect of the spellcraft was still thick and heavy inside her, exhaustion a dark web tangling through her joints and muscles. She ached everywhere, not just from her use of the arcane speed but from the sheer effort she'd expended that day.

But as much as her body clamoured for sleep, she knew it wouldn't come now. There were just too many questions, too many tantalising glimpses of hidden knowledge and secrets. She couldn't forget what she'd heard outside her father's study that afternoon either – that her mother had written of a 'bloody-eyed hound of portent', that Tiberius thought it was back because of Edrea and the fact that she had felt so much kinship with it out there on the moor. She'd *known* it, soul-deep. And been known in return.

'Why is it impossible?' she demanded. 'Father, why? Why can't you see that these things must be linked? The beast and Mother's gheist? She's trying to tell us something.'

'Impossible,' he muttered again.

'Lady Hephzibah's tomb is well protected and guarded, Edrea – you know that,' Tiberius said. 'You are the one in charge of maintaining the wards, after all.'

'Then... then I must have made a mistake,' she said stubbornly, knowing she had not. Runar was confused, but her father and Uncle Tiberius gave her matching sceptical looks. 'Then why that room?' Edrea demanded, changing tack. She'd get some answers this night or die in the attempt.

Aaric was staring at the locket, retrieved from Tiberius and held as if he'd never let it go again. He gave no indication he'd heard her.

'Was that where she died?' Edrea tried, louder this time, unnameable emotions swirling through her. Her father twitched at that, and the lines around his mouth carved even deeper. 'Well?' she demanded, and her voice was shrill. 'I have a right to know. Was that the room where I was born, where my mother died? Is that who put her claws into Mister Skoldofr?'

'No.' The word was soft and belonged to Tiberius. 'But it was where she spent a lot of her time. It was her study, where she practised ritual and developed spellcraft. Her... sanctuary from Aaric and my ramblings whenever I came to visit.'

'But it's a bedroom now,' Runar interjected.

Tiberius looked again at Aaric, but still he refused to speak. 'After her... Afterwards, your father cleaned out the room and converted it. The memories were too painful to leave it full of her things.'

'I couldn't walk past that door every day and know she wasn't in there,' Aaric whispered. The pain in his voice was a distant thing, held at bay by Edrea's own sweeping feelings. By her *rage*.

'You wiped her away,' she said hollowly. 'You swept her out of this house as if she was nothing. As you, Uncle, did just now in this very room, casting her out as if she doesn't belong here.' Her hands were fists now, and she didn't miss how Tiberius shifted slightly to put himself between her and her father. 'You left me nothing but a few portraits and a few stories and shelves of her work I'm not supposed to touch. Tell me, Father, is your heart as empty of my mother as this castle is?'

'*Enough!*' Aaric roared, with such sudden violence that she rocked back on her heels with a flicker of fear, a flicker that was swiftly subsumed with satisfaction. 'You understand nothing.'

Aaric had been a hero of the Blackshore Guard in his youth, in the early years of his marriage to Hephzibah. After her death, he was a changed man, at least according to Tiberius. Not a cowardly man, as such, not when it came to himself, anyway. He still hunted the moors and assisted the other towns and villages of Null Island in the eternal fight against the undead, the constant infestations of restless spirits and other horrors besides. But his daughter was a different matter. He was so afraid of Edrea dying that he'd spent her entire life not allowing her to really live. And, worse, of not seeing – of refusing to see – what that did to her.

What was the point in being able to shoot a rifle if he wouldn't let her hunt the moors with it? Or even go onto the moors without an escort? The castle courtyards and gardens were not enough space when she was growing up, let alone now she was an adult. Market day, the town temple, the green for funerals and weddings. They were all so *small*. There was an entire realm out there, and he wouldn't even let her walk the five miles to the Blood-Rock Peaks, the rite of passage every child of the Hollow completed to prove their courage. As for meeting someone to spend her life with, it appeared Edrea's destiny was to remain trapped in Gothghul Hollow until Aaric fell down dead.

'I understand nothing? Perhaps that's because you won't tell me anything,' she struck back. 'You throw me crumbs of my past and expect me to be grateful. Even now, even here in this situation, when we are plagued with a ravening creature that is killing the townsfolk, when Mister Skoldofr is meeting the spirit of my mother – the *angry* spirit of my mother, I might add – you tell me nothing! You won't even let me hold her locket, as if I am six years old and might break it.' She stepped up to Tiberius' shoulder and pressed her fingers against his arm until he took a step sideways. 'What is it about me?' she asked quietly. 'You wish I'd died and she had lived? You hate me that much?'

The priest winced. Her father stared at her, glittering eyes in a pale face. 'Of course not,' he said, the words cracked and broken – and a beat too slow. Too hesitant.

'Why was the window in her room enchanted?' Runar asked loudly before anyone could say anything else.

'It is?' Edrea demanded. Something else she hadn't known.

'Hephzibah placed a loose spell upon it so that no one and nothing could open it, either from inside or out,' Tiberius said. 'It was the same with the lock on the door. What she kept in there – not just her books but her experiments and tools – was too valuable, and too dangerous, to leave lying around. She wouldn't even let the servants in there to clean, did it all herself. The enchantment remains on the window.'

'But not the door?' Edrea asked.

'No. That one was broken... during the last days before your birth.' Tiberius looked suddenly wary, and Edrea felt a flash of suspicion lance through her stomach, swiftly followed by nausea. She was so tired.

'And how did you break an enchantment my mother herself had crafted?' she asked.

'It doesn't matter now,' Aaric said, finally breaking his silence. 'Your mother was deeply ill by that time and we just needed the door open. It was for the best.'

'And then what? Did you rifle through her personal possessions yourself or just confiscate them? You clearly didn't use them to save her. So you... what? Waited for her to die and then threw everything out? Sold it? Burnt it?'

'Edrea,' her father began, pain lacing his voice. 'Please.'

'Please what? Please stop blaming you? I don't blame you, Father. I've never blamed you. I only wish you could say the same about me.' She held up her hand as he began to protest and noted, dully, that it was trembling. 'Get out. All of you, out. If you won't tell me the truth, then I have nothing more to say to you. Except you, Runar. You stay.'

'Absolutely not,' her father started, but Edrea had had enough.

She advanced and shoved him in the chest, and he stumbled back a pace. 'Don't pretend to care about me now, *Aaric*,' she said viciously, and shoved him again.

Tiberius slipped between them, gripped her father's elbow and steered him from the room. 'You both need your rest,' he said. 'Don't forget.'

'Out.' Her voice shook. The door closed with a soft click and took Edrea's strength with it. She stumbled to the foot of the bed and sat. Runar backed carefully to her workbench and leant a hip against it, his arms folded across his broad chest. Divested of most of his clothes and all of his weapons and bandoliers, he seemed smaller, more vulnerable, though that might have something to do with being ordered to remain in her bedchamber in the middle of the night.

'Was it really her?' The words came out in a whisper before she could stop herself.

He pressed his lips together into a thin line and then nodded. 'The miniature... I believe so. Yes.'

'And she led you here, to my room?' Another nod. 'Then why did she allow herself to be banished? She's my mother – why come to you? Where's her message for me?' Edrea had thought her tears for her mother had been cried years before, but it seemed there was an inexhaustible well of them buried deep somewhere within her soul, and they surged up her throat, tightening it, and stung her eyes and overflowed. She turned her face away from Runar and let them run, silent, unwilling for him to see.

'Ah, Edrea,' he murmured, his voice so soft she barely heard it, and she remembered with a rueful sigh that he was a sharp-shooter; his gaze missed nothing. 'I myself asked Mister Grim to secure the room. If I'd known it was your mother... but your father is a complicated man, I think. Intensely private. I don't believe he means to hurt you.'

'And yet you say yourself you barely know him.' She sniffed and scrubbed at her face. Then she barked a humourless laugh. 'For years he tried to prevent me harnessing the magic of this realm, and would have succeeded if I hadn't started accidentally blowing up parts of his study. That's one of the first times I met Uncle Tiberius – he gave me a grimoire and helped me read it. Father could have at least sat with me and helped me understand what the basic terminology meant, but he wouldn't. Even then he had no interest in me, preferring to spend all his time out on the moors, gone for days, sometimes, leaving me in the care of Young Aethelwych, our housekeeper. If not for the need for me to learn to control the magic I could access, I'd be as much a shade in this castle as my mother apparently is.'

Runar shifted against the workbench and Edrea realised how uncomfortable she'd made him. 'I'm sorry,' she said slowly. 'You don't need to hear this. But...' She glanced at the door, then rose on unsteady legs and crossed towards him. She didn't miss the slight tension that tightened his shoulders at her approach. 'But I want to get out of here,' she whispered when they were barely a foot apart. 'When this is done, when it's all over, take me with you.'

Runar's mouth dropped open.

'Not for good, don't worry,' she said hastily. 'Just take me to somewhere I can get set up, find a place to lodge. I know more than enough spellcraft that I can get by selling potions and amulets for a while, but I want to go somewhere... big. Like Lethis. Maybe enrol at the Collegiate Arcane, even.'

'Have you ever been to Lethis?' the sharpshooter asked her. He held up his hand before she could reply. 'Sorry, of course you haven't. But... you don't want to go there – the place is a cesspool. It might be safer than the wilds, but the things you will be asked to do, expected to do, even, especially...'

'Especially what?' Edrea demanded, angry and defensive and a little bit desperate.

Runar shifted, uncomfortable. 'Especially being as beautiful as you are.'

She stared at him, nonplussed, heat crawling into her cheeks. 'Well,' she managed, 'the Collegiate Arcane might be a better choice then. Just think about it, all right? Please? Give me a way out that isn't...' She trailed off and turned away, fresh tears blooming in her eyes.

Runar's big, warm hand landed on her shoulder and tightened, painfully hard. She gasped. 'Isn't what? Suicide?' he demanded, his voice rough with anger and not a little alarm.

She stared up at him with cold eyes, jerking out from under his palm. 'Just because my father hates me doesn't mean I hate him, not truly. I would *never* hurt him in such a way. I am speaking of a way out that isn't me attempting to hitch a ride on an export cart that my father will find out about within the hour and come to fetch me back.' She stepped decisively away from him. 'I had hoped you might help, but if you have so little regard for me, then–'

'Wait. Just stop talking,' Runar interrupted her, for once disregarding the supposed difference in their statuses. Edrea was so surprised that she did as he ordered. 'All that could well be a long way away. Who knows what's really going on in Gothghul Hollow? Is the beast gone? We don't know. Was it your mother's shade I saw or something else? We don't know. Can we concentrate on the events we're in the middle of before we start making plans to flee the town?'

Edrea stared at him and then blushed, biting her lip. 'You're right, of course. Forgive me. There is just… There is a history in this house I have never been allowed to understand. There are secrets in every painting and behind every door, it sometimes feels. The castle is mortared in silence and I learnt a long, long time ago that it is my fault, and that only my own silence could possibly make my father happy. It is – it was – a heavy burden for a young child.'

'It would be a heavy burden for a woman grown, too,' he said softly, and she wanted his hand on her shoulder again. On her face. 'Do you… want to examine the room where I was led?'

'I do, but he'll be there now, I can guarantee that. I'm more interested in why she'd come here and then allow herself to be banished.'

'She wanted you to have the locket, perhaps.'

Edrea grimaced and took a casual step forward again, into his space. He didn't move back this time. 'And yet I do not have it, and you were almost shot by my father. I'm sorry about that, by the way.'

The corner of his mouth quirked, the candlelight catching the edge of his stubble and highlighting it in gold. 'Not as sorry as I'd have been, I can promise you that. On reflection, bursting into a maiden's chamber in the middle of the night dressed like this' – he waved a hand at himself – 'was not the cleverest thing I've done in a long list of not-clever things.'

Edrea cocked her eyebrow and her smile became mischievous. 'Maiden, you say? I'm afraid that ship sailed some time ago, though for all that's holy, don't tell my father or Uncle Tiberius.' She laughed when Runar gaped, and she stepped closer again, put her hand on his arm. He stilled beneath her touch, a wild animal tamed.

'What do you think is going on, Mister Skoldofr? Really, I mean? I've been in every room in this castle a thousand times. I've crawled under and bounced on every bed as a child. I still visit random rooms now when the... Well, it doesn't matter why. What I'm saying is, how can that locket have suddenly appeared when it wasn't there before?'

He sighed and slumped against the workbench again, and she remembered his wounds; his exhaustion must be as acute as her own. 'I wish I knew, I truly do. What does your learning tell you? If it is your mother's spirit, can she have manifested the locket somehow?'

Edrea felt a prickle of pleasure that he had asked for her opinion. 'I have read of such things. Particularly with strong spirits, fuelled by emotion enhanced by the moment of their deaths – usually negative, like resentment or anger.'

'Bladegheists, Tomb Banshees, yes,' he said. 'I've had the misfortune to encounter them all. Your mother's shade was... different. Far too controlled, too focused. Usually it's a simple fight to the death with a Nighthaunt, but this time, while I was clearly in danger, while it was – forgive me – vicious and frightening, it also had a purpose.'

Excitement twisted in Edrea's stomach. 'Yes. A purpose, as the beast has a purpose. Do you see? They must be linked. If my mother died mad – not mad as in insane,' she added defensively, 'but mad with anger, that my father and Uncle Tiberius weren't understanding her, weren't allowing her what she needed – then yes, it's possible she could have moved the locket. But that doesn't tell us where it's been hidden all these years. Father said he hasn't seen it since the night she died. And even in the depths of his initial grief, I can see that. Because surely – *surely* – she would have wanted me to have it. Tiberius would've known that, even if Father was too lost to think of it. I'd have grown up knowing it was mine, not being ignorant of its existence entirely. So where has it been?'

Edrea broke off and smiled ruefully. 'Sorry, I'm thinking aloud. Probably not making any sense.'

Runar shook his head. 'You make perfect sense,' he told her quietly, and she felt another bloom of pleasure in her chest. 'So we need to know how the locket disappeared in the first place, and how it came back. Neither seems particularly obvious.'

'Could it have been stolen by a servant in the aftermath of her death? It looked expensive?' she asked, because they had to dispense with the mundane reasons first. In her heart, Edrea knew it was more than that, but she had taught herself to be methodical in everything. While her magical abilities were more intuitive than most, they still required precision if she wanted to avoid an unpleasant, messy death.

Runar frowned. 'It could be as simple as that. Do any of them still work here who were alive back then?'

'Two. And the children of three others, Young Aethelwych included. Though that still doesn't explain why they'd put it under the bed, unless they were wearing it and it slipped free as they cleaned the room.' She yawned. 'Perhaps it really is that simple,' she added with clear scepticism and then busied herself at the shelves. 'Sit on the table.'

'What?'

'Sit. I may as well check your wounds again while you're here, and deal with those fresh scratches. Just because you're not cursed doesn't mean they don't need cleaning. Your intuition, Mister Sko–'

'Hadn't we agreed it's Runar, Miss Gothghul?' he asked as he hopped up onto the table.

She sniffed. 'Hadn't *we* agreed it's Edrea, Runar?' she replied tartly. 'The truth is I dislike "miss" as much as "lady"'

The sharpshooter grinned and ducked his head in acknowledgement. 'Perhaps not in front of your father, though. So, let's assume the locket has a mundane story behind its reappearance. That doesn't change the fact that the spirit appeared in the immediate aftermath of the beast vanishing. Although it makes no practical sense, I agree that the two events – the two apparitions, for want of a better word – are linked. The beast didn't attack me when it saw the Gothghul crest pinned to my jacket. It didn't attack you at all. And then the spirit led me to your mother's locket.'

'The bloody-eyed hound of portent,' Edrea muttered as she unwound the bandages from Runar's left hand.

'Eh?'

'My mother... Before she died, but during her illness, she wrote, over and over again in one of her journals, about a bloody-eyed hound of portent. I overheard Father and Uncle Tiberius discussing it before I came out to find you yesterday. Tiberius thinks the beast might be the same creature, that it's come back for a reason.' She held his hand up to the light and turned it over gently, lips pursed at the puffy, weeping flesh. 'And then for my mother to appear, who knew of the beast, it's too much coincidence. Of course they're linked.'

Runar was silent while she cleaned and redressed his wounds. The heat was in her cheeks again as she wiped a damp cloth over his chest, and the sharpshooter seemed barely to be breathing. But when she would have carried the tray of medical supplies away, he stopped her. 'What are you planning, Edrea?' he murmured.

Her face twitched. 'I'm wondering, why you? The beast didn't kill me, no, but it didn't kill you either. For which I am very grateful,' she added hastily. 'But then my mother appeared to you. Out of all of us. Why doesn't she want to see me?'

'Ah, Edrea,' he murmured, chafing her arms gently with his palms. 'I know little about spirits and apparitions other than how to destroy them. I wish I did. I wish I had an answer that would bring back your smile.'

She looked up at that, startled, and found his dark, piercing eyes fixed entirely upon her. Unwavering and intense and seeing her in a way no one ever had. Her own hands alighted softly on his forearms, and she bit back the quip that sprang to her lips – silly, light-hearted words that she used to build a barrier between herself and the world so that it couldn't see her or her pain. Breath shuddering in her lungs, she let him look at her – and looked in return. It was more frightening than any ritual or spellcraft she'd ever attempted – and more liberating.

What would he do if she leant in now, her lips parted for his kiss? Want, and the fear of it, were held in an exquisitely painful balance within her chest. They paused on the cliff edge, and then drew back.

'Do you grieve for your hunters?' she asked, and then flushed. Of course he did. He nodded and answered her anyway, as if the question wasn't foolish.

'I'd known Aldo the longest, and by extension Karl. Aldo and I used to track for the Blackshore Guard on occasion. That's how I know Mister Grim. Afterwards, he came to me when he had quiet work he needed doing, and through him, your father. They were a good crew. Even Karl. None of them deserved what happened to them.' He paused, his hands still so warm through the thin silk of her robe. 'But that's what we're paid for, to take the risks others won't. We all signed up knowing it would mean our lives one day. It's the job.' He smiled wanly.

'Not this job,' Edrea said fiercely. 'Not you.'

Runar found a slightly warmer smile for her and squeezed before letting go. 'Well, I certainly have no intentions of either drawing your ire or standing between you and the subject of it.

As for what you said earlier...' He paused and puffed out his cheeks, and she felt a flash of unfamiliar panic. 'Yes. Of course I'll take you away when this is over, *if* you still want to go.' His voice was low, and she felt the weight not just of those words but all that was unspoken behind them. 'You're too... alive for this place. And don't forget, the shade did come here to your room. Perhaps you will get to hear her message one day. But you should sleep now. You're exhausted.'

Edrea clicked her tongue, though she couldn't deny the truth of it. She suppressed another yawn even as his words triggered a wave of exhaustion that swept through her and left her feeling weak and faintly nauseated. 'And you're wounded. Take the chaise longue, it's very comfortable. There's a blanket in the wardrobe there. No, Runar. You're not going back to that tiny little room in the servants' wing – you should never have been placed there on your arrival, let alone now, after everything that happened today. Besides, you might still end up with a fever. This way, I'll hear you if your sleep is disturbed.'

It was an easy lie, and one he couldn't refute, but the remedy she'd spent so much energy and blood creating would see off any but the most virulent illness caused by his exposure to the storm. Still, he didn't need to know that. Reluctantly, he did as she requested, and she climbed back beneath the bed-clothes and lay there listening to him rustle and turn until he was comfortable. There was a small smile on her face as she drifted back to sleep.

Her rest didn't last long. Barely two hours had passed when she was woken, unexpectedly, by icy fingers trailing across the side of her face and then digging in, bruisingly hard. Gasping, Edrea shied away and opened her eyes, just in time to see a slender figure slip through the door. For a bare instant, she thought it was Runar, but a quick glance at the chaise longue showed him huddling uncomfortably upon it, feet hanging over the end. There was a crease in his brow, but he slept deeply and she didn't wake him. She knew, instinctively and with a jealous satisfaction, that this was for her alone. Her mother had come for her.

Edrea slid from the bed and dragged on a pair of boots over her bare feet, then retied her dressing robe and took the knife from beneath her pillow. Just because it was the shade of her mother didn't mean she was wandering the dark castle unarmed. Not with everything that had happened that day and in the weeks preceding. Not if Hephzibah and the beast were somehow connected – and being sent by the same powerful entity. Besides, her face stung from the strength in those icy fingertips.

The candelabra Tiberius had brought in was burning low, but it would last long enough – she hoped – so she lifted it from her workbench, hesitated, and then slipped a packet of blinding powder into her left pocket and lung-seize into her right, then added a stimulant in a separate tiny jar. She wondered for a brief moment what her father would do if he knew she'd even made such items, let alone had every intention of using them should the need arise. A sly smile crossed her face as she stole from the room and into the corridor.

The spirit – her mother – was drifting towards the servants' stairs, and Edrea hurried to catch her, candelabra streaming flames, dagger warm and familiar in her fist.

Music. Edrea's feet slowed a little and she held her breath to listen. No, not music, but a sort of... distant chanting, perhaps? A lone voice, dark and wanton and hungry. It wasn't loud enough for her to discern the language or intention but was just present enough to make her cautious. Edrea herself could chant rituals in eleven different tongues, depending on what the spell required. While this one didn't have a familiar cadence or series of syllables, it felt dangerous.

The spirit disappeared into the shadows of the stairs. The

voice didn't change or echo – it wasn't coming from the shade itself then. And, now that she thought back, she hadn't heard it when she'd met the beast. Aaric had been right: Edrea did keep her mother's tomb fully warded. It meant that Hephzibah's body couldn't rise, but someone had circumvented the wards enough to raise her shade. The chanting must be part of the ritual to bring her under control.

What had the Gothghuls done to draw such a powerful spell-caster's ire? Using Hephzibah against them seemed particularly cruel. And, of course, the townsfolk were surely innocent. If this was some long-held grudge against Aaric, then the sorcerer's control of the beast, at the very least, was incomplete. Perhaps that was why they had sent the spirit as well, although, as Runar had pointed out, this particular Nighthaunt didn't seem to have their destruction as its only aim.

Edrea reached the stairwell and slid through, cautious, the candles lighting the plaster a warm yellow. The stairs were narrow, dark, steep and creaky, and she crept down them as best she could. She hesitated at the guest level, but the faint chanting continued and something drew her, inexorably, on down to the ground. Back here, it was a warren of storerooms and kitchens and the servants' private living quarters, but out where the unfinished plaster became dark wood panelling and expensive rugs and tapestries, it was the library, the studies, the dining room and all the rest. Her world. Her prison.

She knew she'd discomfit the servants if any of them found her wandering around here, so she was relieved, and somewhat apprehensive, when the wispy figure dragging its cloak of barely audible chanting glanced back – eyes as dark as Edrea's own, she saw with a lurch of her heart, though she could see little else – and then vanished through into the ballroom.

'Wait.' The word was both soft and involuntary, but the figure had already gone. Edrea rushed after it, heedless, two of the candles blowing out and dimming the light, but she didn't care – that was *her mother*.

Her features had been indistinct in the gloom, but the magnetism of those eyes was undeniable, and the chanting almost seemed to spiral, for an instant, into something on the edge of familiarity. Still dark, still almost feral, but it made Edrea's heart quicken nonetheless as she burst through the door into the ballroom.

The vast, dark, echoing ballroom. The empty ballroom. 'Mother?'

Edrea's voice was barely there, skating on the tail of her breath, quieter even than the chanting that rose all around her without a source. She tried again. 'Hephzibah Gothghul? We found the locket you sent us. Is there a message to go with it? A message that the beast tried and failed to convey?'

This time the words echoed back from the walls, though they did not draw a reply. Where was her mother? Why bring her here and then vanish? Why not stay – why not *speak*?

'Mother?' she whispered again as she wandered through the empty dark. There was movement at the very edge of her eye and Edrea jerked her head in that direction. Another flicker of pale skirt, by the wall between two of the immense, draped windows.

'Ah.' Fingers tight around the candelabra, Edrea hurried over. She was suddenly flooded with energy, and though she knew it was fool's energy – those last bitter dregs before the inevitable collapse – she welcomed the purpose and clarity it brought her.

She knew what lay on that wall, shrouded in white cloth. She reached out with her knife hand, stretching onto her toes to grip the bottom edge of the cotton and pull. It was thick and heavy, securely wedged behind the top of the heavy gilt frame, exactly tight enough to prevent easy access. She tugged again, and then a third time, but the cloth was stubbornly fixed in place.

Edrea held her little finger over a candle flame until the skin blistered and there were screams painting her tongue, and then released her breath in a single long rush of syllables and a wisp of magic, fed by her flesh. She flicked the burnt hand at the shrouded painting and a ripple of air followed it, lifting the edge of the cloth and sweeping it up and back. A cloud of dust billowed from its folds as it tore free and fluttered heavily to the floor before her.

The flames guttered as she staggered under the toll of the magic-debt, still unpaid from the day. She held the candelabra carefully until the flames steadied and buttery, yellow light gleamed over the vast canvas, then placed it on the floor below the painting and stepped back so she could view it all at once.

Aaric and Hephzibah, larger than life, painted in the months after their wedding, when her mother was at her most powerful and most vibrant – a sorceress beyond compare. As a small child, Edrea had studied the portrait for hours, staring up at her parents, imagining Hephzibah stepping out of it to sweep Edrea up in her arms and carry her back into the portrait – back into the magical land where her father smiled and had that lightness in his eyes that she'd only ever seen here in this one image, and never in life. A land of peace and safety away from monsters and fanatic cultists, secure in the love of both her parents, where the war against Chaos and the unquiet dead couldn't touch them.

Hephzibah was the only person who'd ever made her father look like that – as if life was worth living.

Aaric had had the painting covered over when she was six, when he grew tired of finding her sitting or lying beneath it, staring up, talking to it. Talking to the mother she had never known. 'Well, what did you expect?' she breathed now. 'It's not as if you ever spoke to me.'

Edrea swallowed the familiar bitterness and concentrated on the portrait. She wasn't that child any more, and she'd resigned herself to Aaric's indifference almost two decades before. Now, she searched for whatever it was that had made her mother's spirit lead her here before vanishing. What was she supposed to see that she'd never before noticed?

As always, she'd thought she had the portrait memorised until she saw it again. Even in the dark, lit only by the fitful glow of too few candles, the colours were so vibrant they almost hurt.

Hephzibah, dark eyes glittering from the canvas and seeming to dance, dressed in a loose white shirt and fitted riding trousers, her left hand cupped below a globe of golden light, even the scars of her spellcraft showing upon her arm. In a sudden rush of insight, Edrea understood why. Her mother had not been posing for some idea of herself, for some stylised version of the woman she was. She'd been painted as she lived, wild and unapologetic, her hair tumbling from its combs and her clothes tailored so they didn't encumber her. The scars on her arm were a source of fierce pride, not something to be concealed by sleeves or make-up.

The painting of Hephzibah was of her as she moved through the world, at ease within it, within her skin and within her marriage. That was why Aaric's smile was so wide, why his eyes were alight with love and excitement. Hephzibah had *lived*, with every fibre of her being.

Edrea's eyes stung with hot tears. She'd been so beautiful and so alive, and she'd died maddened and agonised only seconds after her daughter was born. No wonder Aaric had done all he could to curb Edrea's impulses and wildness. He'd been terrified she would become too much like her mother – a bright, roaring flame consuming its own tail until it guttered.

'And yet look at her,' she whispered, the words running around the edges of the ballroom to mingle with that ghostly chanting. 'She was so beautiful. So vibrant. She lived every second with joy and purpose, even if she did die young. If I do the opposite, I'll be dead inside long before my body withers. Perhaps I already am.'

She snorted quietly. She'd always had a predisposition to melo-drama, but it seemed her exhaustion exacerbated it. She stumbled as she stared upwards, a wave of dizziness breaking over her head and fatigue a red-clawed shape at the edges of her mind.

Swaying, Edrea slid her hand into her pocket and dragged out the stimulant. It would probably give her an hour of almost normal functionality before the crash took her. Surely that would be enough to find out why her mother had brought her here and do anything she needed to do?

It was thick and bitter in her throat, but she swallowed it down, her mouth twisting at the taste. She'd only had occasion to use it a few times before, always at the tail end of some great crafting she was attempting on the roof or in the castle grounds. She'd never used it just as a means to keep going, to stay awake against the demands of her body and Shyish's magic.

Hephzibah chuckled against the skin of Edrea's throat, icy breath ghosting over her. Edrea jerked, but there was nothing to see, not even when fingers tangled in her hair and jerked it cruelly hard. *Hurry, daughter. Hurry to understand.*

'I will,' she breathed, unsure if she'd imagined the command or not, but as soon as she felt the first flickers of new energy – even rawer than the fool's energy from before, and far more toxic – she examined the painting again. She worked carefully, quartering the massive canvas as she'd been taught to examine the ground for game when hunting.

There was nothing to see in the bottom quarter but the per-fectly realised backdrop of the moors. And there was nothing on those moors, no figure or tomb marker, certainly not the Blood-Rock Peaks. The top quarter showed Hephzibah's left hand and the glowing globe floating above it, a moody sky dark with clouds, a few bands of light breaking through in great lilac sweeps. The curve of her hand was familiar but not special, a simple cup, even though the globe didn't sit within it.

In the centre of the painting, Hephzibah's and Aaric's bodies stood close, his arm around her waist, hand resting on her hip. Hephzibah's right hand was near her throat, holding her necklace. Above that...

Edrea's eyes returned to the jewellery, and her gasp was loud in the stillness, drowning out the ghostly cadence of the voice. That was the locket. That was the exact locket that Runar had found. The stimulant was speeding through her veins now, and she let it, ignoring how grubby it made the inside of her skin feel.

She ran to the storeroom off the servants' corridor to drag out a set of heavy wooden ladders. The noise they made as she pulled them across the highly polished floor was enough to summon the beast down on them, and she knew there would be servants trembling in their beds, convinced death was stalking them. She'd apologise in the morning, but for now she just didn't have time.

Edrea opened the ladders in front of the painting and made sure the central struts were locked in place, then snatched up the candelabra and ran up one side as if it was a set of stairs. She wobbled to a halt level with the painted locket and her mother's hand, because that was something she'd noticed dozens of times – for a painting that was so perfectly rendered, for figures that were so lifelike, that hand was twisted strangely. Now, leaning precariously off the side of the ladder and holding the candelabra as close as she dared without setting the canvas alight, she squinted at the locket. It was definitely the same one, and... Hephzibah's hand was contorted because her thumb and first two fingers were touching three points on the pattern engraved on the front. What she'd always thought were paler brushstrokes turned out to be veins of light running down her hand and wrist, matching ones in her left hand and pooled in her cupped palm below the glowing orb.

'Nagash,' she swore. 'It's powering the orb? *It's powering the orb!*'

There was a faint tinkle in the music, as of laughter, and Edrea wobbled on the ladder, scanning the darkened ballroom. There. Her mother. The shade nodded once, perhaps in approval. 'Aaric,' she said, her voice floating over the dark chant, and disappeared through the ballroom door.

'Wait!'

The figure didn't, and Edrea's boots were too loose without socks, and she had to take the rungs of the ladder slowly so she didn't fall and break her neck. As soon as she was down, she ran after her mother, the candle flames streaming behind her and then one by one winking out. The ballroom was plunged into darkness just as the far door slammed open and Runar came in, armed.

'Edrea?'

'Come on,' she shouted, uncaring now how many people were woken by her racket. 'I saw her, come on.'

He ran heavily towards the sound of her voice as she wrenched open the door Hephzibah had vanished through. 'She said my father's name,' she said breathlessly, 'so either his study, the library or his bedchamber. Unlikely to still be in the guest room at this hour.'

'Let me light the candles,' Runar said.

'No time, no time,' Edrea muttered, determined not to lose her mother now. Not again. Not when she was so close to answers. She ran along the long corridor, hoping to see the spirit's pale form, but there was nothing. She slammed open the library door – empty, the embers in the fire burning low – and then Aaric's study. It was also empty, though this time the fire flared into uneasy life at the draught.

'Bedchamber then,' she said to herself, and then stumbled. Runar caught her beneath the arm and took the candelabra from her.

'No,' he said sternly. 'You're exhausted. You have to rest.'

Edrea broke his grip and summoned her best, most Aaric-like glare. 'Do not presume to lecture me,' she snapped. 'I am bubbling with energy.' And it was true, but that didn't mean her limbs were miraculously more coordinated than before. Still, she made her way to the staircase and began to climb as Runar wasted time lighting the candles. Edrea didn't need them now; she knew where her mother was going, and she'd lived in this castle all her life. She could navigate it blindfolded.

Runar caught her up on the middle landing and then pushed ahead, lighting the way with his rifle half brandished.

'You won't need that,' she told him confidently.

'What's wrong with you?' the sharpshooter hissed, a deep line appearing between his brows as he glared back at her.

The drug was making her giddy, and Edrea took a deep breath in through her nose. 'I took a stimulant. Probably got about forty more minutes before it wears off. So let's hurry.'

She ignored his muttered complaints about her recklessness and bounded up the stairs to the family floor. They reached Aaric's room in time to hear him cry out in fear. Runar pushed Edrea against the wall and then burst in first. Edrea followed. She closed her fingers around the packet of blinding powder just in case. Aaric shouted again at the sudden intrusion and then abruptly quieted when he recognised Runar. Apparently, him lunging into this bedroom didn't cause as much of a stir as when he'd entered hers.

'What's going on? Where is she?' Edrea demanded from behind Runar, though she didn't squeeze past until he'd given the all clear. 'Father? Where's Mother?' She stared around the room. Aaric was pressed to the far wall, as far as he could get from the dresser that had once been Hephzibah's. The items littered across the top had changed over the years, brushes, cosmetics and jewellery slowly vanishing and being replaced by a shaving kit, a dish for coins and oddments, and a clear space for books to be piled.

One thing had always remained, though, one thing of Heph-zibah's that Aaric had never quite had the courage to hide away. Her scent bottle. Even now, every year Aaric sent off to the near-est city for a fresh vial of the perfume, emptying out the old and replacing it with new. Edrea knew that in his most melancholy moments, he would sit at the dresser and breathe it in. She'd done it herself, countless times, trying to get a sense of the woman from the components of her favourite perfume.

'She indicated the bottle, didn't she?' Edrea asked now, and noted that it was in the middle of the table, not at the back where it usually sat. 'Did she move it? Was she corporeal? Runar and I thought that maybe she'd brought us to the locket, too. If she moved the bottle...'

Aaric couldn't speak, but he managed to shake his head.

Edrea deflated. 'You put it there?'

'Yes,' he croaked, slowly peeling himself off the wall. 'And the locket.'

And that was all the half-permission Edrea needed. Her father was trembling and had finger scratches down his right cheek similar to those on Runar's chest. She didn't care. She swept the locket up into her hand and turned towards the lantern. As much as she wanted to examine the engraving, she popped the clasp and separated the halves to study the miniature of her mother. It was an image she'd never seen before – there were a handful of smaller portraits scattered through the private areas of the house, and one in Edrea's own room, but this was new. Just her face, serious but with a hint of a smile at the corner of her mouth and her dark hair tumbling around her jaw.

Edrea's heart twisted within her and her breath hitched, but she made herself examine the other miniature. This was Aaric as she knew him best – remote and distant. Unsmiling. She closed the locket and brushed her fingers over the engravings as Runar and Aaric spoke quietly behind her. She avoided the three spots that the painted Hephzibah had been touching – even with the stimulant racing through her, she was not in the right frame of mind to even examine the locket's aura, let alone activate anything upon or within it.

She undid the clasp and put the necklace around her throat. When Aaric noticed, he lurched forward. Edrea met his eyes. 'Don't. You're not the one to wear this. You're not the one who deserves it.' She took the perfume bottle and pocketed it. 'This you'll get back, once I understand what Mother is trying to tell me. Now where is she?'

'It's not your mother,' Aaric said. Edrea scoffed. Who else could it be, gifting them the locket, bringing her to the painting and then indicating the perfume bottle? Of course it was Hephzibah. No random Nighthaunt, especially one that *wasn't* bent on wholesale slaughter, would present them with so many clues to help identify it.

'The stench of blood woke me, and then cold breath across my face and neck. When I opened my eyes, the shade was... sitting on my chest. It attacked me' – he indicated the cuts on his cheek – 'and then moved to the dresser while I retreated to the wall. It fled as you opened the door.'

Edrea snorted. 'Retreated. You ran away from your own wife.' She started to say something else and then stopped. Even with the stimulant, she was weary down to her very soul, weary of her own endless resentment, of her father's disappointment and his cowardice. Weary of the castle and its secrets. Weary of always wondering and never knowing, of not being trusted. Even more than the solitude, it sapped her of strength and will.

Runar shifted, uncomfortable but not getting in between them. Then he winced and drew something out of his pocket, stared at it in numb confusion. 'Oh.'

'What's that?' Edrea asked, because Aaric seemed unable to take charge of the situation and her mind was crystal bright and razor sharp – for now. Anything and everything could be of significance, and she needed to gather as much information as she could before the spellcraft claimed its looming toll.

'When I was first woken, I reached for my revolver and picked up this instead. It's the beast's claw. I cut it off.'

Edrea's heart gave a lurch, and she crossed swiftly to his side and snatched it from his grip. 'Yes,' she breathed. 'I can craft with this. I didn't think it was a ritual because we didn't have life... but now it will work.'

'What ritual?' Aaric demanded, sharp and worried.

'The locket – metal and memory. The claw – life and will. The perfume – liquid and breath. Fire I can bring, of course, and earth. No, it's about how to combine them now, how to bring them together, infuse them with magic so that–'

'No. No, Edrea, I forbid it.'

'Oh, Father,' Edrea said, and she knew there was a manic edge to her voice – she could hear it, feel it even. It was the stimulant burning through her final reserves and burning, too, through the last of her restraint.

'I don't care what you forbid. Don't you understand? You've kept me from the knowledge of my mother all these years and yet I learnt it anyway. I can speak dead languages and tame creatures that would frighten you to death. I can talk to the past and see glimpses of the future. I can use magic, and blood, and lore you've never even heard of, and you have never been *able* to stop me. I just *let you* stop me. And I will let you no longer.'

Aaric's eyes were wet with tears but hard as granite. He opened his mouth to speak but Edrea crossed to the door and left. The fourth visitation would, of course, be Tiberius. Her father said something behind her, some soft-voiced protest that was easy to ignore, so she did. She'd probably regret many of the things she'd said later, but for now there was no time to consider Aaric's feelings or even her own. Hephzibah had a message for them, and Edrea needed to learn what it was.

She knocked on Tiberius' door, aware that Runar and her father were behind her. 'Uncle Tiberius? Has she come to you yet?' she called softly, and then twisted the door handle. He wasn't there, but the room was cold despite the fire, so the ghost had been here – and not long before.

'A way to bring them all together,' she repeated under her breath. 'Of course. The forbidden shelves.' She hurried back down the stairs yet again, the men following more slowly. Edrea felt a pang of regret that Runar was doing so much running around when he was wounded, but she trusted him to know his own limits the way she knew hers, and if he wanted to push them, that was his affair. There were still some doses left of the remedy she'd crafted that would speed his recovery.

The library door was open and golden light spilt from it. Tiberius must have come here only moments after she'd checked the room for her father. *Like rats in a maze, we've all been running around in the dark.*

When Edrea pushed the door wide and walked in, she saw Tiberius first and the shade – her mother – second. The priest startled at the sound of her feet, his eyes wild.

'Show us, Mother,' Edrea said softly, but the apparition and the haunting, mournful chanting on the edge of hearing were both already fading. Panic flooded her. 'Stop! Please come back, please,' she begged, rushing forward. She pushed into the sphere of cold air and tried to close her hands on the pale skirt or dark hair, anything to stop her leaving. There was a sharp, burning sting in her hand, making her cry out, and then the apparition was gone. 'No. No! Why would she go? Why leave me again? *Mother!*'

Tears began to well up, and abruptly the stimulant's potency was over. The abyss of her exhaustion began to yawn at her feet – she didn't have more than a few minutes.

Tiberius reached her side. 'Edrea, what are you doing awake? You're exhausted, you should– You're bleeding!'

She looked down at her hand, numb, and saw her finger was gashed open. Mechanically, she drew it to her mouth and sucked away the blood, revealing a small puncture. The spirit – *her mother* – had drawn her blood, too. Had marked her.

'Did she scratch you?' she demanded with the last of her willpower. 'Uncle? Did she?' Wordlessly, Tiberius showed her the back of his hand. 'All of us, then. All of us to bring her home.' She licked away the welling blood again and then hid her hand in her pocket when Aaric and Runar came in. 'Now, please, which book?'

'What?'

Edrea sighed. 'My mother's spirit guided you here, likely to the forbidden shelves. She has guided each of us to something vital to the ritual – Runar the claw and the locket, Father the perfume bottle, you a book, and me to the painting to put it all together. So, which book?' His glance flicked over her head, and she knew he was silently asking Aaric for permission. 'It's very likely I can work it out for myself, but this would at least make things quicker. Please, Uncle. There's nothing either of you can do to stop me, so you may as well just tell me.'

It wasn't strictly true – all they needed to do was wait and she'd be unconscious in a matter of minutes. And… Runar knew that. She threw him an anxious glance, but there was no subterfuge in the sharpshooter's face. A protracted whine began in her ears, and below it, almost masked, she thought she heard the voice again. The hungry, smoky chanting. She waited for her mother to reappear.

'Uncle,' she managed as a wave of dizziness crashed over her. She held herself carefully upright, breathing slowly. 'Which book?'

'Tiberius, as soon as the sun rises, I want you to perform a cleansing of the castle,' Aaric said abruptly. 'I want all foul and invasive spirits and entities banished and new talismans put on every window and door. Stronger ones. Then–'

Edrea's dizziness rolled over her again, and she was suddenly kneeling on the rug before the bookshelves, her still-bleeding hand down to steady herself.

'She took a stimulant,' Runar said quickly. 'It's wearing off, that's all.'

'The shade bit her before fleeing, Aaric. She's bleeding,' Tiberius added, and even as Edrea was falling into unconsciousness, she heard her father's panicked denial.

'Bit her, when the rest of us were merely scratched?' Aaric sounded strangely terrified. 'No. Please, Sigmar, please not her, too.'

'What?' she tried to ask, but only a hoarse croak made its way out of the sudden dryness of her throat. All the places she'd drawn her magic from – the cuts on her arm, her blistered finger, the inside of her mouth and most of all her head and chest, seat of will and spirit – were aching, a fierce pulling as the magic toll began to be paid.

Hands slid under her shoulders as Edrea toppled forward, both craving and fearing sleep. She looked up, vision blurred, and saw Runar's worried face as he cradled her. She had time to wonder why, out of the three of them, he was the one holding her. Behind him, Tiberius picked up a book and handed it to Aaric. She squinted, trying to make out the cover or the title, but there was no stopping her slide into sleep. The cover was faded blue, possibly leather, but she could see no more.

Why is he scared of you, Mother? Edrea thought, the small puncture wound on her finger beginning to ache in time with the rest, as if it, too, was connected to magic. It was her last coherent thought.

She could hear the voice again, barely there but closer, somehow. Which made no sense. Heard it not through the ears but the skin, or the blood. As if it was inside her. Edrea tried to move, to open her eyes or call out, but nothing happened. *Oh*, she realised, *I'm asleep.*

But it didn't feel like a dream; it felt very, very real. Her body was trapped in the heavy, suffocating immobility that only came with the debt that followed prolonged magic use, but her mind, which was usually just as fatigued, was wide awake. Edrea had no sense of where her body was or what she was lying on. No sense of the physical, the *real*. And yet this, too, felt real. Painfully so.

She knew her father would have had her moved to her room, and Young Aethelwych would be watching over her. Uncle Tiberius would probably have forced some water or cold tea into her, and they would continue to do so every few hours until she woke. They'd been through this before, and, no doubt, Aaric would have dealt with similar crashes with Hephzibah. They had this in common, Edrea and her mother: a commitment to magic and truth and ritual that would quite literally leave them drained to the point of unconsciousness.

In the past, when she'd overtaxed herself, she'd been truly unconscious, whereas now she was paralysed but awake. It was new, different and deeply unpleasant, because no matter how much she trusted the others to watch over her, she didn't – couldn't – know for sure that she was safe. Her physical form was a distant, unknowable thing that she couldn't reach. Cut off.

And the voice, low and melodious and somewhere inside her, as if her very bones were singing. As if she was made of music. Its beauty frightened her, and so she did what she did best – she fought it.

Hello? she asked, feeling faintly ridiculous. The haunting chant didn't change, but Edrea could suddenly see. Not with her eyes – her body remained unresponsive – but images began to assault her, confused and rapid and frightening, as if her question had solidified some link between her and the singer.

One after the other, the pictures tore at her. The beast. Runar, bleeding. Her bitten hand. The locket. The painting. The beast again. A blue-covered book. A distant, blurry figure with billowing dark hair. *Mother?* The perfume bottle.

Emotions accompanied the images – fear and pain and frustration, rage and a terrible, red-edged hunger – battering Edrea's mind as it lay trapped and helpless in the prison of her body. She wondered whether there were any physical signs of her distress, whether anyone would notice and perhaps try to wake her. Whether they'd succeed. Whether she wanted them to.

Mother? Hephzibah Gothghul? Please, Mother, answer me!

Her mother's spirit had fled each time she'd drawn near to it, merely showing her the painting and then moving on to visit Father and Uncle Tiberius. Only Runar had spoken of hearing a voice loud enough to be called such, and only in the study, in the dying moments of Edrea's consciousness, had Hephzibah interacted with her, allowing her daughter to step into the sphere of her influence where she had... drawn blood and fled once more. Hephzibah had drawn blood from all of them.

She's blood-locked to us now, she realised, but while that made sense in the context of the other three, she didn't understand why her own mother would need an extra layer of connection to Edrea herself. The images assailed her once again, and again they were accompanied by fear and confusion and a ravenous, gnawing hunger that ripped at her. *Mother? Talk to me, please. Tell me what you need, what the message is that you and the beast have for me. Or... anything. Tell me anything. Everything. Let me know you, at least a little. At least give me that.*

Please give me that.

The emptiness was silent, even the dark chanting fading, the images falling away to be replaced with... Edrea didn't have words for where, or what, or who she was as she was battered from all angles, all her senses attacked at once and her mind twisting like a bird in flight, desperate to escape the eagle's talons.

Teeth and blood and screams were the only common theme in each momentary place she fell into before she was wrenched away to the next, and the next, and the next, all played out against a backdrop that was both everything and nothing at once, enough to sear pain through her mind as she tried and failed to comprehend it. Faces that were human, faces that had never been human and things that should never have been born gibbered at her, tearing at her consciousness, trying to eat their way inside and possess her. Daemons, gods, a premonition of a future when Chaos infiltrated the Hollow... Edrea didn't know. Tried to close her mind to knowing.

Mother? Please?

A thousand malformed spirits screamed her words back at her, cackling and jeering until their mockery flayed her open.

She was seeing the raw, untamed spaces between the realms, perhaps, or the heart of Chaos itself, and all the horrors such places spawned. Creation and destruction and the horrible mangling of both together in an endless howl of frantic entropy.

Was she screaming? She should be screaming.

A hand, so bitterly cold that it froze her flesh, gripped her wrist. Agony lanced through her arm and a web of frost, blue and black, grew across her skin. Her sight fizzed and went black. She couldn't see what was holding her. She *couldn't see.*

'Demand the truth. Demand the tale of your birth. The tale of the Fourth.'

The voice chimed like bells and smoked like brimstone, imperious and savage, as hard as the hand crushing her flesh.

Edrea strained her senses, but there was just more of the same nothingness and everythingness and wrongness. The quiet sobs of the damned, the enraged wails of the desperate and the maniacal cackling of the mad.

The hand released her, fingers tracing lines of ice so cold they burnt up to her elbow, and Edrea began to fray beneath the onslaught of sounds and sensations, strands of her soul fluttering free like a wind-torn flag. Terror piled on panic piled on hurt and there was no way out, no way back. She was trapped.

The sorceress screamed – silently.

'The Fourth. Ask about the Fourth. And the place of shadows – the death-place.'

CHAPTER SIX

Dawn had been only a few hours away when Edrea was finally settled to Aaric's satisfaction, and he had set Young Aethelwych to watch over her and Runar, who once more took the chaise longue in her room.

Runar had pulled the blanket up over his ear, and, despite the strangeness and the fear of all that had happened – and the constant, ever-present bite of grief for Aldo, Karl, Einar and Moll – he had slept deeply and well, his rifle tucked in his arms like a child. His rest was better than Edrea's, it seemed, who despite lying as still as the once quiet dead, had spent the last five hours whimpering and breathing too fast.

'Nightmares,' Young Aethelwych had told Runar when he woke and saw Edrea, sweat sheening her brow. 'Been like it all night, but she hasn't stirred, not properly.' The housekeeper paused, biting her lip. 'She's not normally like this, though, sir,' she added quietly. 'I've sat with her when she's overtaxed herself before, and she just slept, didn't move, didn't make a sound.

This is more like a fever. My mother, Old Aethelwych – Nagash rest her – watched over Lady Hephzibah when I was a lass, and she never told me anything like this happened either. Least not till that last night. Oh, but we're not to talk of that, Lord Gothghul's orders.' She glanced nervously towards the door.

Runar grunted.

'Right to-do though, isn't it?' Young Aethelwych continued. 'All those dead – oh, I am sorry,' she added, as if belatedly remembering that four of the dead were his.

'I'll watch her. You get off to bed now, and if you could have tea and toast sent up, maybe some eggs and fruit, I'd be obliged.'

The housekeeper hesitated. 'Is it... appropriate?' she asked.

Runar gusted a sigh. 'I got torn almost to pieces by a beast bigger than you just yesterday, so I'm in no state to do anything at all, appropriate or not. I'm also trusted by both Mister Grim and Lord Gothghul, but leave the door open when you leave, or send someone else up to watch her, I don't care. Just... breakfast, please.'

Young Aethelwych blushed and nodded, then bustled out.

When they were alone again, open door be damned, Runar shambled across the room, took Edrea's hand and reiterated his promise that he'd take her away if she still wanted that, once this was over and she was awake. It didn't seem to soothe her troubled sleep, and her face was waxy and too pale, dark hollows beneath her eyes and the usual glossy sheen missing from her dark curls. The skin was stretched tight across the bones of her skull, as if she was already dead. He shook off the image.

He was awed and a little afraid at how hard she'd pushed herself, how at no point had she seemed to pause to consider the cost of what she attempted. It was reckless and yet calculated, and he respected it. That respect did nothing to lessen his worry for her.

In the stillness of early morning, in her own stillness, he could see the resemblance – both with the paintings of her mother and with the faint, delicate outline of the spirit in its pale clothes and pale skin and dark sweep of hair. Small and yet fierce, like a hawk.

Runar sent for more tea and then dripped water over Edrea's lips, a little at a time. She swallowed but didn't otherwise react. He murmured to her in his rough voice more used to shouting orders or bantering with soldiers, the gentleness strange upon his tongue. But fitting.

He didn't do her the discourtesy of thinking she needed tenderness because of her title as Lady Gothghul; he just used the same voice he'd used with Einar as he lay dying, though he prayed to all the gods that Edrea's life would not be similarly cut short. All that potential wasted.

He took the beast's claw back out of his pocket and examined it. The flesh clinging to the bone was beginning to turn, a smell rising from it. Carefully, he pared it away into a bowl until he could snap the tendons holding the toe joint together, leaving just the end knuckle with the claw growing out of it. He rummaged through Edrea's shelves until he found an acid he knew and melted the last of the skin, fur and muscle from the claw until it was pristine – white bone, black talon.

He put the mess of flesh and acid on the breakfast tray and warned the servant to dispose of it carefully, then swung open the windows to clear the stink from the room. Edrea hadn't stirred even as the soup of meat and chemical bubbled and steamed into the air – he'd have been impressed at the strength of her stomach if it hadn't reinforced how deeply fatigued she must be.

Stripped, the claw was beautiful in its elegant lethality, and he considered, idly, keeping it as a trophy once this was all done, though Edrea had spoken of some spellcraft that she needed it for. Still, if it remained intact in the aftermath... The beast had nearly killed him – and had killed his squad – after all. Surely

Mister Grim could fashion a powerful protection amulet from such an artefact.

Runar stretched and paced, testing the limits of his injuries and the constriction of the bandages still wrapping much of his body. His hands were the most affected, punctured and torn by the beast's teeth, making his movements clumsy and his grip weak. It had taken everything he had to control his rifle the night before. After that abuse, they were even more swollen, the flesh puckering and pulling around the stitches, and the side of his face was hot and puffy where a fang had nearly taken out his eye. He drank more of Edrea's remedy, wincing only a little at the bitterness. Soon enough he felt the aches dissipate, and the weariness in his limbs faded. His wounds began to itch. Would the remedy help Edrea?

He rang the bell for a servant and left her with another woman, this one prone to fluttering and chattering, then went to find Tiberius and Aaric. They were in the library, hunching over the book that Tiberius had indicated just before Edrea fell unconscious. He knocked and then entered, pretending not to hear the furiously whispered argument he was interrupting.

'My lord, Mister Grim, forgive my intrusion. I thought one of you might know whether Miss Gothghul's medicinal potion could perhaps be diluted and used to help her?'

He held up the nearly empty jar. It had perhaps two doses left, both meant for him, but he'd happily forego one or both to see Edrea come out of her faint. He had a feeling they'd be needing her unique skills more than his sooner or later.

Tiberius hesitated and then ran his hands across his face. His palms rasped against stubble, and he looked as tired as Aaric, his normally impeccable hair loose so that strands of silver curled at his brow and nape. Runar wondered whether either of them had returned to sleep after all the commotion.

'Well, it wouldn't hurt, but I'm not sure how much help it

would be either. She's exhausted rather than injured. Rest is the best thing for her, and that remedy was made for you and your encounter with a supernatural entity. No doubt she'll have tailored it to target curses or undead attacks.'

Runar nodded and eased himself down into a chair. 'Very well. Then may I know our next move?'

Again, the two older men exchanged glances. 'We were just discussing that,' Aaric said eventually, stiffly. 'We have not yet come to a decision.'

'Miss Gothghul is of the opinion that the spirit of her mother and the beast are somehow… trying to convey the same message.'

'It isn't Hephzibah,' Aaric said yet again. Runar made a non-committal noise but didn't refute him. If he needed to believe that in order to reconcile himself to the fact that Tiberius was going to exorcise the shade from the castle, and that they might need to take more drastic action to destroy it entirely, then the sharpshooter wouldn't deny him the comfort.

'With regard to the message itself, though,' he tried, 'do you believe the same? That the beast and the apparition are trying to tell us – tell Miss Gothghul – something? And if so, what steps can we take to learn what that message is?'

'Tiberius is about to start the cleansing. Once that is done, we won't need to worry.'

Runar frowned. 'You're… My lord, you plan on ignoring it? What if that forces the beast to return? Even if the castle is safe, what about the town? I no longer have my hunters, and I'm not facing it alone. Not again. I'm sorry, but–'

'We'll stand with you,' Aaric said, as if that solved everything.

Runar's gut lurched and he looked to Tiberius for aid. The old priest, the old *soldier*, looked uncomfortable. He understood. 'Then we'll die. I'm sorry, I don't doubt your ability, but neither of you has confronted that creature. It's… beyond anything I've ever faced, and my squad was the best. If we fail to understand

its message and it decides we're of no more use to it, then it's
going to tear us to pieces. You saw what it did in the Peaks.'

He winced and pushed away the images of blood and teeth
and Aldo, pleading with his eyes to be saved. 'Could we instead
allow Miss Gothghul to do what she says needs to be done?' he
ventured. 'Her knowledge, her skills, seem–'

'No.' Aaric's tone was implacable. 'She has no idea what we're
dealing with.'

'And you do? Forgive me, my lord, but if you know something, I need to know it too. You hired me to protect the town
and the castle, to protect you. I can't do that unless I have all
the facts. Please.'

Tiberius looked torn. Whatever the lord of the castle knew, he
was aware of it too. And he could see the sense in Runar's words.

The sharpshooter's eyes fell on the book again. 'Is there anything in there that will help us defeat the beast if it returns? And
can either of you wield whatever spells are required for victory?'

'What did the spirit say to Edrea?' Tiberius asked instead of
answering.

Runar clenched his fist on his knee and then relaxed it. Again,
he understood Edrea's frustration with the secrets that were
kept in this castle. *I half believe these men would rather die of
tight-lipped stoicism than reveal the truth of what we face.*

'I don't know,' he said instead of voicing his thoughts. 'I woke
up and she was gone. When I came to find her, she was fleeing
the ballroom in pursuit of her, of the shade. She'd already taken
the stimulant – she was manic, not making a lot of sense. She just
said that she knew it would visit Lord Gothghul next. And it did.'

'Did you pull down the drape over the portrait in the ballroom?'
Tiberius asked, but he already looked as if he knew the answer.
Runar just shook his head. 'And she took the locket from you,
Aaric. She's worked it out. Perhaps–'

'Cleanse the house,' Aaric said. He took the locket that had been around Edrea's throat out of his waistcoat and held it up to the sun streaming through the window. Runar's eyebrows lifted, and the old lord had the grace to look a little shamefaced. 'She has no idea of the power in this. She has no idea what it is she's contemplating. It's best I keep hold of it.'

'She seems extremely capable to me, my lord,' Runar said carefully. He waved one hand. 'And this... whole situation seems geared very much towards her abilities, not yours or mine. I know you're a scholar and your knowledge is vast and that Mister Grim's training in the priesthood is of huge importance, but Miss Gothghul is the one with the, ah, practical experience in harnessing Shyish's magic. She communicated with the beast, which is more than the rest of us managed. She has conceived of a ritual to learn the message.'

Aaric lurched to his feet, spots of hectic colour in an otherwise sallow face. 'I will not lose my daughter the way I lost my wife, and that is an end to it.' His voice was as cold as winter, as hard as steel. Runar flinched and nodded quickly. That avenue of conversation was firmly closed.

'Mister Grim, can I be of assistance during the cleansing?' he asked after an awkward pause. The other men were waiting for him to leave in order to continue their whispered argument, but Runar had been hired to defend the castle and that gave him a measure of authority, regardless of whether Aaric liked it – which he did not.

'Ah, yes, if you don't mind carrying supplies for me. There's not much you can do practically.'

'That's fine,' Runar said, and stood up expectantly. Tiberius exchanged another glance with Aaric and then closed the book and slid it back onto a shelf. He made a complicated gesture and there was a pop, and a ripple of light, like oil on water, flashed across the shelf. The sharpshooter assumed that was the prayer-binding that prevented Edrea from accessing her mother's works. He barely managed to repress a snort – he didn't think the sorceress would be in any danger from whatever was contained therein.

'I want this place scoured,' Aaric said, and his tone brooked no dissent. Tiberius nodded, and Runar followed him out and into the kitchen in silence. On the table were packets of herbs and other ritual items: metal shavings in a glass jar; pieces of blood-dipped wood; symbols carved and painted onto the bones of lizards, snakes, bats and owls; and a stoppered clay vessel. Runar gathered them all onto a tray and then buttoned his jacket, checked that his revolver and knives were secure and followed Tiberius out of the house. He'd been delighted to have the weapon restored to him that morning, having feared it lost with his prized sunsteel rifle up on the Peaks.

'And this will prevent the beast getting inside, will it?' he asked, shivering as the air cut at him.

'No.'

'But it will stop the shade from returning?'

'Theoretically.'

'And if it's still in the house?' he persisted.

Tiberius sighed, the white plume of his breath ripped away by the wind. 'Then we'll trap it in there with us if we do it wrong.'

Runar was quiet for a few seconds. 'And is that Aaric's plan? To trap the spirit of his wife in the castle with him? Some sort of reunion?'

'It's not his wife,' Tiberius said, and Runar snorted.

'You too? Fine, if you say so. It doesn't sound to me as if you much believe in this cleansing though, Mister Grim.'

'Fortunately, as a priest of Sigmar I've done this hundreds of times, and so I'm confident that it won't get trapped. Instead, we'll force it out of the last available exit and it won't be able to get back in. Besides, Aaric is... dealing with a lot. If this brings him a measure of peace, I will not begrudge him that. Now, I need silence for the next while.'

They had reached what was Hephzibah's old herb garden, which Edrea had taken control of as a girl. It was laid out in a complicated design that itself conjured magic into the herb beds, increasing their potency. The garden was bordered with a tall hedge of witch elm that obscured the black stone of the castle walls. Statues peered from among the twisted boughs: grinning skeletons and indistinct gheists, Nagash and Sigmar, and a delicately carved figure that might even have been Hephzibah herself, although, inexplicably, the statue's head had been smashed in.

Runar studied it, shivering, as the priest wove his long, thin fingers over the items on the tray, muttering under his breath. The wind whipped at Tiberius' steel-grey hair until he took on a slightly deranged appearance. Runar checked their surroundings again, for danger this time. Edrea's potion had loosened the stiffness of abused muscles and torn flesh, muting the sharp clamour of pain into an incessant whisper he could ignore. The herbary was windswept but otherwise empty. No glowing red eyes watched them from the tops of the walls or the depths of the shadows. No pale gheist drifted among the witch elms. He started at a whirl of leaves that scampered past, the items on the tray rattling slightly as his hand flinched towards his holster.

When he glanced back up, Tiberius was watching him with understanding and a little sympathy. 'Are you all right?' he asked softly.

Runar blew out his breath and relaxed his grip on the tray. 'I am. Apologies for distracting you.'

'It's fine. You don't have to accompany me.'

'Of course I do. Capable as you are, sir, I'm not having you wandering around out here alone when we have no real idea what we're dealing with. Or I don't, anyway,' he added pointedly. Tiberius grimaced. 'Mister Grim, please. We've known each other for years. I've saved your life, you've prayed over me when I was nearly dead. Since the Necroquake, you've called on me more and more – that has to mean you trust me. Tell me what I need to know to keep you all safe. Please.'

'The... story isn't mine.'

'But the death might be. Or it might be Edrea's. And I can promise you now that I'm not going to let that happen. But it'd be far easier to protect her if I knew what I was facing.'

'These items are charged now. Let's begin the cleansing.' Runar didn't move. Tiberius scrubbed his hands over his face, crazing his eyebrows to match his hair. 'Let's cleanse the house. By the time we're done, Edrea may have woken. If she has, it may be that the story gets told anyway. I don't think that young woman is prepared to wait any longer for the truth of her origins.'

'Origins?' Runar demanded as he hurried after Tiberius.

The priest waved away his question. 'Not my place to say,' he said. 'I have a part in it, but I'm not at the heart. I'll say no more.'

And he wouldn't. Runar trailed him in frustrated silence as Tiberius methodically visited every door and ground-floor window, where he muttered a lengthy invocation and tied a tiny bundle of metal, wood, bones and herbs to the latch and dripped a single drop of liquid from the clay vessel upon the whole. Each time he did so, the hairs stood up on the back of Runar's neck. He'd been around some crude displays of magic during his career, but still it left a greasy taste in his mouth and a faint ache behind his eyes. By the time they'd circled back around to the front door and completed the first layer of protection, his wounds were aching and his throat was dry and scratchy with thirst.

Tiberius didn't seem much better, his voice a rasp as they moved inside and up to the first floor to repeat the process on the windows there. 'The aim is to drive anything inside up and up and eventually out – we'll open one of the windows in the dome. Like steam out of a narrow-necked flask, there will be nowhere for it to go but through that exit. And then we seal that last window and the castle is safe. Clean. Protected.'

Runar didn't respond, instead balancing the tray on his left hand and letting his right find the comforting smoothness of his revolver's grip. He didn't doubt the priest's abilities, but the shade had been different enough from other Nighthaunt that he worried this standard ritual wouldn't work on it. And that it would do nothing at all if the beast returned.

His hand lingered on the gun as he followed Tiberius from room to room, ignoring the old man in favour of checking the angles and corners of rooms, the shadows and the gaps behind doors and between furniture. A creeping uneasiness grew beneath his skin as the sun climbed towards noon and Tiberius' voice became more and more hoarse. The ache behind Runar's eyes blossomed into pain.

'I feel,' he began when he couldn't stand it any longer, 'I need another dose of Miss Gothghul's remedy.'

'It's not physical,' Tiberius said, a thread of something in his voice. He paused and glanced back, and Runar saw both strain and anxiety in his face. 'The gheist is here in the castle. It's fighting back. Stick with me and we'll drive it out. Can you?'

Runar took a deep breath and nodded. 'Absolutely. Anything you need.'

He stayed close behind Tiberius after that, murmuring encouragement as the old man slowed, his chest heaving as he poured more and more of himself into the cleansing.

Eventually they reached the top floor – the family floor – and Edrea's room. It was well into the afternoon and she was still sleeping, sheened with sweat, eyes dancing beneath their lids. But when Tiberius' muttering was complete and the charm was hanging from her window, she seemed calmer. Aaric was with her, and Runar clearly heard his sigh of relief as she relaxed down into her bed. He dripped water into her mouth, and for the first time she seemed to respond, lips parting for more. The room's charged atmosphere seeped away, replaced with a father's overwhelming relief at the safety and health of his child. If only Edrea was awake to experience it.

Lord Gothghul smiled at them both as they exited, and Runar thought he hadn't seen an expression so light on the man's face since he'd arrived. It added a lightness to his own step and seemed to lift some of the fatigue that clawed at him.

By the time dusk was pinking the clouds to the west, Tiberius was staggering on his feet. He stood beneath the dome with Runar a few paces behind, chanting the last words of the ritual and fixing the last bundle of magic to the window latch. 'Brace,' he muttered, and Runar didn't have time to ask why before a wind tore up out of nowhere, out of the castle's very depths. A scream rode its back and the wind had claws, ripping at exposed skin and tearing out hair, shredding the sharpshooter's shirt. He grabbed for Tiberius to pull the old man into a protective embrace, but the priest was the one to tuck Runar's head against his chest. He was shouting something almost lost in the maelstrom, holding up a talisman.

Runar got a hand to the amulets at his neck and the other on his gun, but then yelped – the amulets were so cold they burnt against his fingers, and he had to rip them out of his collar before they froze the skin of his chest.

'Don't drop them!' Tiberius bellowed. 'Whatever you do, don't let go of them.' His own hand was white-knuckled on the talisman, which was coated in a thick hoar frost. His breath steamed in the frigid air.

A particularly violent gust sent them both staggering into the banister encircling the atrium, and Runar wound one arm through the iron railing and the other around Tiberius' chest. He had to let go of the amulets, but it was that or they both fell.

The Nighthaunt screamed in triumph and battered at his face, seeking an entrance via eyes or nose or mouth. The priest shouted again and then pressed the talisman to Runar's crown.

The sharpshooter screeched in pain, turning his face into Tiberius' chest to deny the spirit entry. It scrabbled at his back, ripping long gouges through his clothes and skin, but the talisman was powerful and eventually it vanished through the opening above them with a final shriek of rage. The priest hooked the window shut with a loud slam, and stillness fell in the castle.

'Shit. Sigmar's arse, that was close.' Runar realised he was still pinning the priest between himself and the railing. 'Sorry,' he muttered, and forced himself to let go. 'Is that it?' The grey, sweat-soaked head huffed a laugh and nodded. 'Then let's sit you down before you fall down. Come on, right here, just catch your breath.'

Runar took off his coat and wrapped it over Tiberius' shoulders as he sat at the head of the long staircase winding down the four flights from the attics to the ground floor. He took a flask from his pocket and unscrewed the lid. 'Brandy,' he said gruffly, and passed it over. Tiberius' hand shook but managed to get the flask to his lips for a swig, then a second, longer swallow followed by a gasp as the liquor burnt down his throat.

Runar reclaimed the brandy and took a sip himself. They'd been working all day without rest, without food or even water. The liquor was a welcome warmth, but more than a few sips and they'd be asleep. They sat slumped in silence, exhaustion pooling through Runar's limbs and reawakening the fire in his wounds. He'd missed his doses of the magical remedy. He'd ignored Edrea's advice about resting. It didn't matter. Besides, Tiberius must be twice as exhausted – and was twice his age.

But the castle was cleansed. More than that, it *felt* cleansed. It felt safe, and Runar didn't realise how much he'd craved that since his arrival – and how much it had been missing these last weeks even when they weren't out on the moors tracking an impossible monster that vanished into thin air.

'Thank Sigmar,' he muttered, 'and thank cantankerous old priests even more.'

Tiberius managed a croaky laugh, one that cut off abruptly when they heard footsteps on the final staircase up to where they sat. It was Young Aethelwych.

'Lady Gothghul extends her thanks for your efforts in cleansing the castle,' she said. 'As soon as you are ready, please join her and the lord in the library. Refreshments will be provided.'

'Ah, so Edrea is awake,' Runar muttered.

Tiberius groaned. 'And judging from the phrasing, she's angry.' He put his hands on his knees to help him stand, then didn't move. 'I've faced all manner of creatures and enemies during my life,' he added, as if to himself. 'I can face the wrath of one determined young woman.'

Runar opened his mouth to scoff and felt the dryness of thirst and fatigue scratch at him again. He said nothing, and they sat in silence until the clock, so far below in the entrance hall, chimed the half hour. And then another quarter.

The sharpshooter sighed. 'Got any charms against Miss Goth-ghul?' he asked, and Tiberius gave him another tired smile but accepted the hand he offered to haul him to his feet.

'If I did, I'd keep them all for myself,' he sighed. 'Let's go.'

They made their way down the stairs, flight after flight until Runar was dizzy, and eventually to the ground floor and into the library, bright with lanterns and a hearth fire that cut through the gathering chill, savoury with the scents of wood smoke and dinner. Edrea and Lord Gothghul were sitting opposite each other in front of the fire. Edrea was pale, but her eyes glittered. Aaric looked, if possible, even more tired than his daughter.

'Uncle. Runar,' she said softly. 'Please, eat and drink before we begin.' Aaric's mouth turned down and he made a low, grumbling sound in his throat, but he didn't contradict her. Edrea gestured, and they saw that one of the tables had been set for dinner.

Runar's stomach made its presence known, and both men hurried to sit, uncovering plates heaped high with meat, potatoes, root vegetables. His mouth watered, but he poured a cup of water and a glass of wine for them both and downed the first in one, moistening his throat. There was a basket of warm bread and a dish of butter. He slathered the latter onto the former, dipped it into gravy and began to eat.

When the initial edge of his hunger had been blunted, Runar pulled the copper jar of remedy out of his pocket and sipped, washing it down with a deep red wine that tasted of summer and sunlight. He put the jar away and buttered another slice of bread, balancing it on the edge of his plate as he attacked the pork and parsnips and carrots.

Slowly, the food and medicine worked on him and the headache vanished, taking some of his tiredness with it. 'This potion is a marvel, Miss Gothghul,' he said without thinking. 'I can't thank you enough.'

He looked up and she met his gaze. The line between her brows smoothed out and took with it the brittle intensity of her expression, softening her edges. 'I'm glad,' she said in a low voice.

'There's still a dose left if you'd like it,' he offered, starting to get up.

She waved him away. 'No need. Sleep and food of my own have done much to restore my energy. Please, finish your meal.'

Runar glanced at Tiberius and found him looking slightly pained. A moment later he understood why; father and daughter were both now watching them eat, the weight of their gazes a physical pressure on their skins. Aaric's fingers beat a slow tattoo on the arm of his chair, his expression stony.

Runar managed half a dozen further mouthfuls but then couldn't stand it any longer. Regretfully, he put down his knife and fork and leant back in his chair.

Tiberius poured them both more water and wine, and the sharpshooter returned the favour by buttering them both some more bread – he could eat that even with Edrea's black, intense gaze focused on him. He put the slice in his mouth, picked up cup and glass, and slid from behind the table into the slightly more comfortable chair set near the fire – between Edrea and her father. Tiberius took the other.

'The cleansing felt thorough,' Edrea said as soon as they were settled, feet stretched towards the fire. 'Something was definitely forced out. My mother's shade, I assume.'

'It's not your mother,' Aaric said automatically, and then flushed and looked at his hands, fingers knotted together in his lap.

Edrea took a deep breath. 'About that,' she said quietly. 'I'm curious as to why you're so very sure it isn't her. So I'd appreciate it if you'd tell me the truth about my birth.'

Aaric looked up. 'Truth?'

'Yes,' she said, calm and self-possessed. 'Tell me about the Fourth.'

PART THREE
THE LIES

CHAPTER SEVEN

There was a long, pregnant silence, and Edrea watched her father and Tiberius hold a silent conversation.

'What do you mean, the Fourth?' Tiberius asked eventually.

Edrea didn't look at him, didn't take her eyes off her father's face. 'The Fourth was at my birth. Who, or what, was it?'

'I don't know what you mean,' Aaric tried, but she could hear tension wound tight as a spring in his tone.

Edrea let one corner of her mouth turn up in mockery. 'Yes, you do. Tell me of the Fourth.'

'You were the Fourth, obviously,' Tiberius tried. 'Me, your parents and you.'

Edrea slammed her palm down on the arm of her chair. 'Enough games!' she snarled, and Runar, sitting next to her, jerked in his seat and then sat up straight. She could feel his wariness as he used his body as a shield between her anger and the others – and perhaps he was right to try and protect them. She felt almost wild with the force of her need to know the truth. 'Tell me who it was. What they wanted. What they did.'

'Edrea, please be calm,' Tiberius said. 'This has been difficult for all of us. What makes you think—'

'Mother told me. While I slept,' she interrupted. 'Before you drove her out.'

'It's not your mother,' Aaric said, and Edrea threw up her hands and jumped to her feet. Runar stood too, reaching out and placing a gentle hand on her arm. Not restraining her, just urging caution.

'Why do you keep saying that?' she shrieked, restraint be damned.

Aaric leapt up, too. 'Because she isn't dead!' he roared back with equal intensity, equal rage and despair and grief.

The library fell still and very silent, as if even the fire was holding its breath. Edrea and her father were toe to toe, eye to eye, the air between them twisting, tightening. Sound slowly returned to her: the crackle of the logs; Aaric's harsh panting; the rustle of silk cushions as Tiberius tipped his head back and closed his eyes.

Slowly, her legs barely under her control, Edrea lowered herself back into her chair. 'What?' Her voice was a croak, a dead thing tumbling from her mouth. Runar sat again too, but not Aaric. Her father turned around, braced his forearm against the mantelpiece and dropped his head onto it.

'Zib... didn't die after your birth.'

There were tears threatening now, but she blinked them back, savage. 'You said... Ever since I was young enough to ask... you said she died.' The words came out with strange stutters and stops, outside of her control. Jagged, bitten-off phrases.

'It was easier than the truth,' Tiberius said softly.

Edrea faced him. 'You,' she said quietly. 'Not another word. I will have that truth, and I will have it from *him*.' Her finger stabbed towards her father's back. 'So the Fourth person, whoever it was, took her away?'

A laugh, bitter as poison, cracked from Aaric's chest. 'In a way, yes, that's exactly what happened.'

Edrea realised he was crying, silent sobs shaking his form, his face hidden in the crook of his elbow. Something unfamiliar surged in her then, and it took her a moment to identify it. She'd spent so much of her adult life angry with Aaric that this thing – this love – felt alien. But all-consuming. She got up and crossed to the fireplace, close enough that her legs prickled at the heat and her trousers were in danger of catching light, but she put her hand on her father's back, and he turned and buried his face against her neck, his arms crushing her tight, squeezing a shocked gasp out of her. Tears fell on her skin.

'I'm so sorry,' he sobbed, just as she said the same words to him. They clung to each other, and Edrea couldn't remember the last time she'd felt his embrace, or the last time she'd craved it so badly. It was warm, it was familiar – if smaller than she remembered; had she grown? Had he shrunk? – and it fixed a hole in Edrea's chest that she hadn't known was there until now. She still needed – wanted, *demanded* – answers, but she needed this too. Just for a moment. Just a little while.

'Will you tell me now?' she whispered after long minutes. 'Will you tell me all of it? For both our sakes?'

Aaric pulled back, finally, and scrubbed his sleeve over his face. His old eyes were red-rimmed. 'I will.' He looked around the room. 'We will. Though there is a lot to tell.'

'Then start at the beginning,' Edrea said, guiding him back to his chair and then pulling her own a little closer.

'I should go,' Runar said, pushing up onto his feet.

'No,' Tiberius and Aaric said at the same time. 'No,' the priest repeated. 'Whatever's coming for us, coming for the Hollow or all of Shyish, maybe, you need to know about it. You're under oath and under contract to protect this family – to protect Edrea. Stay.'

Runar looked at her, and she reached over to squeeze his forearm. 'Please. For me.' He nodded, perhaps a little awkwardly, and sank back into his seat.

Aaric rose and crossed to the table, returning with the wine bottle. He poured them each a measure. He sat and sipped, then sighed. 'Start at the beginning? Where's that? Long before your birth, I suspect.'

He looked at Tiberius, who nodded. 'With the words.'

Aaric sighed again. 'Yes. It starts with the words. Everything starts with the words in the book.'

Gothghul Castle, twenty-six years ago

'Hephzibah? Zib?'

Hephzibah's head jerked up, hair tumbling to fall over one eye. 'Stay where you are!'

Aaric halted, knee-deep in heather, and Hephzibah spun and then released the magic out into the moor in the opposite direction. It blasted out of her, a purple-edged flare that limned every leaf and twig and branch and blade of grass. In its aftermath, the shrubbery sparkled – and then grew. Taller, faster, gorse spines getting longer, sharper, curling wickedly towards the Gothghuls. Reaching for them.

'Back up,' she called, feeling backwards across the springy ground with her boots. The shrubs were shoulder height already.

'Zib?'

'Should be fine, my love. Just another few seconds.' She projected confidence into her voice, but the spellcraft cut in her arm was throbbing, as were her temples. Aaric's interruption had broken her focus at the last second and the spell had sucked out more energy than she'd been prepared to give, powering the magic into something far larger than she'd planned for.

And yet, as predicted – as hoped – the growth slowed and

then, eventually, stopped. Gorse, heather and grass stood higher than their heads, the usual pale amethyst darkened to violet and indigo and edged in black. Something chittered within.

'Oh,' she murmured, and drew the rapier at her hip.

'Zibby,' Aaric said plaintively as he unslung his rifle. She could hear the long-suffering pout in his voice.

'Shouldn't have disturbed me then,' she replied tartly, not taking her eyes off the monstrous tangle of vegetation. She heard him cock the rifle and a warm rush of love swept through her. That one use of her name was his only complaint, and then – as always – he was there at her side, standing ready to face down whatever was coming for them.

Hephzibah couldn't help the grin that tugged at her mouth. 'We might be lucky,' she murmured as the overgrown shrubs began suddenly, visibly, to wither. The chittering got louder, more frantic, and the thick stand of grass shivered. A gorse-rat, charcoal-furred and thigh-high to Hephzibah, ran at them with a hungry squeal, its bald grey tail lashing and yellow incisors dripping foam. 'Or not.'

Hephzibah lunged and thrust at the same time that Aaric's rifle kicked. Bullet and blade went into the oversized creature and it squealed again, thrashing. As it stilled, its flesh began to fall in on itself as muscle wasted. Its fur paled and thinned, and a tooth fell from its gaping mouth. Film covered its eyes, and behind it, the giant shrubs continued to age and shed and die and rot – all in the space of a few minutes.

They waited until there was nothing but a rotten slurry of slime and bone before putting away their weapons.

'Well,' Aaric said, his tone equal parts exasperation and amusement, 'do I even want to know what you were trying to do?'

'Speed up plant growth,' she said absently, already scribbling notes in her journal.

'Congratulations. You definitely did that.'

She gave her husband a narrow-eyed stare. He was laughing at her. 'If *someone* hadn't interrupted at the crucial moment, it might have actually worked this time. As it is, I've wasted a week's worth of preparations and a lot of energy.'

Aaric limped closer and ran a gentle thumb across the cuts on the back of her forearm. 'I'm sorry,' he said, brushing her hair back and kissing her temple. 'I'd been standing there for ten minutes while you just stared through me – I was getting worried something had gone wrong. You've been using a lot of magic lately. Yes, I know you know your limits, and no, I'm not trying to stop you,' he added as she glared again. 'But surely I'm allowed to worry? Cultists have been sighted on the moors, and with you focusing so intensely, they could walk straight up to you and cut you down and you wouldn't even notice.'

Hephzibah shrugged. 'I have wards in place against strangers. And yes, of course you're allowed to worry. Not that that'll stop me. Lord-commander of the Blackshore Guard. Hero of the Bone-splinter War. How is your leg, by the way?' she added with sweet malice, and laughed when he began to splutter.

He had broken his leg in three places and punctured a lung in battle. The company's healers had done their best, but he was looking at months of convalescence.

'I'm simply pointing out that your own occupation isn't without risk, my darling. And besides, this is all your fault. If not for that conversation you and Tiberius had last time he was here about quick-growing rations for soldiers, I wouldn't be out here turning gorse-rats into, into...' She waved her stick of charcoal.

'Really big gorse-rats?'

Hephzibah swatted him, and he drew her against his chest, laughing. 'You know how much I appreciate your work, my love. If anyone can do it, you can. If anyone can change this realm for the better – all the realms – it's you, Zib.'

She felt herself blush and ducked her head against his chest. 'Flatterer,' she said softly, pleased.

'It's my job as your husband,' he answered. 'Now, are you done? With that much energy expenditure, you're going to make the cook earn her wages again, aren't you?'

Hephzibah's stomach chose that moment to growl, and they both laughed again. Aaric took her hand and they walked together back to Gothghul Castle, stopping at the graveyard to offer prayers for the restful dead. There were signs of discontent and disturbed earth around one grave, so Hephzibah lit a corpselight that would alert the temple down in the town and spared the spirit a few drops of her blood to placate it.

Aaric's position as lord-commander and status as a war hero, combined with the vast sums of money he donated to kit out the company, afforded him the privilege of infrequent trips back home. Despite this, he still spent years away, and Hephzibah spent his absences deeper in study, in experimentation and spellcraft up on the moors of Null Island, distant enough from Lethis to go unnoticed by the Collegiate Arcane, which was exactly how she preferred it. The Collegiate had too many rules and restrictions for her liking. Hephzibah preferred her learning to be organic, growing wild and tangled, travelling as many paths as her curiosity and imagination could find. She was a collector, a magpie of magic, taking what aided her and discarding whatever held her back. She crafted her own tools and artefacts, she conducted her own experiments, and she lived wild and free, far from the Collegiate's strict rules.

Aaric had abandoned his own scholarly pursuits upon joining the Freeguild, but he left all of his vast library bar a few select tomes for Hephzibah's use. She had an incredible number of spell books, scrolls and grimoires at her disposal, and more than enough pursuits to keep herself occupied during his long absences.

After the catastrophe that was the massacre of Blood Meridian, in which two-thirds of the Blackshore Guard were annihilated by a daemonic attack, Tiberius could no longer continue within their ranks. He spent months recuperating in Gothghul Castle, keeping Hephzibah company, before returning to Lethis once a year to offer his experience and training to the next generation of warrior priests.

Every time he visited the city or travelled further afield on some secret quest of Aaric's, he would scour bookshops and magic vendors for anything that might interest Hephzibah.

It was in one of these randomly gifted books that she first came across the reference to the Fourfold Herald. The book was an old, mostly useless compendium that Tiberius had sent her during his travels near Necros, and the phrase sat alongside a confused mess of fragmentary legends, half-understood prophecies and badly written rituals.

The castle was quiet but for the wind whining around the eaves. The servants were occupied elsewhere, and Hephzibah was sitting with her feet on her desk in the library, flipping through the book and making the occasional note when she first saw the phrase, and it gave her pause. 'Aaric?'

Her husband hummed acknowledgement from the chaise longue they had moved into the room so that he could recover surrounded by his books.

'Have you ever heard of the Fourfold Herald?'

The scratching of his pen stopped. 'No, I don't think so. Why?'

Hephzibah hesitated and then slid her feet off the desk, the chair's front legs thumping down onto the rug. 'I don't know. It just feels... familiar. As if I've read it somewhere before.'

Aaric grinned. 'What's the context?' he asked, smelling a mystery.

Hephzibah snorted. 'Unclear. The rest of the book's a mess, and the spell work that it lists is incorrect. If someone used this to attempt to imbue a talisman with movement, they'd likely end up imprisoning their own consciousness in it instead. Which... could be interesting, if it could be bound so that the effect was temporary.' She paused to scribble herself a brief note while Aaric waited, a fondly exasperated smiled on his face. 'But this,' she added, and her finger tapped the faded writing, 'there's something about it. I know this. Or I know of it.'

Aaric sighed and leant back, a brief grimace twisting his features. 'And you're not going to be able to rest until you've worked out where you've read it before,' he said. He got up, ignoring her protests, and limped over to one of the shelves. 'Start with the library index, Zib.'

She scowled. 'That's no fun,' she protested. 'I like... roaming the shelves.'

'Roaming the shelves takes three times as long because you're as easily distracted as a kitten,' he said, handing her the thick index journal written in both their hands and listing all the books and scrolls in their collection and the main topics they covered.

'So rude,' she murmured, but without heat – it was true, after all. Aaric knew her too well. He pressed a kiss to the rumpled curls tumbling about her face, and the corner of her mouth turned up. She swatted him – gently – away. 'Now who's easily distracted? Back to your dusty tomes and your rest, husband. I have a reference to find.'

He laughed under his breath and returned to the chaise longue with a relieved groan, propping up his leg on a pile of cushions. The library fell into companionable silence but for the riffle of pages and the scratch of pens. And, increasingly, Hephzibah's sighs of frustration. None of the topics listed a 'Fourfold Herald', meaning it wasn't the main theme of anything in their collection. Perhaps she'd read it somewhere along the route her family had taken when fleeing the charred remains of their home town for Gothghul Hollow. It was a memory Hephzibah did not enjoy reliving, and she framed it now exclusively in terms of the literature she had read along the way in the few houses and libraries she had been able to visit while her parents negotiated the next stage of their journey. It was easier than remembering everything else.

Hephzibah closed her eyes and let the tantalising familiarity steal over her. It was tied to this place. If she'd read it or heard it spoken of, it was here in Gothghul Hollow. To be certain, she pricked her finger on the tip of her dagger and muttered a quick memory aid. Yes. She'd seen it written, not heard it spoken. Not necessarily within the castle, though, but definitely within the Hollow. Which was... interesting. Still, she'd start with the library; it was the most logical place. Perhaps she'd taken a book onto the moors or into town with her to while away an afternoon, and that was why the words weren't memory-linked to the castle.

They didn't have any books from Necros itself – the vampires guarded their knowledge too fiercely – so she gathered a selection of texts related to heralds in general instead. 'Where are you?' she muttered under her breath. 'Where have I seen you before?'

Aaric lasted all of an hour as Hephzibah flicked through the books, her muttering getting louder as she tapped her feet in frustration. Then he stood, quietly gathering his own research and the skull-carved walking stick, and limped into his study to work in peace. She barely noticed him leave.

It was dark by the time she'd exhausted the books featuring heralds and prophets, and even the two on divination and fortune telling. She had a headache from squinting at the pages in the fading light and the library was chilly. Hephzibah sat back with a groan, stretching out the kinks in her neck and back and massaging her temples. She knew where it wasn't but had no idea where it might be.

Hungry and tired, she wandered out of the library and to Aaric's study, bright with warmth and light. 'Any luck?' he asked as she entered. 'Supper's nearly ready,' he added.

'It's... elusive,' Hephzibah complained. 'And it's annoying me.'

Aaric stretched in his chair and then closed his own books and journals. 'Well, then. We can't have my wife annoyed. I'll join you in your search tomorrow, how about that? We'll find it soon enough with the two of us looking.'

Hephzibah smiled and sat on the edge of his desk, stroking the edge of the leather-bound book he'd closed. 'You're a treasure,' she murmured. Then she gasped. 'Why are you in here? You're supposed to have your leg up.'

Aaric laughed. 'You think your muttering and cursing is good for my recovery?' he demanded with a mock scowl. Hephzibah began to protest. 'It's fine – I'm fine. And I'll help you tomorrow because I have a very advanced survival instinct, even for an injured old soldier. When my little Zibby is angry–'

'Don't call me that,' Hephzibah said, and he laughed again.

'Point proven,' he teased, and she managed a rueful smile.

It didn't take a day. It took a solid month, and by the time Hephzibah finally found it, she was close to losing her mind. Aaric had helped with the search every couple of days, and they'd been delighted when Tiberius showed up unexpectedly, though the priest had been somewhat surprised when Hephzibah leapt on him and immediately began an interrogation about Necros and his travels.

His mental and physical health were still delicate in the aftermath of the massacre, but dry research seemed a safe enough option, and he willingly joined her in her pursuit, sure that he'd personally never come across the phrase before. He examined the reference in the book he'd sent her, and they spent long hours musing on its meaning. Was the Herald itself fourfold, or did it herald four of something? They debated and researched the meaning of the number in legends and folktales of Shyish and then other realms. Did it foretell an end to the war? Whose would be the victory? And over and over, like an itch they couldn't scratch – four what?

And then she found it. Maybe. '"The Path of the Fallen Four",' she read aloud, and Tiberius made an interested noise, putting his finger on the text he was reading to save his place and looking up.

'The what?'

'The Path of the Fallen Four,' she repeated. 'I don't know, it could be nothing, but it's the closest I've come so far.' She scanned the rest of the text. 'It's an old story, but it's bound up in a second, more elaborate tale of hauntings and possessions here in Shyish.' She whistled and sat up a little straighter. 'Someone's conducted extensive research. According to this, every twenty-five to fifty years, there's a short spate of... occurrences, somewhere across Shyish, in which the victims nearly always end up dead.'

'That's... not exactly unusual, Zib,' Tiberius said dubiously.

Hephzibah snorted. 'All right then, priest, but how about this? The first victims are just slaughtered, but as time goes on, a few live long enough to convey a message, which varies but is usually along the lines of "Do not take the Path of the Fallen Four." Others speak or write a word' – she squinted, frowning – 'that looks like... "Mhurghast". Even if they survive, they are changed – damaged, it says here – forever.' She blew out her cheeks. 'Mhurghast. Ever heard of it?'

Tiberius shook his head, but his eyes were sparkling with curiosity. 'It's not from any language I know, I don't think. Is it an entity?'

'It doesn't say. From context, it could be what these Fallen Four are collectively known as. Or perhaps "the Path of the Fallen Four" is an imperfect translation of this word, and that's why it doesn't quite correspond to the Fourfold Herald?'

'You're presuming the two are linked,' Tiberius mused, and then shrugged. 'The Mhurghast. Well, it's something else to look up, I suppose. I've got a couple of volumes of dead languages back at home. I can have them sent here, see if any of them reference this word, or even a diminutive or child word that's grown out of it. The mystery grows, my dear. And it might even be enough to pique Aaric's interest again.'

Hephzibah snorted at the light of challenge in his eyes. 'Mysteries always do, I find. But thank you – those books could be valuable indeed.' There was a curl of excitement in her belly, like a plant growing towards realmlight. She couldn't stop thinking about it. About the Fourfold Herald, the Path of the Fallen Four, and now Mhurghast.

CHAPTER EIGHT

Gothghul Castle, the present

'To say she became obsessed would be an understatement,' Aaric said softly, breaking the spell he'd woven with his tale. Edrea blinked, coming back to the room slowly. She'd been almost able to see her mother, a whirlwind of energy out on the moors, a coiled spring here in this very library, only her curiosity and lust for knowledge pinning her in her chair long enough to read and study and learn.

'I should have seen it,' Tiberius said mournfully.

Aaric tsked gently. 'We both should have. You were still recovering. And she was my wife.'

'And so you were used to her fancies,' the priest contradicted, almost aggressively. 'My duty is to see people's needs and their weaknesses, to nurture them through illnesses, physical and spiritual. In this I failed.' They spoke as if they'd had this argument hundreds of times before. As if Aaric's guilt was an old friend – or an old enemy. 'You'd become desensitised, almost, to how intense her focus could become. And you were recovering too. It made sense for me to work with Lady Hephzibah while you healed and dealt with correspondence from the Guard, so the responsibility was mine to see when she began to spiral out of curiosity and into something... darker.'

Edrea didn't say anything to comfort either of them. It sounded very much like one of them should, in fact, have noticed if her mother's research had taken a turn into compulsion. Especially for a sorceress as powerful as she knew Hephzibah to have been. Obsessions among spellcrafters often led to catastrophe. Edrea had a sudden, uncomfortable inkling that that explained her father's concern over her own studies. *And yet I am not my mother. Her intensity is not mine.*

She resolutely didn't think about how far she'd pushed herself only in the last day and night in order to reach this point. It wasn't the same thing at all.

'It took weeks for my books to arrive from home,' Tiberius continued when it was clear Edrea wasn't going to give either of them the comfort of a denial. She focused back on the conversation. 'We had more than enough here to keep us occupied during the wait, and we found several other references, some to the hauntings and killings across Shyish, others to the number four. None of them appeared linked on the surface, but when taken together, it was clear there was a pattern emerging.'

'Is this to do with the Curse of Null Island?' Runar asked.

Tiberius rocked his hand from side to side. 'Yes and no,' he said. 'The curse is simply this region's connection to the wider pattern of activity.'

'What pattern?' Edrea asked hoarsely.

'According to the research your mother found, the initial lives taken served to strengthen the apparition, the spectre, or whatever it was,' Aaric said, taking over the narrative. 'All the accounts and legends concurred that only once it had gathered its strength through the killings could it impart the message of the Four. Or the message of Mhurghast.'

Edrea felt her stomach writhe unpleasantly. 'Is that,' she croaked, and then gulped at her wine. 'Is that what Mother... Is that what the apparition meant during my dream? Ask who the Fourth is?'

'Perhaps,' her father said. 'But it does also relate to the circumstances of your birth.'

Edrea started. She'd been so caught up in the mystery, she'd almost forgotten the reason they were having this talk in the first place. 'Tell me,' she whispered.

Gothghul Castle, twenty-six years ago

'Are you sure?' Aaric asked for the third time.

Hephzibah smiled patiently. 'Absolutely,' she said. 'The child will be born just before winter arrives. Please plan your wars accordingly.' She winked, and then Aaric was in her arms, dragging her out of her seat and into a tight embrace before abruptly releasing her.

'Are you all right?' he asked, anguished.

Hephzibah laughed. 'Oh, I can see I'll be able to take shameless advantage of this,' she murmured. 'And to answer your question, I am in perfect health and a hug will not change that. I don't plan on changing any of my activities for some months yet, all being well. I'll be careful,' she added, seeing the concern flicker across his face, 'and I'll do nothing to harm myself or the child. But I also won't be cooped up in the castle for the next seven months. I'll have murdered everyone before the summer is over if you make me stay inside.'

Aaric let out a long-suffering sigh. 'Of course not. I trust you to know your own limits. I always have. But too much heavy spellcraft, even in the early stages–'

'There will be no heavy spellcraft,' she promised him. 'Some light crafting, on the other hand, yes, but nothing that taxes my body or my energy unduly.' She indicated the piled books and the thick, soft leather-backed journal in which she and Tiberius were recording their discoveries. 'Besides, we still have a mystery to unravel. Surely even you cannot find fault in me spending most of my time diligently reading old scrolls?'

And he couldn't, of course, though his eyes moved over the chaos on her desk with something like alarm. 'I have asked the cook to prepare something special for tonight,' she said to distract him. 'Shall we tell Tiberius, my love?'

Another smile, brighter by far than Hysh's realmlight, broke across his face. 'At dinner,' he said, catching her hand and pressing a kiss to her knuckles. 'I want to marvel in you and the promise of our child for a while before anyone else knows.'

Hephzibah stood and pushed him into her chair, then sat on his lap and wrapped her arms around his neck. Gently, as if she might shatter into pieces, he laid one hand on her belly. 'It's still so flat,' he whispered wonderingly. 'Are you–'

'Aaric Gothghul,' she said with mock severity. 'Husband of my heart. I am pregnant. Do not doubt me.'

'Never,' he said fervently. 'Never.'

Hephzibah leant her head against his, relaxing in his warmth, and let her eyes rest on the books on her desk. She could feel the itch beginning again, the urge to read, to discover, to know, creeping beneath her skin. She pushed it away with an effort. Aaric and she deserved this moment, this stillness. This joy. A child to brighten the cold, quiet halls of Gothghul Castle. A legacy to inherit Aaric's steady, studious nature and Hephzibah's wild, impetuous curiosity.

'When,' she began, and then paused, running her fingers idly through his hair. 'When will you have to go back?'

Aaric shifted her on his lap, wincing at her weight on his healed leg. 'I don't know. I'm almost well enough to fight again, and I don't think they'll let me delay my return until after the babe is born. Let me think about it and see if I can come up with a solution.'

She pressed her face into his neck and kissed it. The thought of being alone aside from the servants through the months of her pregnancy, through the birth and through who knew how long before he returned prickled like blood-rose thorns across her skin.

Hephzibah made herself think of pleasanter things and laughed softly. 'This child will be the most insatiably curious creature ever to walk the Mortal Realms with us as its parents,' she said.

'And able to defend itself whether with logic, devastating charm, magic or weapons,' her husband replied. 'It'll get the charm from me, naturally.'

Hephzibah snorted. 'You wish.'

The weeks passed quickly, and the news spread through the castle and then through the town. Aaric developed a mysterious malaise that kept him at home for a few more weeks, but eventually he had to leave. The farewell was bittersweet, tempered only by Tiberius' promise to remain until the babe was born.

Hephzibah's studies and experiments continued, though she kept her word and reduced her magic use, developing spells and rituals to practise once the child was safely born. Her fingers itched to try them, but instead she allowed the scar on her arm of this year's ritual craft to heal, thick and purple and slowly fading to red. That itched, too, in a different way, but her passing fancies were easy to ignore as her belly rounded and her studies led her deeper, and the Rule of Four, as she began to think of it, consumed her every waking – and many dreaming – thought.

She and Aaric wrote to each other a few times a week, and Tiberius added his accounts of the progression of the pregnancy to the expectant father. Aaric's own letters were cheery and decidedly lacking in detail – she knew he was keeping the horrors of the war to himself. Despite that, she worried, even more than usual. The only thing that could distract her was immersing herself in the mystery.

The placement of the visitations at first seemed to have no real pattern, until Hephzibah got hold of the town records of Null Island and nearby Mute Island. And then she saw it.

'Tiberius!' she shouted, and the priest sprinted into the library, alarmed. She heaved herself up out of her chair and waved the parchment excitedly. 'I've worked it out.'

'Sigmar preserve us,' Tiberius murmured faintly, his hand pressed to his chest. And then, 'Are you well, Zib? Nothing's the matter?'

'What? Oh, no, no, I'm fine.' She realised, belatedly, what she'd done and managed an embarrassed grin, her free hand rubbing over the mound of her belly. The child was due in a few months now. 'Sorry, please rest assured that we are both in excellent health.' He looked only a little relieved.

'But I've worked it out. Look here – look. Every town where a visitation has occurred in the last century and a half – where there's been mention of the Fourfold Herald, or the Path of the Fallen Four or the Mhurghast itself – all of them have had a strong spellcrafter residing there. The magic-user themselves wasn't targeted, and so it seems the messenger needed to ensure, as far as possible, that someone would understand what it was trying to convey and so chose those locations specifically.'

Tiberius paused and then laughed. 'Are you talking about the Curse of Null Island? My grandmother told me those tales, but that's all they are. Towns that forgot to honour their dead and were punished for it. And rightly so.'

'I think it's more than just stories,' she said, feeling the familiar frustration building in her stomach. 'And it's across more than just Null Island. Mute Island too, and further afield. There are references that prove this extends across all of the Prime Innerlands. If my calculations are correct, there should be an occurrence due soon. We could draw it here and end its threat once and for all.'

The air in the room froze with indignation and then anger. Tiberius' face tightened. 'Draw it here. To you, presumably, and your unborn child? Or newborn child. Or never-to-be-born child because you end up dead? Not to mention how many towns-folk would have to die first in order for it, as you yourself have hypothesised, to grow in strength enough to impart its message. And you'd do all of this without Aaric even knowing? Do you want to bring another Blood Meridian down on us?'

Hephzibah's face fell. 'I would never put the baby at risk,' she said, and heard the approaching winter in her voice. 'You dishonour me to even suggest it. And of course I would inform my husband – I am not reckless. But with all this evidence, this wealth of knowledge we've gleaned and everything still in our library that could corroborate it, we could finally understand what the Fourfold Herald wants. What its message is. In order to *prevent* deaths.'

Tiberius pulled at his lip, his expression plainly disapproving. 'Listen to me,' she snapped, slapping the parchment down. 'It needs to increase its strength in order to make contact. But if I am already expecting it, if I know it's coming, then it won't need to try and attract my attention, will it? It won't need to kill – not innocents, and not the spellcrafter it is seeking to communicate with. I can draw it into a protective circle and speak with it. No one need die. Especially not me or my child.'

'Has this been tried before?' the priest asked when the silence had stretched long. 'Do the records you've got suggest such a ritual was attempted or succeeded?'

'No,' she admitted reluctantly. 'But that's only because no one else has seen the pattern. It's spread out across Shyish. No one would even think to look for it. I wouldn't have, if not for the Fourfold Herald mentioned in that old book of yours.'

'Yes, that reference you say you'd read before and yet we have found no evidence of,' he continued, and there was something implacable in his voice that Hephzibah didn't understand. 'You've been through every book here and haven't found it again. You can't have read it before. You're seeing patterns where there are none, my lady. And you're suggesting something so dangerous that even if you weren't pregnant, Aaric wouldn't allow it. Sigmar, I won't allow it.'

Hephzibah gasped. '*Allow* it?' she asked very softly. 'I am a sorceress in command of knowledge and abilities you cannot fathom, priest. I know my limits and I know the vast depths of my abilities. Mine is the expertise in this, not yours. You are not adept at carefully calculating what and how much you can give at any one moment in a ritual or piece of spellcraft that has never been attempted, has never even been written until you yourself created it. How dare you tell me what I am and am not allowed to attempt. Neither you nor my husband owns me.'

'Zib,' he tried, and she slashed her hand through the air.

'No. You and Aaric marched off to fight, and I wished you good fortune and sent with you my love. When you were broken by that war, did I ever reprimand you for it? No. Never once did I tell you that your actions were too reckless or that you were attempting rituals beyond your capabilities. Because I trusted you.'

'Yes, and look where that led me,' Tiberius snapped. 'A shell of a man consumed more with fear than with faith.'

'And yet never have I asked you or Aaric to stay, to not take the risk. Because you were – and he is – a soldier. I never tried to take your purpose from you. You will not do so to me.'

'I'm not saying that,' Tiberius tried. 'Once the baby is born and you are strong and the child is thriving, of course you can resume your studies. Aaric would never – *will never* – take that from you or require you to give it up. All I'm saying is *not now*. And maybe... not this. Every encounter we've read about has led to multiple deaths. Maybe there has been a witch or sorcerer in every town, but that could easily be coincidence. I'm sure there's a forge-master in every town too. A baker. How can you assume that whatever is attempting to break through into Shyish and deliver its so-called message is doing so to speak with a spellcrafter? And how can you possibly know that you could summon this thing and then constrain it? You sound obsessed. Maybe even possessed.'

Hephzibah was furious. More than that, she was hurt. 'I have exorcised shades and defeated Nighthaunt, priest. I have done things that you cannot even fathom, even with Sigmar behind you. I keep the graveyards quiescent – I keep the quiet dead quiet. I have woken the land and commanded animals to my bidding. I have performed rituals you don't even *understand*. How can you doubt my abilities? Doubt me?'

'I do not doubt you,' he said, and his voice was quiet and reasonable, so calm she wanted to scream in his face. 'What I doubt is the nature of the thing you will summon. You cannot know from any of these records what it is. How powerful it is. You *cannot* know these things. I do not want to have to tell Aaric that you are dead and his child has no mother because you did something foolish.'

'I–' she began.

'You said it comes every twenty-five to fifty years? Well, summon it next time. When your children are grown. You and them, working together to end its scourge.'

'And let it kill indiscriminately during this... attempt to reach someone who can understand its message? I believe the curse to be real, Tiberius, but spread out over far more than just this island of ours. I know you don't believe the same, I know Aaric doesn't, but something is happening. Something not related to Chaos or even the undead. Something else, and we have an opportunity to defeat it. Is it not our duty?'

Tiberius spread his hands, as though his words were eminently reasonable. 'There are always civilian losses in war.'

'This isn't a war.'

'Isn't it? Some creature from another realm, another plane even, attempting to force its way into Shyish and taking life to do so? It sounds like we're under siege, however sporadically. Besides, how do you know what you're attempting to summon isn't a daemon? It would kill you, everyone in this castle, and probably everyone on the island. Are you willing to face all of those people in the afterlife and explain that you caused their deaths?'

'As a former soldier and as a priest, why can't you understand that I have to do this?' Hephzibah tried desperately.

'Zib, you are a prodigy, a genius, but in this you are thinking of yourself as you were before the pregnancy. You are not thinking of what will come with the babe – the responsibilities, the love. This risk is too great. By all means collate your research, by all means send messengers to your contacts far and wide with what you suspect. You could even – in fact, you probably should – contact the Collegiate Arcane with your suspicions. If anyone is equipped to deal with such a manifestation, it is surely them.'

Hephzibah spat. 'Those tower-dwelling, navel-gazing fools? I can think and craft rings around them without even breaking a sweat. Besides, they'd haul me in immediately if they suspect what I've been doing without their sanction – you know that. Not even an anonymous warning would keep me safe from the Collegiate. They'd take me and the babe both if they found out.'

Tiberius dragged both his hands down across his face, looking suddenly exhausted. 'Hephzibah. You're my friend and I love you, but never have your interests become so inflexible, so closed to gentle debate. What is it about this story in particular that fascinates you so?'

Hephzibah was as abruptly fatigued as the priest looked. She lowered herself heavily back into her chair, the small of her back aching. 'It speaks to me,' she whispered. 'The mystery. There's something here, something I need to know. As if all this time it's been seeking me specifically.' She laughed quietly. 'Does that sound arrogant? It does, I know. But it's true – this Fourfold Herald, its warning against following the Path of the Fallen Four, it... resonates with me. As if it has struck a bell deep in my soul. This is my mystery to solve, Tiberius. Mine alone. I cannot let it rest.' She took a deep breath. 'I will not.'

Her friend stared at her in stricken silence. He was pale, his lips colourless as they pressed tightly together, as if trapping words they would both regret being spoken. 'You will not?' he managed in the end, his tone strangled. 'Then I am afraid you leave me no choice. I must inform Aaric of what you are planning.'

Hephzibah laughed, the sound bitter. 'Of course you must,' she said, and made no attempt to hide her mockery. 'Ever the good little guard dog.' Tiberius flinched, but would say no more. He stalked out of the library, and she could see the anger in the tense set of his shoulders. She did nothing but watch him go. And then she bent again to her books. He wouldn't stop her. Neither of them would.

Gothghul Castle, the present

'Things got... complicated after that,' Tiberius said in a low, apologetic tone. 'I wrote to your father, and he called in every single favour he'd ever been owed and managed to get back here within a few weeks. Even during that short period, your mother deteriorated. She refused to talk with me about anything, especially not her research. Despite the pregnancy, she was losing weight, spending hours from dawn until well beyond dusk in here, poring over books and increasingly muttering to herself. She wouldn't eat, wouldn't leave the castle. She began holding conversations with something that simply was not there. As if she was speaking to the entity she was convinced was coming. There seemed nothing I could do to stop her.'

'And of course, I only made matters worse,' Aaric said.

Edrea snorted very gently under her breath, but Runar glanced over with a mild frown anyway. She felt the slightest curl of shame and pushed it away defiantly. Her father's shortcomings were obvious to all.

'I arrived home in a panic and a towering rage. We got into an argument in less than an hour, and I said things that were ill thought out. I told her that I would not hinder her research, but that she was *only* to do research until you were born, Edrea. I pointed out that there was no way to predict with any accuracy when the manifestation would take place, or where, or what entity she might summon. I said... I said I hoped she could spare me and our child at least these last few months to ensure that you were born safely. But that after that, if she wished to commit suicide by way of daemonic possession, I would not stand in her way.'

'Ouch,' Runar said quietly.

'I didn't see her again for three days,' Aaric said bleakly. 'And when I did, it was too late. She was... deranged. Possessed in truth, I think. I'd told her there was no way she could guarantee it would come to the Hollow, and she seemed determined to prove that it would. Within a week there were reports of attacks on the road, of restless gheists. A two-headed dog was seen on the moors and an entire family was killed in their home – torn apart – with no culprit ever discovered.'

'Wait,' Runar said slowly. 'Are you saying *she* did these things in order to draw the creature here?'

Tiberius shook his head. 'We believe it was just an awful coincidence. The hauntings and killings were the beginning in the same way that the beast attacks this time are the beginning.

But I have to admit, the changes to Lady Gothghul herself were such that the thought did cross my mind.'

Edrea let out a long, slow breath. 'What changes? Just because she didn't have much of an appetite doesn't mean she was possessed.'

'She scratched incantations on her study wall with her ritual knife in a language neither of us have ever been able to translate. She set part of the library on fire because she said the books were watching her. She slashed her own face out of as many portraits as she could get her hands on. All of these could be the sign of an unbalanced mind, it's true, but whenever she spoke of the Fourfold Herald, there were...' Aaric trailed off and gulped at his wine.

'Her eyes went red.' The words were Tiberius', and they were spoken so softly that Edrea would have thought she had misheard if not for Runar's gasp in the chair next to her. 'Just for a second, but bright red. Like blood.'

'I thought that with time, once her anger and obsession cooled, she'd come around to my way of thinking and give up her research. That she'd understand I was just putting her and the– and *you* first, Edrea. But she didn't. She never understood. And she never forgave me, I think. Not truly.'

Edrea nodded helplessly. Her father's words were laced with pain and regret. 'Did she summon the entity?' she whispered, her voice almost lost in the crackle of the logs in the fire, it was so quiet.

Aaric closed his eyes, leaning his head back against the armchair. He gestured for Tiberius to answer.

'We don't know. We'll never know. By this point, really, it no longer matters. It's done. Your father has lived with the not-knowing, with the guilt and the pain, ever since. All we can say is your mother's illness progressed. Intensified at an alarming rate.'

Aaric drained his wine and Runar silently topped up everyone's glasses. Her father took another sip and then looked at her. Edrea's throat was tight; he was so open, so raw and vulnerable. She'd never seen him look like this, not once.

'It's... not pleasant,' he murmured. The sorceress grimly gestured for him to continue. She'd come this far – she'd learn it all, no matter how ugly.

'Things began to escalate in the Hollow. Disturbed graves, infestations of diseased rats, the well water turning to blood. Every visitation, every wild tale or spirit sighting, made Zib a little more manic, a little louder in her protestations that the entity was pushing through and she had to meet it.

'A girl and a boy were sacrificed up at the Blood-Rock Peaks by people too frightened to listen to reason. The ringleaders were hanged on the gibbet as a warning, but... it was as if madness had taken hold of the entire town, and your mother the most. She tried to get up to the Peaks herself, and Sigmar only knows what she'd have done if she'd managed it. When we stopped her, she said that all the deaths that were to come were our fault and our hands would never be clean again.'

Aaric looked down at his calloused palms as if they were, in fact, soaked in blood.

'She locked herself in her study and never came out except to eat and sleep. When she did sleep, it was in the guest bedroom next door to her study. At first, she said it was because the pregnancy made her uncomfortable and she didn't want to disturb me. She began taking her meals there, too. And then the trays were left untouched, the baths unused, the bed not slept in.'

'But I... I wasn't even born yet,' Edrea whispered. 'What about me?'

Aaric rubbed his face wearily. 'Something was controlling her, Edrea. It wasn't that she didn't care. She was in the beginnings of possession, compelled to uncover the mystery and summon whatever was controlling her. She would never have hurt you.'

'Forgive me for somewhat changing the subject, my lord, but why wasn't the Blackshore Guard clamouring for your return?' the sharpshooter asked, as if recognising that Edrea needed a moment to collect herself.

'They were, but by then the town was under supernatural attack, and that allowed me to elect to remain here with Tiberius and combat it.'

'You were lucky they allowed that,' Runar said. 'The Freeguilds' restrictions are why my squad and I only ever hired ourselves out as trackers to them or hunters for towns that needed our help. I want to be able to go where I'm needed, not ordered.'

'You'd sound more rebellious if you hadn't kept turning up to help the Guard whenever we needed you,' Tiberius said wryly. 'But here, things were escalating further. We were more than worried about Hephzibah by then. We were scared. For her. For you,' he added to Edrea.

He reached out and put his hand on Aaric's. 'In the end, when she had taken a rare break to get some fresh air outside, we… we broke into her study and confiscated everything we could find.' His voice was low but unapologetic, and his gaze was frank and open.

Edrea gasped. Even Runar looked shocked.

'You have to understand,' the priest said, now with a tinge of desperation, 'she wasn't eating. She wasn't sleeping, unless she did it lying on her study floor or sitting up in her chair. She was so thin we could see the muscles in her jaw. Her collarbones jutted out. She was harming herself, and she was harming you. There were apparitions in the castle, ones that she attempted to befriend rather than remove. Foul smells drifted from her study, smokes and acids, even small explosions were heard. The only reason she left her room that day was because it was the first snowfall of winter and Zib always loved snow. Always. Even then she left by the servants' staircase, as if she didn't want us to know she'd gone out. It was our only chance to help her. She was a month away from giving birth, but I truly believe neither of you would have lived until then if she'd fallen any deeper into her obsession.'

'She wouldn't have... She couldn't have wanted to hurt me, could she?' Edrea said with a wobble in her voice. 'I know you said earlier, but... I was the thing that was stopping her summoning the entity, so maybe she did. Maybe she hated me that much. I was just another thing holding her back. Trapping her.'

It was as if every monument she'd built in her mind to the mother she'd never known was crumbling, preparing to shatter around her ears and leave her with less than nothing. Not even the singular pain that was the absence of a mother, but instead the horrific possibility of a mother who'd never loved her and had resented her very existence. Who had actively attempted to kill her.

Aaric scrambled out of his chair and knelt next to hers, seizing her hands. 'Never,' he gasped, 'she would never, *ever* do that. Edrea, my precious daughter, *Zib loved you*. Carrying you was the greatest thing she ever did – she told me so herself, and I believed her. I still believe that. She was sick, she was possessed, but she loved you. And so we had to act.'

'What happened then?' Runar asked when it appeared none of them had the courage to continue.

Aaric laughed bitterly and sat back on his heels, then hauled himself to his feet and returned to his chair. He leant his elbows on his knees and spoke to his feet. Edrea shifted forward to hear him.

'She was always cleverer than me. When she went out into the snow she took at least one journal with her, and various magical items and ingredients. Her ritual knife, naturally. I specifically

looked for it when we were emptying her study, but I hoped –
like the fool that I am – that without her books she could do
nothing with it even if she did have it.'

Edrea felt a prickle go down her back. She understood her
mother's decision to keep her knife with her even as she despaired
at it. Edrea's own was currently sitting in its ornate sheath on
her belt, but then, Edrea wasn't sick, possessed or deranged. Nor
was she eight months pregnant.

'Please tell me she didn't attempt a previously unknown or
invented ritual based solely on her memory of it?' she whispered.
Aaric and Tiberius just stared at her. 'Of course she did. So even
if she wasn't possessed before, she was afterwards?'

The priest shrugged. 'Again, we simply don't know,' he said. 'I
know that's not what you want to hear, but it's all the truth we
can give you, I swear. When your mother saw what we'd done,
she flew into a rage like nothing I'd ever seen from her before.
Her eyes turned bright red and things flew off shelves, paintings fell from walls, and the face on her statue, the one in the
herbary – Hephzibah's own face – shattered under some invisible force. She'd come back in looking relaxed, looking healthier,
the cold bringing colour to her cheeks. Perhaps we should have
taken the opportunity to speak with her, instead of… of doing
what we did.' He heaved out a sigh.

'Perhaps, and if only and maybe,' Aaric muttered.

'Sigmar knows we've spent enough time reliving those decisions, playing what if. We did what we did, and Zib… she took
one look at her study, screamed us out of the room and slammed
the door in our faces. She bound it shut with an enchantment,
the window too. She locked herself in there without food or
water, and she was *eight months pregnant.*'

Edrea's heart was somewhere in her throat, blocking it so
securely she couldn't speak.

'So what did you do?' Runar asked for her, and she flashed

him a glance, part plea, part thanks. She didn't want to know –
she *needed* to know. She was rigid in her chair, pain creeping
up the back of her neck from the tension in her shoulders, but
she couldn't force them to relax. She was getting everything
she'd always wanted, and learning just how much her father had
done to try and protect her from the knowledge. Childishly, she
wondered if she could ask him to stop, or if this wound, for so
many long years festering, would continue to be lanced no matter
what. She suspected this flood of poison couldn't be stemmed.

'Zib did it for us,' Aaric said.

CHAPTER NINE

Gothghul Castle, twenty-five years ago

The world was on fire with knowledge and secrets and power, power, *power*. All of it just beyond her fingertips, almost within reach. If she could just stretch that little bit further and seize it, there would be nothing she could not accomplish.

Hephzibah had sealed the chalk circle so that the castle was safe, but somehow the explosion had broken the enchantment on the door and also set it on fire. It didn't matter; nothing mattered but the power and the knowledge that the entity could give her. It wasn't fully here – it hadn't made it into the circle in any meaningful way – but she could see its outline, and even though its form wavered, its knowledge was vaster than anything she had experienced before.

She was lying on the floor, a sharp sting in her elbows and the back of her head that told her she had fallen. She put both hands on her stomach and patted the secret life within. 'All will be well, little one,' she murmured as the shade she had summoned knelt over her, one clawed hand stroking her cheek with a tenderness she did not expect. The other was loose around her throat and cold, so cold.

She was barely aware of Aaric and Tiberius as they battled to put out the flames on the door. All she could see was the red eyes of the gheist; all she could feel was its fingers on her flesh. 'Tell me who you are,' she murmured. 'You have been trying to break through into Shyish for so long, haven't you? I can help you. I can bring you the rest of the way if only you tell me what you need.'

The hand on her throat flexed and tightened, its cold searing through her skin until she gasped and exhaled a plume into the suddenly frigid air.

Dimly, as if from a vast distance, she heard Aaric's shouted plea. She ignored it, unable to look away from the ruby gaze.

The sealed circle began to crackle and buzz and hiss, its magic straining against her skin. It hurt, and it hurt the spirit as well, which grated an inhuman screech. Its claws dug into her neck and her face. 'No, please, don't go,' Hephzibah begged. She tried to gather the entity close, but although she could feel the tiniest amount of resistance, her hands and arms passed through it.

The circle was bulging inwards now, its power fluctuating wildly and concentrating in the area where it was slowly, inexorably being breached. Hephzibah looked up. Aaric, his face set in a rictus of agony and determination, was forcing his body through the magical barrier.

'Stop, my love,' she breathed, the strength of her voice stolen by the gheist's clutch on her throat. 'Stop, or it will kill you.'

Even if Aaric could hear her, she knew the stubborn look on his face all too well. Pain was nothing when set against his implacable will, and eventually the circle shattered. Her husband fell into the centre, barely managing to catch himself on his hands before he collapsed on top of her. The spirit screamed in her face and fled.

Hephzibah screamed too, as the magic rebounded from her circle into her, cutting like knives, and then she fainted.

The sorceress woke laughing, jammed with new knowledge and new strength. There was more, far more, but still it sat just beyond her grasp. Soon, though, she would have it. Soon she would have everything.

Her eyes opened to the bedroom she shared with Aaric, though it was different. No bed hangings, no dresser littered with ornaments and books and perfumes. A ridiculous profusion of talismans and protective charms, even individual pages torn from holy texts, were hanging from every wall and surface. So many it was funny, and Hephzibah laughed some more.

'Aaric?' she called when she had her breath back, but there was no response. Grunting, she heaved herself into a sitting position, her lower back protesting the movement and her knees splayed to accommodate the mound of her belly. Absently, she ran one hand over the drum-tight skin and felt the child within twist and kick, up under her ribs and into a lung. She grunted again.

'Tiberius? Aethelwych?' Hephzibah grumbled at the lack of response and slid her feet into her slippers, then crossed to the door. It wouldn't open. She stared at it blankly for a few seconds, and then tried the handle again. 'What?'

Hephzibah bent forward, her centre of gravity shifting dangerously as she did. She kept her hand flat on the door to steady herself and peered through the keyhole. 'Hello? Aethelwych, what in Sigmar's name is going on? I can't open the door.'

There was no reply, so she pounded on the wood and shouted some more. She'd have kicked it, too, but she was only wearing slippers. Eventually, her noise was rewarded by the slow clip of boots moving along the corridor.

'Aaric? Aaric, what is going on?' she demanded, because she'd recognise that measured gait anywhere. 'Why have you locked the door?'

'Zib?' His voice was almost painfully tentative. 'How do you feel?' She almost paused at the question because her husband himself sounded... terrible. Weak and pained, as if sick. But then the reality of her predicament hit her again.

'How do I feel?' she demanded, a strange, formless anger building in her chest. 'Right now, bloody angry. You've locked me up as if I'm some sort of criminal. *Explain yourself.*' The last two words cracked with a command that shocked her. It hadn't sounded like her voice at all.

'You had an accident, a few days ago. You've been unwell ever since. Violent. A danger to yourself and the baby. We thought this was the best way to keep you both safe.'

Hephzibah snorted. 'Well, it isn't. What happens if I faint, or fall over, or go into labour?'

'There are wards in the room,' he said. 'They'd alert us if you were in danger.'

Hephzibah stiffened. 'Wards? How dare you,' she breathed as that unfamiliar anger twisted in her, heating her skin. She turned from the door and scanned the room, found the first piece of the warning spell easily enough, up above the main window, and tore it down.

'Zib? Please, you really haven't been well. You've been having nightmares, or hallucinations maybe. You've been shouting nonsense.'

She paused in the act of searching for the next part of the ward and glanced at the door. 'What sort of nonsense?' she asked, despite herself. Aaric sounded closer, as if he was leaning against the door, pressed against it to get as close to her as he could.

'About enemies and presences, creatures and–'

'The bloody-eyed hound of portent.'

There was a long silence, then, 'Yes. That, too.'

Hephzibah retreated to the bed and sat down. The bloody-eyed hound of portent. The words, the name, sat in her mind like a lead weight, drawing all her attention. They were one fragment of that seemingly endless knowledge that was a breath, a heartbeat, a wisp of magic away. So close and yet so distant. But if she could remember this, if she could reach for and seize this scrap of knowledge, then surely the rest was within her grasp. She just had to learn to access it.

Aaric was still speaking through the door, but she ignored him, narrowing her eyes as she searched the room for anything useful. In the end, she settled on the white pillowcase, stripping it and carrying it to the window seat, where weak winter sunlight glared through frost-webbed glass. It had snowed again and the courtyard far below was a white, unbroken blanket. No one had been in or out of the castle since it had fallen.

The angle of the sun told her it was mid-morning, but on what day? Aaric had said an accident, had mentioned a few days had passed since whatever had happened. She paused for a moment at that, cataloguing her body. Her elbows were tender, as if she'd knocked them against something. Had she fallen? On instinct, she drew back the sleeve of her thick, long nightgown. The scar of her ritual work had been reopened, and deeply. For the first time in eight months. That would never have been done by Aaric or Tiberius – she'd done that. She'd done it to herself despite promising she would perform no magic until after the child was born. It must have something to do with all of that hidden power. Fortunately, her body and her child were both in rude health. 'No harm done then.'

Aaric paused his low-voiced monologue, as if he'd heard her, and she wondered briefly whether the wards had been calibrated to pick up every noise she made. That would make things awkward, but she was nothing if not resourceful. Besides, judging by the length of time between her banging on the door and her husband's arrival, either the talismans were weak or the transmission to the receiving ward was faulty. Whoever had made them had little skill in the art.

Either way, she didn't need long.

All right then, harbinger of infinite wisdom, let's see what you've got for me.

Hephzibah dug her thumbnail into the scab on her arm until it began to bleed again, then dipped her forefinger into the blood and began to draw on the pillowcase, murmuring the spell as quietly as she could without it losing its efficacy.

The magic crackled and smoked as the imperfect materials struggled to contain it, and Hephzibah bent all her will and focus to the spell, ignoring Aaric still speaking through the door, his voice sharper now, a loud imperative she wouldn't have answered even if she hadn't been otherwise occupied. She wasn't one of his soldiers, his to command.

The spell was simple, a search and bind that would connect her to any spirit, entity or manifestation within the circumference of her strength. Hephzibah had long since attuned the spell to ignore Aaric, Tiberius, the castle staff and the inhabitants of Gothghul Hollow. It sometimes snagged on visitors – traders, merchants or family members – but she'd learnt to identify the energy signatures of the living, sentient races of Shyish, as well as the quiet, harmless dead. The others, the malignant corpses and undead monstrosities, would all be revealed to her witch-sight. And what she was looking for this time, what she cast her mind and energy and spirit out in a net to find, was something other. Something new. Or... four of something.

The memories of the hours and days preceding her so-called accident rushed back, and Hephzibah let them settle into her mind without disturbing her focus or low chanting. The sigils on the pillowcase were complete, curling and writhing as the magic woke them and was in its turn bound to their will. She opened herself to the magic, took it in, swirling through her limbs and blood and bones, and then cast it out, wide and deep and true. Further, and then further still, feeling the drain begin in her mind and then, soon after, in her muscles. Still she searched, her breath short and rasping, sweat breaking out across her face and down her back.

The babe kicked, sudden, as if annoyed, and Hephzibah laughed and stroked her belly. 'Magic,' she crooned to it. 'Flowing through us both, little one. You'll be born understanding it, able to harness it. You'll be so powerful, my child.'

Even that couldn't distract her, though. Hephzibah had spent her life learning control, discipline. She could wield her will as a surgeon wielded a scalpel. And so she searched, out from the castle, out into a circle that took in the moors and the town and further, along the roads, towards the Blood-Rock Peaks, and, *oh*. *Oh*. There it was. Just a sliver, less than an echo, and yet familiar.

'I feel you,' she breathed. 'Fourfold Herald, bloody-eyed hound of portent, I feel you. Come to my breath, my being. Come to my blood. Deliver the message you have held and yearned to pass for so long. I am here. I hear you.'

There was a flicker at the edge of her consciousness, a tiny brush as of fingertips across her mind, tantalising with promise, with secrets and knowledge and things as yet unknown. She gasped. Oh, but it was beautiful. By all the gods and the honoured dead, it was beautiful. Smoke-dark and cruel as it began to curl through her. Powerful and shimmering and endlessly, mindlessly hungry. Reaching for her as she reached for it, spirits yearning towards one another, knowledge forming, words whispering, edges touching, flickering, tasting, like lovers coming together for the very first time. Hephzibah gave herself up to the hunger. Threw herself into that dark cruelty without hesitation. Offered herself as the vessel for that knowledge, the recipient of secrets and powers she could not begin to imagine.

And then the door burst open behind her.

'*Come to me!*' she screamed, now that there was no need for quiet, for stealth. 'Come, Herald of the Fallen Four, come and fill me with your message, your wisdom. Tell me who you are, what you–'

'*Hephzibah Gothghul!*' Aaric bellowed, his tone and the volume of his voice pitched to cut across the mayhem and carnage of a battlefield. 'You will cease this instant!'

At the same time, someone – she couldn't see who as her surroundings faded, obscured by the swiftly growing presence of the Fourfold Herald, smoke and shimmer, red-edged with hunger – tore the pillowcase from her hands and tossed it into the fire.

The backlash from the spell ripped the Herald from Hephzibah's mind and flung it violently away. In a last, desperate attempt to maintain contact, the sorceress let the entity tear a scrap of herself free to take with it. A wisp of spirit, wrapped in her being, her breath and her blood. A promise. *Follow it back, follow it back to me, Herald. I am here. I will know you and your message.*

And then the rebound hit her, and she was lost beneath an onslaught of scarlet claws of pain as the spell that had driven outwards coalesced back into her body in crashing waves that threatened to drown her. It mingled sickly with the toll from the spellcraft until Hephzibah didn't know where one started and the other ended. Didn't know the faces before her or her own name. Only pain – and then nothing.

Hephzibah didn't wake laughing this time. She woke screaming. She was in two places, her consciousness, her reality – perhaps even her spirit – split and existing independently in separate locations. One was... She squinted against the pain tearing her open. One was home, the castle, the bedroom she shared with Aaric. The other... the other was a liminal space, a nothing space where evil and mayhem reigned side by side with agony and fear. Dimensions and distances made no sense, a thousand million faces twisted in agony battered at her, and her ears were assailed by screams and groans and noises no sentient being could possibly make.

She screamed again, saw movement in the bedroom, movement in the... other place. The death-place. Hands touched her body, her face, and over the hiss and shriek of dying stars and planets, she heard a voice. Voices.

'Zib! Zibby, it's me, it's Aaric. Can you hear me?'

Fallen... Fourfold... Mhurghast.

Red eyes coalesced, close – too close – mesmerising, terrifying, and behind and also over them was Aaric's face, Tiberius and Aethelwych with him. She was seeing two places at once, and it made nausea spike in her throat and pain rip through her skull. More hands on her body, more tearing in her chest, and then lower, into her belly. A sudden convulsive pain, quite distinct from the others. A bodily pain, not one of the mind or the spirit. Hephzibah groaned and clamped her hands to her belly.

'My lord! My lady, is it the babe? Is the babe coming?' Aethelwych cried.

'*What?*' Aaric bellowed, so loud and so close that Hephzibah winced and shied away. 'No, it can't be. She's early, she's a month early, it can't. *Not now.*'

Aethelwych shoved him unceremoniously out of the way, and it would have been funny if not for the pain or the red eyes or the gaping wound in her soul. If not for being in two places at once and dying in both of them. The housekeeper ran her hands over Hephzibah's stomach. 'It might only be a practice pain,' she said, but her voice was grim.

'I'll fetch the healer,' Tiberius began, backing away.

Hephzibah cackled, a wild, grating laugh. 'No,' she managed, and the voice wasn't hers, didn't belong in her throat. It had harmonics she'd never heard before, and yet which were somehow familiar. Known. 'No, it will be just the four of us, I think.' She gestured and Aethelwych's face went slack. Her hands fell to her sides as if she were a puppet, and she turned and walked to the window. She jerked it open and then kept going, toppling out head first and falling without a sound. The men just stared in shocked incomprehension at the open, empty window. Hephzibah gestured again and the wood of the bedchamber door burst into furious life, driving roots down into the stone floor and branches through the walls and up into the ceiling. Sealing them in.

'No,' Aaric said, and Tiberius rushed to the door, pulling fruitlessly at it even as the new, green growth thickened and browned. 'No, Zib, no. You have to let us out. Let us fetch the healer, someone to help you.'

'Just the four of us,' she repeated. Or the thing that was using her voice repeated, anyway, its strange double harmonic – a voice both hers and not hers – sending weird flutterings through her chest. She smiled, feeling its unnatural pull, showing far too many teeth. 'Nice and cosy.'

The bedroom faded out of existence for a while, and Hephzibah was back in the heart of the death-place, where everything was shaded in tones of rotten blood that assaulted her eyes, where dimensions moved through each other with a sound like violence, like tearing. Like the void given voice. It was everything and nothing, and all of it hurt. And in that place-that-was-not-a-place, something besides her stirred. Moved. Crept closer, drawn by the splinter of her spirit that it carried, coming to reunite it with the rest of her.

'You did this,' she screamed wildly as another pain rippled through her core, tightening all of her muscles and leaving her trembling, panting, in its wake. She forgot, for a moment, that she had gifted the messenger with that splinter. But she hadn't meant *this*.

Message... the Fallen Four are... Mhurghast will bring... of everything.

'I can't hear you!' Hephzibah shouted, no idea whether her body in Gothghul Castle was tearing itself apart or whether she was screaming the words there as well – screaming them, it would seem, at Aaric and Tiberius. 'Come to me. Find me. Tell me and then let me go. *Please.*'

More pain, more nausea, more cracks appearing in her mind as it strained to understand not only the place a part of it was trapped within, but that it was split at all. Perhaps if she was fully in whatever space this was, it would be easier. But she was not, and Hephzibah knew with utter certainty that she would rather lose her mind and her life than allow her unborn child to be subjected to this. And so she did what she was best at: she searched for the heart of the mystery, the component that would link everything together – blood, magic, breath, ritual. She would hold it within herself until the situation made sense, and then she would proceed with full and certain knowledge of what would happen next. What she would make happen next.

She was in – *she was* – ritual itself. She was *inside* magic, though of a sort and with a power she had never before experienced. And Hephzibah was good at magic, better than anything else she'd ever attempted in her life. Better than marriage, or friendship, or conformity. There had never been a ritual or a piece of spellcraft she had not mastered. This would be no different.

Hephzibah lost track of the presence within the madness when her awareness was ripped back to her body. She blinked open her eyes to the sound of shouting. Tiberius yelling down into the courtyard, his hands white-knuckled on the sill as if he thought he might fall – or be pushed. A winter storm, full of teeth of ice and hail and wind, was screaming in through the casement. All of the candles had guttered and the hearth fire was a bright, roaring thing in the corner of the room. The sorceress could barely hear the priest over the howl of the gale.

'What?' she gasped, and Aaric leant over her. He was pale, his eyes huge.

'Zib? Zib, can you hear me, see me?'

'Of course,' she managed in a rasp. 'Thirsty.'

Aaric's face flashed with anger so intense it stole her breath. 'There are no supplies in here but a single glass of water. No food, no medicine, no hot water or pain relief. You have sealed us in, Zib. Do you remember that? You need to reverse it. *Now.*'

Hephzibah watched his mouth move, let his words sink into her mind but made little sense of them. 'What are you talking about?' she asked, and he reached out and snatched her shoulders, then seemed to remember himself. Gently, he lifted her up to sitting and then pointed at the door. It was… no longer a door. She gasped. 'Me?'

'You,' he confirmed. 'Tiberius is calling for the servants to come up here with axes, but we don't know whether the spell will hurt them or whether the door will keep growing. You have to undo it. Please, my love.'

There was sweat trickling down the nape of her neck now that she had lifted it away from the pillow, and she became aware of a fatigue that was more than just from using magic. Hephzibah looked away from the door, away from her husband and Tiberius and down at herself. The sheets beneath her were soaked. 'Oh,' she said faintly.

Aaric seized on her moment of realisation. 'Yes,' he breathed, his grip on her shoulders tightening. 'The child is coming early. Now do you see why it's so important that we get out of here? Zib, Zibby, please, please. *Open the door.*'

Tiberius glanced back. 'Or at least ensure the spell on it won't activate when the servants start cutting through it. It might be less of a drain on her strength,' he added to Aaric. 'She's still got to give birth.'

'Help me up.' The two men eased her up off the bed and towards the door. Hephzibah put her hands against the wood and closed her eyes, forming the connection. The magic wasn't hers. She'd suspected as much, but it still sent a cold prickle of unease down her back. Whoever the messenger in the death-place was, it wanted her here. Wanted her all to itself, excepting Aaric and Tiberius.

'Get me a chair.' Aaric took both her elbows while Tiberius dragged the armchair away from the window. She sat next to the door – or the tree that had once been a door – with her palms and her forehead pressed against it. She couldn't undo what had been done, but perhaps she could siphon the energy out of it. The magic. Use it to restore her own levels for the labour to come. Tentatively, Hephzibah let a thread of energy sink into the wood, seeking the magic that had brought it to life. Found it. Tasted it and recoiled, then tasted it again. It was foreign and unpleasant, and it almost seemed to taste her in turn. She had a sense it was hungry, as the presence in the death-place was hungry, and if she wasn't very, very careful, she suspected it would devour her.

She was about to begin when a contraction seized her in its grip, drawing a long groan from her chest. A fingernail bent backwards as she clawed suddenly at the wood.

'Breathe, Zib, that's it, come on now, just breathe.' Aaric was rubbing soft circles against the small of her back, and Hephzibah managed to suck in air in deep, shuddery draughts. It seemed to last an eternity before fading.

'All right,' she croaked when it was over and she had possession of her thoughts again, however fragmentary. She began to chant, a slow and steady stream of words and invocations that settled her mind and centred her power and reached out to entwine with that in the wood. Slowly, as if trying not to wake a sleeping monster, she spun it around the golden ball of realm-magic and drew it inside, moulding it and shaping it until it merged with her own, its foreignness and unpleasant-ness rejected and only its pure power retained. Like straining tea. Only nothing like straining tea, as more sweat gathered at her hairline and slid down her back and ribs, her breath short-ening until the words were panted, gasped, the pauses between phrases growing longer. Until she could do no more and slumped back, too weary to even open her eyes and yet thrumming with stolen energy. A twisted, unnatural combination of sensations that made her muscles twitch.

'Zib? Hephzibah?' Tiberius' voice seemed to come from very far away, though there were fingers pressed to the pulse in her wrist. 'Open your eyes, Zib.'

There were boulders sitting on her eyelids, weighing them down, but there was another one sitting on her bladder that was far more important, so she did as he asked. The door was... mostly unchanged, and her breath left her in a long, frustrated groan, but then she saw where Tiberius was pointing and squinted, leaning forward. Aaric carefully held her shoul-ders again, as if she might fall out of the chair. The way she swayed, belly pressing into her thighs, it wasn't an impossibility.

The wood around the edges of the door was thin and dry, almost grey, as if the slender branches and tendrils of roots were long dead and a simple touch of a candle would send flames licking through them.

'You did it,' Aaric breathed against her temple. 'Up you get.' His arms were implacable as he forced her to stand and shuffle away from the door. As soon as they were clear, Tiberius drew a knife and began sawing at the dead wood, tearing at the thin-nest branches.

A smile ghosted across Hephzibah's face, but then her vision narrowed, narrowed and vanished, sucked into the silent cacophony of that other dimension. She heard a shout, felt hands tighten on her, and then she was once more only connected to her body by the flimsiest thread.

'...four. You must tell... ghast is the... listen. Listen to me, you–'

This time the words were shrieked, screamed across a distance unknowably vast and just behind her. Hephzibah spun to the voice, but the space moved with her, oily and alive, sliding and writhing over, beneath and through itself, until neither her eyes nor her mind could make sense of it.

'I didn't hear you,' Hephzibah cried. 'Say it again. Tell me. Come to me. Touch me, so that I can understand you.' She flailed hands she didn't possess in this place, stretching and straining to move, turning again and again as the void turned with her. Mocking her. Increasing her disorientation and her distress. The pain of trying to comprehend where she was began to grow again, a corresponding pain building at the core of the body she was only barely linked to.

'...Fourfold Herald. *Heed my warning...*'

There was more than desperation to the voice that faded in and out. Madness rode it and hunger drove it, cruel and demanding and utterly uncaring of who or what it hurt in order to deliver its message.

'What is your warning?' she screeched as somewhere far, far away, her body clenched on itself, muscles standing out in stark relief. It was hard to demand like this, hard to focus when everything in her pulled towards her child, yearned towards it with a fierce, desperate intensity the likes of which she'd never before felt. It was more primal, more urgent and more right than any lust for man or magic she'd ever known. She wanted, she needed, to be in her body and with her body and to see her child enter the world.

My baby. Aaric's child. I must go home to them. I must.

'Mhurghast.' The voice was a low growl that trailed off into a sobbing laugh.

She steeled herself. 'Yes? Who is Mhurghast? What is it?'

'Beware...'

Hephzibah again felt herself slip back towards her body. 'I will not come here again!' she shouted, defiant. 'If you would give me your message then follow me, follow me home. Now.' As she sped towards her body, something shifted in the maelstrom, a thing that held a vague form and didn't warp or change like everything else. Something dark. And as she'd commanded, it followed.

Gothghul Castle, the present

Edrea's chest was heaving as if she'd just used her arcane speed again. 'I don't know how much more of this I can listen to,' she muttered, so low that only Runar heard her. The sharpshooter leant over and put his hand on her forearm, squeezing lightly, his thumb rubbing tenderly over her sleeve and then down onto the delicate skin of her inner wrist. She shivered, a tiny sliver of her awareness on him even now.

'You're strong enough, Edrea,' he murmured, and she lifted her eyes to his. He smiled and bobbed his head. 'You can do this.'

She snatched up the goblet to drink. Runar squeezed her arm once more and then sat back.

'If you don't mind me saying, my lord, there appears to be no visible evidence around your bedroom door of the magic Heph–Lady Gothghul employed,' he said politely. It wasn't important, but Edrea thought he might be doing it to slow down the pace of the narrative once more, find her a few precious seconds in which she could breathe. Gratitude bloomed amid the disbelief and ancient hurt tangling in her chest.

'Afterwards, after... we got masons in to smash out that whole wall and rebuild it, put in a new door. Paid them well not to speak of what they saw. I couldn't stand to look at it, much less squeeze through the destruction.' Aaric, too, seemed glad of the momentary reprieve.

'But I was born in that room,' Edrea said as she put the goblet back down. 'Wasn't I?'

Tiberius nodded. 'You were. We broke through and got the door open. I sent the cook – I don't know if you remember Old Man Ba? – I sent him into Gothghul Hollow for the healer, but there'd been three accidents that day because of the ice. The healer told Ba that if your mother's labour had only just begun, he would come up once he'd treated his other patients. He said that we'd have hours, especially with it being Zib's first baby.'

'Of course, we hadn't told Ba about any of the other stuff that was happening to pass on to the healer,' Aaric said when Tiberius seemed to run out of words. 'How could we? "Hello, Lady Gothghul is possessed by dark forces and unable to control her abilities, and in labour – can you come and assist?" The whole town would have come up here with pitchforks and guns. So when he said he'd be delayed by a few hours, we didn't have a plausible excuse to get him here faster. We needed a willing healer, not a kidnapped one. And we weren't going to move Zib with the storm raging. So, yes, we stayed in our bedchamber, with your mother raving and screaming and a shattered door that had tried to become a tree and a corpse beneath the window. And the...' He paused and sighed, and Edrea saw how he knotted his fingers together in his lap until his knuckles showed yellow.

'And the what?' she pressed.

'The growing presence of whatever – whoever – the Fourth was,' Tiberius said softly.

'You could see it?' Runar asked in a horrified whisper.

'We could see it taking over Hephzibah,' Aaric said heavily. 'Her appearance and her mannerisms were changing. Not just the strange timbre of her voice, but her eyes would go red. Other things. The way she moved, how her hands clawed...'

Edrea licked her lips. She wondered what the growing magic would have tasted like, what her mother's magic tasted like, but neither man would have been able to sense it. Would the power from another dimension, or a being from another dimension, taste anything like the amethyst magic of Shyish?

'And was she still' – Runar paused and waved his hands helplessly – 'travelling back to that "death-place" she kept mentioning? During her labour?'

'She was,' Aaric said, 'and with increasing frequency. There seemed nothing we could do to prevent it, even with Tiberius in here tearing through every book we had that might give us a clue of how to anchor her here, somehow. We'd have done anything, attempted any ritual despite the risks. We'd have given what was needed. But in the end, we were helpless. Useless.'

Edrea noted with dull detachment that her fingers were trembling. 'Was she doing it on purpose?' she asked, and then grimaced. Every question she had seemed to paint her mother more a monster, and she didn't mean it like that, but she also had to understand. She had to, and not just because it was Hephzibah Gothghul, her mother. *Because I fear it is happening again. I fear that my communication with the beast and what I know of Mother's – of the shade's – message is leading me to make the same mistakes. I've been to that death-place, after all. I've been spoken to by whatever is trapped there. Am I destined to bring destruction and madness upon this castle as she did?*

Her throat clicked as she swallowed hard. *And do I have any other choice?*

Aaric's mouth twisted. 'I don't know. By then, the labour was progressing fast, the storm was getting worse and we weren't sure if the healer was coming at all. I sent Ba down a second time to hurry him as the evening wore on. She wasn't often coherent, but when she was with us we gave her water and broth, and bathed her face. Did everything she wanted, but the contractions were getting quicker, and then suddenly, she'd be gone again. For minutes, longer.'

'And her behaviour when she was gone? Was it like me, in my sleep earlier, when I was in… that place?'

Aaric tapped long, gnarled fingers on the arm of his chair. 'Yes and no. She slept a little, mainly through sheer exhaustion, and during those times it was clear her dreams were plagued. That was similar to how you appeared. And the place you spoke of, well, I think we can all agree that it's the same. That you described it as you did before I'd mentioned anything about your mother convinces me of that much.'

He paused and licked his lips, anxiety flaring bright in his expression. 'When Zib was awake and… went away… it was very different,' he continued eventually. 'Her voice changed and she had a conversation with someone we couldn't see, begging it for answers, begging it to come here. But also begging it to let her go. She spoke of you, Edrea, told the thing and the place that held her that she needed to be here in her body, to welcome you to the world as you deserved. As you needed. As was her right.'

Edrea's breath got tangled around the obstruction that was suddenly choking her. She heard herself wheeze and felt her cheeks burn with unnameable emotion, eyes stinging.

'She loved me then,' she whispered, almost to herself. 'I know you said before, but she really did. Didn't she?'

'She really did,' her father said quietly. 'She was desperate. I think she thought that if she couldn't escape it, then bringing it here would at least reunite her consciousness with her body. That if she was here, in the heart of her power – even in the middle of childbirth – she'd be strong enough to deal with whatever it was. She had a mother's instincts – she'd have faced down Nagash himself and denied him. And she'd have had us standing at her side, too.' He exchanged another look with Tiberius, and Edrea braced herself.

'What?'

'But sometimes it wasn't her talking at all – it was the thing itself. And when that spoke directly through her, that was when her eyes changed – her hair and body too.'

'Her body changed?' Edrea's voice was barely above a whisper.

'The way she moved, the... way she touched us, caressed us. She bit me. At first I thought it was the result of a contraction, that she was simply out of her mind with pain, but then she did it again, and it was when she was channelling this Fourfold Herald.'

'It's hungry,' Edrea said. 'The beast was hungry, the shade was hungry – it drew blood from all of us, remember – and the death-place itself is hungry. Whatever has existed in there must have absorbed that hunger. Must be mad with it.'

'The changes – her voice and the way she moved despite being in labour, the frenetic energy and the red eyes, the biting – all pointed towards daemonic possession.' Tiberius' voice was carefully flat. Neutral. 'We theorised that perhaps it chose Zib because of you, Edrea.'

The room seemed to flicker, the edges of Edrea's vision growing dark. 'Explain,' she managed, though she already knew what they were going to say.

'If it was something trying to break through from another plane, we thought that perhaps it was made of pure spirit, that it was incorporeal and–'

'And that it would be born into my body if it could latch on to my life essence. Yes, I see. It's a reasonable assumption. And of course, the only way to deal with that would be to kill me in the first seconds after I was born, before the daemon could settle into my flesh.' Edrea felt strangely detached from both the words and the images they conjured.

Tiberius' mouth fell open.

'No!' Aaric squawked, his voice high with shock, with vehement refusal. Even Runar jerked in his seat as if she'd slapped him.

'Gods, no. Never. Even if that had happened, Tiberius and Hephzibah would have done all they could to banish it. We knew that. We just wanted to be prepared.'

Edrea didn't reply.

'And could she have dealt with it, even in the middle of childbirth?' Runar asked.

'Yes,' the sorceress replied, without even pausing to think, stung on her mother's behalf by Runar's scepticism and grateful to find something else to seize on.

'No,' Tiberius said. He held up his hand, stilling her. 'It was changing her, speaking through her more and more. Stripping away what made her human, let alone what made her Hephzibah. Every part of her mind that was here in Shyish was consumed with giving birth, and by the time she needed to push, the part of her that was in the death-place was, I think, entirely under the entity's control. She couldn't have defeated it. She didn't defeat it, because when she did drag it through to Shyish it... took her away.'

There was long, thunderstruck silence. 'What?' Edrea demanded. Too many shocks, too many secrets laid bare, had stolen her voice, her words, until that was all she could manage, and then barely.

Runar asked the question she couldn't voice. 'Lady Gothghul is there, in the death-place? Physically there?'

Edrea's mind was racing and she couldn't sit still, jumping up to stalk to the other end of the library and back, fingers clenching in the fabric of her trousers and jacket as she moved. 'Is that why I felt her when I was unconscious?' she asked as she spun to face them at the other end of the room. 'It must be – she's been in there for twenty-five years. I have to get her back!'

Aaric stood too, patting the air to still her and shooting Tiberius a stern, disapproving glare. 'She may not be in there,' he said. 'But the daemon is, as far as we can tell. That's what's been speaking to you. That's likely what sent the spectral hound, what sent the shade.'

'That's not how daemons work, Father, and you know it. And even if it was, that doesn't mean Mother isn't there too, waiting for us to rescue her.'

'That is a distant possibility,' Aaric allowed. 'Or she may be somewhere here in Shyish. We don't know – we cannot know.'

Edrea experienced a moment of such intense vertigo that she staggered, and Runar leapt out of his seat and across the room to put one hand under her elbow and the other around her waist. Her father, too, scrambled across the carpet towards her. 'My mother's alive and might be in Shyish? I thought, when you said she wasn't dead, I... I hadn't got as far as thinking of where she might be. I couldn't allow myself to. Now you're saying she's here somewhere?'

'We're getting the story muddled up,' Tiberius said in a soothing tone. 'I know this is important to you, lass, but please, let us tell the rest in order, up to that point. It may help us all to understand it better. And understand what it is we need to do next.'

'I want to know,' she whispered as Runar led her back to her chair, Aaric hovering awkwardly on her other side until she gestured him to his own seat. She didn't sit straight away, instead dragging her chair further from the fire and closer to Runar's. She was so hot, her face burning. It was hard to breathe. *She's alive and in Shyish. She's here. I can go and find her.*

'We'll tell you everything, I promise,' the priest said.

'No more secrets,' Aaric added. 'Though it was all to keep you safe.'

'I just want to be sure I understand,' Edrea said slowly, still standing. 'Mother was plagued by what you think is a daemon, and you were worried it would possess me either in the womb or upon my birth, but you weren't going to kill me no matter what happened, and then my mother vanished once I was born?'

'Clinical but accurate,' Tiberius said.

Edrea barked a sharp laugh. 'Clinical is the only way I'm going to get through the rest of this, I think,' she said bitterly.

'Perhaps we should take a break then?'

'No. No, Father, Uncle. Don't you dare. I've waited all my life for the truth. I won't wait further.' She sat down, leaning side-ways towards Runar and the comforting, safe smells of leather, wool and gun oil. He rubbed soothingly at her shoulder. She took a few slow breaths and then nodded, once, for the rest of the story of her birth and her mother's not-death.

CHAPTER TEN

Gothghul Castle, twenty-five years ago

Hephzibah wailed and let the overriding instinct to push take control. She had Tiberius' hand in hers, grinding his bones together as she squeezed, while Aaric knelt on the bed between her knees. 'I can, I think, sweet Sigmar... I can see the head. I think I can see its head!'

Hephzibah felt a savage blush of hope and accomplishment and triumph at his words, used them to lift her up as she panted and pushed again.

The room was far too hot. The fire was a bright incandescence and every lamp and candle they had was lit, adding to the unbearable heat. Sweat stung her eyes and cracked lips, slid past her teeth onto her tongue, bitter, adding to her thirst.

The storm outside must be building, because the fire began to roar in the chimney and all the candle flames flickered and then lay flat, burning parallel to the floor. She only noticed because the light moved and shifted the shadows in the room, but then she screwed up her face and pushed again, and the pain grew and grew into something monstrous, the size of the world and centred at the very core of her. The baby moved, shifted, and the pain got even more intense.

'The head! Zibby, the head's out. I can see it! One more push, sweetheart. Just one. Come on now. Push. *Push!*'

'Why don't you bloody push,' she sobbed, but then took in another breath, gritted her teeth and did what her body demanded.

The room's light dipped and flowed again, and Hephzibah barely registered it. She heard Tiberius swear, heard his quiet 'Aaric', but none of it meant anything. There was nothing else but the burning, tearing need to push, her body at once outside her control and deeply, completely connected to her mind.

Aaric was tense. 'Can you start now?' he asked.

'She won't let go,' Tiberius murmured.

'Then make her.' Aaric's gaze flickered around the room, but then he was leaning forward with his hands outstretched, awe and tears alike shining on his face. 'Again, last time, Zib, last time.'

Hephzibah let out a broken sob and hauled in air. She pushed again just as Tiberius wrenched his hand from hers and leapt to his feet, crossing to the table, where there was a tray heaped with vials and herbs that she'd noticed earlier but not paid much attention to. Pain relief, she'd suspected. Her hand clawed after him and then fisted in the sheets as, with a final convulsion, the immense pressure within her slid free into Aaric's hands.

Hephzibah let her head fall back, sobbing again, for breath, for sheer relief. For exhausted joy. The candles juddered wildly and darkness began to puddle on the floor between the bed and Tiberius. She closed her eyes and tasted metal and oil and hunger. The priest was muttering, his voice rising and falling in a familiar cadence, but there was another voice, too – the lowest, quietest singing at the very edge of her hearing. Or perhaps she was imagining it – she'd never been so tired.

'It's a girl. Zibby, we have a baby girl.' Aaric's voice was awe-struck, hushed with reverence. There were tears sliding down his face. 'You did it. She's... Gods, Zib, she's so perfect.'

Hephzibah closed her eyes for the duration of a single inhale. She let the weariness wash over her, a great, crushing wave she longed to throw herself into, and then she pushed it back and looked at her husband and their daughter, took in every line and angle of them, his bloody hands cradling her, the astonishment in his face, as if he hadn't quite believed it until now. She tucked the image away, deep inside her heart where nothing could ever reach it, not even her terror.

She watched him stroke a cloth across his daughter's body and wrap her up, his movements achingly gentle. 'Give her to me,' she croaked, 'and then help Tiberius set up the wards. It's coming.'

'What?'

She'd recognised the chant now, and knew the names of the items on the tray. 'Help him cleanse the room. It might keep it out.' It wouldn't, she knew. Her own circle of protection had been no match for the messenger despite being a hundred times stronger than a priestly cleansing, but it would buy them – her – precious seconds, and she needed every one of them. The baby was starting to cry when Aaric handed her over, and Hephzibah lowered the neck of her nightgown and pressed her to her skin, her heartbeat.

'The birth cord,' Aaric protested.

'I'll cut it. Help him, my love,' she added, and saw the surprise, swiftly masked, in his eyes. How long had it been since an endearment had fallen from her lips? Days. Weeks, perhaps. 'Help him now.'

Aaric studied them much as she'd studied him, as if memoris-ing every detail of this moment, and then he put his fingertips to his lips and pressed them to her ankle, stood and crossed to Tiberius.

'Little one,' Hephzibah murmured, and gave herself twenty seconds to sink into the joy and rightness and love for this little scrap of life she had made. 'Edrea. My daughter. Know your mother loves you more than the world and all the magic in it.' Her voice cracked and she cleared her throat. 'I love you more than life,' she whispered.

The missing part of her was returning. She could feel herself coming back together, her ability to think and plan and understand intensifying, or it would if she was not so deeply, deathly exhausted. The grandfather clock in the main entrance hall tolled four. Hephzibah glanced out of the window – it was dark, but not the sort of dark that came at four in the morning.

'Work faster,' she grunted at Tiberius and Aaric, and heard the priest's chant become a little strangled as fear sparked in him. They were in a race now, and they were losing. Hephzibah fumbled with her free hand for the thread and scissors to tie and cut the cord. Aaric was ever moving, looking at her, prowling the edges of the room and slapping the talismans against the walls as they were completed. The candles danced around them, their flames moving independently of each other, of the breeze drifting in through the open door. Shadows pooled, blacker than oil, blacker than Hephzibah's hair or the faint coaly wisps on Edrea's head. Carefully, Hephzibah tied the cord, preparing to cut, praying to the warrior Sigmar for time, just a little more time with her family, just a little.

They were losing.

And then, suddenly, they lost.

When it manifested, it wasn't in the centre of the room ready to do battle with a priest of Sigmar as they'd all expected. It was on the bed. It was *on Hephzibah*. Not a weight so much as a presence looming over her. Familiar and awful and seductive. Edrea's thin wail of protest was abruptly muffled, as if a hand had been pressed across a tiny rosebud mouth, a delicate button nose.

Aaric screamed their names. Tiberius' chant broke off and he drew, of all things, a pistol. The report of the shot was obscenely loud, and plaster exploded on the far side of the room as the bullet passed through the dark, smoky outline crouching on Hephzibah's chest. Only the ruby-red, blood-red, life-and-death-red eyes were clear, and she could read madness and a ravening, bottomless hunger in them as the entity bent over them both.

The low-voiced chanting that Hephzibah had been hearing abruptly became clearer, and she cocked her head. Her body began to tense again in an effort to expel the afterbirth, stealing a good portion of her remaining attention, and a jagged laugh broke from her, tinged with hysteria. It trailed off into a groan.

Tiberius fired again as the shape began to shift and solidify and Edrea's cries became screams, surprisingly loud for such a small creature.

'Mhurghast,' the thing of smoke and cruelty growled, reaching for Edrea, for Hephzibah, with hands that became more corporeal with every second. 'Mhurghast is coming. The Four with it. Stop it, you must stop it.'

'I will,' Hephzibah panted as more pain crested within her and the apparition's hand closed on her face. She could feel it, both the hand and its legs pressed to either side of her waist. It was so terribly cold that it burnt against the heat of her skin, and she gasped and tried to paw it away. Dank hair trailed in her face and she felt the imprint of nails – sharp enough to be knives – pressing into her cheek and jaw. It pushed, baring her throat and twisting her head to face Aaric, who was frozen in fear and indecision. Breaking her gaze with Edrea so that it could take her away. Drool, or perhaps blood, pattered onto her neck and chest.

'Zib?' her husband breathed, tense as a bowstring at full stretch.

Hephzibah's hand found the scissors meant to cut the cord. She clutched the handles tight in her fist, her eyes locked on Aaric's even as he began to leap towards her, shouting incoherently. Hephzibah brought the scissors around and down as the entity began to take control, its fingers cruelly tight upon her face.

The scissors bit deep. The thing on top of her reared back with the blades sticking out of the side of its neck and its blood spraying across Hephzibah's face and throat, into her eyes, into her mouth.

'*Leave my baby alone!*' she screamed, infusing the command with every last drop of energy, courage and magic she had. A blast erupted from her, flattening everyone in the room, extinguishing the candles and almost the roaring fire. The windows shattered, glass flying outwards into the storm. The twisted, warped tree-door slammed back against the wall, its hinges splintering.

Blackness fell, thicker than just the absence of candles. Below, the grandfather clock's heartbeat chime struck four, four again, and then there was a crash as if it had toppled over and splintered against the flagstones.

Groans and harsh breathing, the scrape of bodies beginning to move.

'Forgive me, Aaric. Forgive me, my darling daughter. I love you.'

'Zib? Zibby?' There was no answer. '*Zibby?*'

Within the darkness, thin and unsure, Edrea began to wail once more.

Gothghul Castle, the present

'And when the fire flickered back from its embers, she was gone.'

Edrea was rigid on the edge of her seat. Runar was holding her wrist in a soft, reassuring grip, and she was grabbing his arm in turn, though her fingers were digging into skin and muscle and she couldn't have prised them loose if her life depended on it. 'Who was gone? Mother? Or the entity?'

'Both.'

'Wait,' Runar said. 'Wait. How is that possible? Where did she go? Forgive me for the indelicacy, but you clearly said the cord had not yet been cut.'

Edrea laughed, jagged hoots of mirth that were as much stress relief as they were amusement. It stole some of the strength from her grip and she managed to loosen it a little, though she didn't let go. 'I think we are far past any squeamishness regarding the circumstances of my birth, Runar,' she managed.

'The cord was cut,' Aaric said, and that silenced her. She frowned. 'But Runar's right – when the candles all went out, it wasn't. I saw her stab the thing that was on her – on you both – and I saw its blood spray across her face. My ears were ringing after the blast, and I wasn't sure which way was up or down for a few seconds, but I didn't hear anything to indicate she, or both of them, had fled.

'But as Tiberius says, when the fire licked back up, she was gone and you were lying in the centre of the bed screaming. The cord had been tied and cut neatly.'

'What does that mean?' Edrea demanded. 'What does *any of that* mean?'

Tiberius shook his grey head. 'We don't know. We've spent the last quarter of a century trying to work it out. Aaric went straight for you, of course. I ran out of the room and down the stairs, looking for Hephzibah. Nothing. No sign. That's why we believe she must have been taken back to the death-place. There is a remote possibility she's somewhere here in Shyish, as your father said earlier, but we have no way to verify either supposition. All we do know is that she's gone.'

'I looked for her, Edrea. You have to believe me, sweetheart. I looked everywhere for her. In the Hollow, on the moors, up at the Peaks, on the roads in and out of town. Weeks, months, I searched, you either back here with the wet nurse or strapped to my chest.' Edrea blinked at that and felt her eyes sting with fresh tears.

'What is it you think Tiberius does when he travels across Shyish each year?' her father added quietly.

Edrea turned a stunned expression on the priest. 'Aaric needed to be here with you,' he explained with a shrug. 'It was the least I could do after everything. After failing this family.'

Aaric shook his head in denial.

'Forgive me, my lord, but I think we could all do with taking a step back from the... intensity of that narrative and viewing it instead in conjunction with what's happening here, now. If you would indulge me?' Runar's tone was painfully formal, but it cut through the tension still sitting heavily in the library.

Aaric cocked a questioning eyebrow at Edrea. 'There is no more to tell. Hephzibah's story has ended.'

Edrea felt a stab of pain at that. She had at least a hundred questions and more just waiting to be thought of. But there was a reason she'd finally learnt the story of her birth here and now – a reason with red, glowing eyes and murderous intent. Her questions were personal; the beast's ravening and the shade's blood-locking and fragmented message were not. Still, a shudder rippled through her as she forced her mind to classify everything she'd heard as research.

'All right. Let's connect how Mother's disappearance links with the deaths in town. I'm not sure I'm going to have the time to process all this on an emotional level before the next visitation, which, I think we all now know, is what we're facing. It's best to just get on with it now. Thank you, Runar.'

He gave her a sympathetic smile and then sat up straight. 'Very well. So far, we've been assuming that the beast and the shade were sent by the same entity, the thing trapped in the death-place.

The thing that was the fourth... person, I suppose, at your birth. But I can guarantee you that there was no ghostly singing going on during the beast's attacks. I'm not a learned man, my lords and lady, but if something was sending these things to us, why would the method of delivery, so to speak, the magic used to send them here, be different? Why did the spirit and the apparition at your birth require singing, but not the beast?'

Edrea stood. The tail of an idea, the merest breath of a theory, was ghosting around in her mind, and if someone spoke to her now and disturbed it, she'd lose it. She stalked to the far end of the library and stood facing the wall, staring at her shadow flickering across the wallpaper and the shelves.

'Perhaps this is why no one has made the connection between them before,' she said to herself. 'Why the curse appears to have many facets, when in fact the visitations are all linked. But linked how? The beast was the first attempt at contact, but it couldn't speak to impart its message. Instead, it compelled people, as it did Aldo. Compelled them enough to sink a message into their minds. Mother found evidence of that, in the survivors. But it's inefficient and it takes time, so why keep trying it?'

She drummed her fingernails on the nearest shelf. 'Why keep trying when it's inefficient?' she asked again, a little louder.

'Because it requires less magic, or less effort,' Aaric said.

She spun and pointed at him. 'Precisely. So, it's inefficient in the transmission of its message, but what does the beast gain by its appearances? Life force. Through the blood, the draining of its victims, it gains enough life essence to move to the second form of visitation – the spirit. But again, there appears to be a huge power expenditure required to send the shade to Shyish from wherever this death-place is in which the sender is trapped. The chanting that we heard is likely to be that power being channelled.'

'But Zib's research only ever detailed one or the other type of appearance,' her father said, though there was no judgement in his tone. He spoke as she imagined he had with her mother, one scholar to another. It warmed a tiny frozen place inside her. 'As far as we know, here and now is the only time the entity has managed to appear in two different guises. Which surely means it has grown in strength and therefore grown in danger to us.'

Runar muttered something she couldn't quite make out, but it didn't sound appreciative. She didn't blame him. The thought of the messenger being even more powerful now than it had been before made her knees weak.

'Or perhaps it has merely grown in desperation,' she contradicted. 'Not only did it appear in two different shapes, but it also managed to deliver the locket to us.' Edrea had demanded it back from Aaric when she woke, and now lifted it out of the neck of her shirt. 'I'm guessing Mother was wearing this at the time?'

He nodded.

'And the spirit managed to bring it across dimensions for Runar to find. Let's not forget that the beast drew his blood and it was he who found the locket. There's a chance it was blood-locked to him at the time of the attack at Blood-Rock Peaks. First the messenger builds its strength, then it begins to give us the tools needed to summon it, and finally it blood-locks to the rest of us through the spirit's actions. The four of us are connected to it now – there's a pathway between us.'

'What exactly are you suggesting, Edrea?' Aaric asked. He sounded weary. He sounded bitterly sad and, strangely, a little bit proud.

Edrea clapped her hands together once and nodded, more for herself than for them. 'If it is blood-locked to us, then it has already chosen us as the recipients of its message. That leaves us little to no choice. Either we embrace the role we have been given or more carnage is unleashed upon not just Gothghul Hollow but all of Null Island. All of Shyish.'

'But we still don't know what it actually is,' Tiberius said, breaking his long silence. 'What if it's an agent of Chaos? What if it is a daemon?'

Edrea was already shaking her head. 'No. Something about this feels different – its actions feel strained, limited, like the desperate choices of an ordinary sentient being trapped in extreme circumstances. And don't forget the message... It would not have spent decades, possibly even centuries, attempting to break through if its message was not of the utmost importance. It has chosen us for something – we cannot shy away from that.'

'Perhaps it's just its last flash of defiance,' Runar said, and then faltered when the other three all stared at him. 'Forgive me, I spoke out of turn.'

Edrea walked back to the group. 'No, please,' she said. 'Elaborate.'

He still looked a bit uncomfortable, but he straightened in his chair again and put his palms on his knees, as if giving a formal report. 'I've hunted my share of beasts and the undead. You corner something, give it nowhere to go, injure it, and that's when you're in the most danger. You're never closer to death in a hunt than when your quarry is bleeding and you think it's down. When its survival instinct kicks in the hardest, that's when you're most likely to lose it – or lose your life.'

'So you're saying that wherever it is, wherever this death-place actually is, the messenger is in danger within it. That would indicate either it's not in its natural environment or that that environment has been invaded.' Realisation swamped her like a frigid wave. 'The Fallen Four. Perhaps they have invaded its home. Perhaps they, too, seek to push through into Shyish from that place. If the walls there are thin, if the magic can be harnessed, even a gate built...'

Aaric took one look at her face and shook his head. 'You are *not* summoning it. By what you've just said yourself, there is no guarantee you'll summon the entity instead of the Mhurghast itself. The only thing we know of the Mhurghast is that the message warns against it. You don't have anything to focus that summoning onto the right life essence. You could open the Mortal Realms to attack.'

Edrea scoffed. 'Any more than they are already? With everything that's happening here? There are no quiet dead any more – there are only monsters wearing the faces of the people we once loved.' She paused to breathe through the sudden realisation that she'd tended her mother's tomb all these years and that it was empty. Another lie. She blinked it away.

'Besides, I do have a focus for it – the beast's claw. Plus the locket, which has been in its possession for twenty-five years. Plus it is blood-locked to each of us. All that makes it easier for it to find us, but also for us to find it. We're never going to get a better chance, and neither is the messenger. According to your own story, even my mother was averse to letting it rampage through the realm every twenty-five to fifty years. Really, how can it be worse?' She made an all-encompassing gesture that took in not just themselves and the castle, but the town and even Shyish itself.

'It can always be worse,' Aaric said, and for a wonder, the other men both agreed with him.

'You have seen little of the world, Edrea,' Runar tried, and although his tone was respectful, she flushed at the implied criticism.

She turned a murderous glare on her father. 'And whose fault is that?'

'Let's not,' Tiberius said, sounding weary. 'For once, can the two of you not begin an argument? Edrea, I would like to think you are intelligent enough to have learnt much about Aaric from the tale we have woven this night. About why he has treated you as he has. Whether it was right is another question, but I'm sure now you at least understand the why of it.'

Edrea let out a measured exhale, letting her anger go with it. Tiberius was right: they argued far too often, and now, tonight, she found that not only did she not have the energy for it, she didn't have the will, either. Her reaction had been one of habit only.

'I do. Father, I do understand. I don't like it, and gods know I didn't growing up, but I can tell you now that, yes, I understand.' She pointed a finger at him. 'I can also tell you that it ends right now. You need me, in ways you cannot begin to imagine. I may not be my mother, but I am far stronger than you know. The summoning was beyond her, and there is no guarantee it won't be beyond me as well, but, as I've already stated, the messenger has chosen us. Surely it is better to prepare for its arrival than fight against it. And with that in mind, I think it's time I was officially allowed access to the forbidden shelves.'

She didn't wait for his answer or for Tiberius to rise and cancel the holy binding. Instead, she went to the shelves she'd stared at for countless hours as a child. She held her mother's locket in her palm and bit down on the finger the shade had bitten the night before, then muttered a few words under her breath. She snapped her fingers. The binding on the shelves shattered into a million splinters of light and then faded. She ignored the gasps of surprise and pushed away the curl of satisfaction in her belly.

She disregarded all the books she'd already read and searched for one with a blue cover. 'This one?' she asked, holding it up. Tiberius nodded. She'd thought it a printed book, but it was another journal, and Edrea recognised her mother's handwriting from the pages of the library index. She took a second to run her fingers reverently over the faded ink.

There were other books she would probably need, so she piled the most likely on top of the journal, to Aaric's increasing horror and Tiberius' growing amusement.

'Just how long have you been able to access these books?' the priest demanded in mock outrage.

'Years,' Edrea said shortly, and then managed a contrite grin. 'After being blown across the room a few times by failed attempts to bypass your binding. Oh, and almost catching fire once, too – that one was memorable. You did a good job, Uncle – it's a very effective spell.' She glanced at her father and lifted one shoulder. 'I was an adult before I attempted it, don't worry.'

Almost an adult. Close, at least. Fairly close.

'How many have you read?' he asked, eyes wide.

'Not as many as I'd like. It wasn't easy, sneaking in and getting them and then putting them back before you might notice they were missing. So only a few. I went for the ones that were obviously lore and spell books first. The ones most likely to broaden my knowledge. The journals…' She broke off for a second. Her heart hurt where it thudded beneath her ribs. 'I always wanted to savour them, and I'd only ever be able to do that if I took them with your permission. Or if… if you ever went away on business again.'

Aaric pushed himself to his feet, then waved Tiberius back down when the other man looked ready to protest. Edrea watched him cross the library towards her, her chin up in defiance at first, but her father's expression was open and sad. Not angry. He reached past her and stretched up to the highest shelf, dragged down a stack of thick leather-bound books.

'Then start with these. Once we've dealt with the current crisis, that is.' He added them to the pile of books in her arms. 'They're mostly diaries and her own experiments. You'll learn more about Zib in there than I could ever tell you.'

Edrea juggled the books against her chest until she could free one hand and then put it, carefully, against her father's cheek. 'And what if I'd rather hear you talk about her?' she asked.

Aaric blinked and inhaled, ragged. 'Then I will talk about her,' he said, and she felt warmth steal beneath her ribs to soothe the hurt. 'And as for the current crisis, well, there's no one I'd rather fight the murderous, mysterious entity that stole my wife with than someone who can shatter a prayer-binding with one snap of her fingers. You're a little bit frightening, Edrea Gothghul. And you're so much like your mother right now that it hurts.'

He took a breath and a decisive step backwards. 'The blue journal is the one we recovered from her study. It contains all the research she did into the Fourfold Herald, all the links she found with the Path of the Fallen Four – real or, ah, or imagined – and the information from the town records. It... degenerates some-what as it goes on, as she became less coherent. It finishes, I assume, with the attempt at summoning. I've never read the last pages myself, though Tiberius has.'

Edrea's skin suddenly felt too tight, her breathing too shallow. She looked at the priest.

'I couldn't understand most of it, and I've read my share of complicated lore. You'll understand the magic better than me, but the rest? Well, she was more troubled than we ever suspected, I think. It's not easy reading, Edrea. Just don't judge her too harshly. As your father said, if we had time, I'd have suggested you read her diaries first. The blue journal, well, you're going to read her at her worst, lass. Just be aware of that.'

'I will,' she said. She looked at them all: Aaric a few steps away, his eyes shining with unshed tears; Tiberius, tired but fiercely proud; Runar twisting in his chair to face her, concerned but trusting in her strength.

'Do you think she's still alive?' she blurted. 'Here, or in that other place?'

'I don't know,' Aaric said. 'Sometimes I hope she is, and other times not, because whatever happened, whatever was done to her, I don't think we'll find Zib the same woman she was even during those last days. The sheer fact that she vanished in the seconds after your birth – that she had the strength to do that – doesn't bode well. I'm sorry.'

Edrea tightened her grip on the books and pushed away all thoughts but for what they needed to do. She straightened. 'All right, let me study the ritual she attempted and see if I can work out where it went wrong, or at least craft something to patch up any obvious errors.' She huffed a little laugh. 'I suppose we'll see whether I really live up to her skill or if I've just been deluding myself all these years.'

'The first one,' Aaric said, and if his attempt at faith in those abilities he'd previously hoped to discourage was a little transparent, well, she appreciated the gesture anyway.

'Perhaps, but once I've done that thoroughly and safely, I say we summon this messenger, whatever it is, and listen to what it has to say. If it's the only way to stop it killing people, especially our own townsfolk, then we have a responsibility. And then...' She paused, fingers tightening on the books even further and her voice going cold and flat. 'And then, for what it did to Mother, I say we kill it.'

PART FOUR
THE TRUTH

CHAPTER ELEVEN

There was little Runar had been able to contribute to the long, twisted tale of Hephzibah Gothghul and the entity, but now things were different. He watched as Edrea cleared the big table and put the stack of books on one edge. Then, carefully, she placed the beast's claw, her mother's locket, the perfume bottle and the blue journal in its centre. She beckoned, and they gathered around the table.

The rain that had been falling in sheets all day showed no signs of stopping, its force if anything increasing as the violet light of Hysh left the sky. The wind blew gusts of rain to shatter against the windows of the library, and the fire in the hearth roared and fluttered, a wounded beast attempting to escape the ravages of the weather.

'What are these?' she asked quietly.

'Three of them are Zib's,' Aaric said. 'Arguably, the claw is the odd one out.'

'And gathered accidentally,' Runar supplied. 'I can guarantee it did not sacrifice that claw to the cause willingly.'

'And yet it is a link, nonetheless,' Edrea said. 'They are all links. To each other, to me, to the messenger. It is not without the realms of possibility that the acquisition of the claw led to it sending us the locket. A locket that, because my mother was wearing it at the time of my birth and it vanished with her, is likely connected to me and also to whatever took her. It could even be spirit-locked, meaning it is attuned to me specifically, but not only that, it's a repository. It both stores and focuses power.'

Runar leant forward and stared at the heavy gold but didn't touch it. He'd handled a few magical artefacts before, but only if they'd been drained or disabled, or their owner had made them safe first. He wasn't entirely sure who owned a locket that had potentially been in some distant dimension for a quarter of a century, and despite the fact it had done nothing to him when he'd first picked it up, he wasn't willing to repeat the experiment. 'How do you know?' he asked instead.

'I can feel it,' she said simply. 'It's empty at the moment, but there's a feel to that emptiness that's hard to miss. But not only that – it features on the portrait in the ballroom, and I could never understand why Mother held it as she did.' She picked up a quill and gestured with the tip. 'In the painting, she's touching these three points and there's a golden orb floating above her other hand. We haven't had a repository in the castle before, so I've never been able to do more than read the lore about them, meaning I didn't make the connection until I actually touched it. It… it sucks at my power. I can feel it wanting to draw it out of me.'

'And you're sure it's empty?' Tiberius asked. 'The messenger didn't send it back to us with an unpleasant surprise hidden inside?'

Runar's hand dropped automatically to the polished wood of his revolver's grip, and he stood up, moving away from the necklace.

'I'm sure,' she said with a small smile, and he relaxed again. 'Did she ever let you touch it?'

Tiberius shook his head, but Aaric nodded. 'I did. But of course that means nothing – it wouldn't have affected me anyway. But if you say it's empty, I believe you.'

Runar didn't miss the tiny smile that hovered at Edrea's lips and remembered, vividly, the pride and pleasure he'd felt on the rare occasions of praise from his mother when he was younger. There was a twist of regret in him at the knowledge that Edrea was only feeling that now, possibly for the first time in her life. *But at least she is feeling it.*

'And you can wield it?' Tiberius asked, bringing the sharp-shooter back to the room and the sheer audacity of what they were going to attempt.

'Once I understand its properties, yes, and I expect those will be in Mother's journals somewhere.' She raised a questioning eyebrow, and Aaric held up the library index.

'I can't remember which one. I'll find it for you.' They exchanged another smile, and Runar couldn't help but echo the expression. It was far pleasanter to be around them when they weren't trying to craft words into weapons to stab at each other.

'Thank you. The point to most repositories is to increase both the focus of a spellcrafter's power and how much they can channel. In our case, this means that the circle I cast will be stronger with the locket's aid. Even if I don't fill it and then wait to replenish my strength, I can focus the power I use more tightly, like a lens intensifying sunlight. Deciding when we want to proceed will allow me to gauge how much magic I can transfer to the repository without being drained for the start of the summoning.' She picked up the locket again and studied it, contorting her fingers but not placing the tips against the metal. Then she nodded, as if confirming a suspicion.

'From what you told us, Father, I think the problem with Mother's circle was that she cast it around herself. She was in there with the entity. That's not what I'll do. I'll cast it around the focal point of the summoning, which in this case will be the claw and some embellishments. I'll draw the entity to that specific spot and cage it in with the circle. We'll all be on the outside.'

Runar exchanged relieved glances with the other two men as some of the tension trickled out of his neck and shoulders. He'd have done – would still do – whatever was needed, but the tale Aaric had woven of Hephzibah in the circle with the creature had not been one he'd wanted to re-enact.

'All right,' she said briskly, a faint blush staining her cheeks at their palpable relief. 'As I said before, the bottle, the claw and the locket represent most of the elements needed for a complex spellcrafting to summon the entity, because the entity itself indicated them and has probably blood-locked itself to us. The locket is metal and memory. The claw is life and will, and is also intrinsically tied to the entity – it will have had to expend a part of its own essence to create the beast, and we now have that essence in our possession. The perfume is both liquid and breath, for the scent lingers on the air. Fire is intention and transformation, and earth is stillness and new life. I can bring those to the summoning easily enough through common magical ingredients. And lastly, the book will contain the knowledge to enact the summoning. Plus, it ties us to Mother, another thread that will convince the entity we mean it no harm but want to understand its message.'

'Well, aside from the fact that I shot at it and your mother stabbed it with scissors,' Tiberius said carefully. 'And that in the last two days, the three of us have attacked it repeatedly. In fact, the only person who hasn't is you, Edrea. With all that in mind, I would be remiss not to ask – so far, we've discussed the practicalities, but are we all actually agreed that summoning this thing is the only way forward?'

'I'll hide the three of you around the corner so it doesn't know you're there,' Edrea said with a wave of her hand.

'How dignified,' the priest murmured, but they both subsided at Aaric's quelling look.

'The question is important,' he said in a severe tone. 'We are existing on assumptions more than hard knowledge. We speak as if the ritual will be successful, yet we cannot guarantee that. We don't know how much strength it has used to appear twice in different guises. It may simply not be strong enough to appear for a third time, no matter the power of your summoning, Edrea. Alternatively, perhaps it has spent the last twenty-five years growing in power, and the energy it has expended so far is negligible. It may appear in your circle with ten times the strength it had before. We can guarantee nothing except that we will all be in the most perilous danger.'

'Everyone has always resisted the visitations. Fought them,' Tiberius added in the heavy, brooding silence as Aaric's words sank in. 'Until Hephzibah. Despite how that ended, despite the awfulness of that entire night, she learnt more than anyone whose accounts she read. And while that knowledge is lost with her, what we do know is that she did it all without guidance.' He gestured. 'Whereas we have guidance, at least of a sort. We have objects belonging to the entity, objects to increase our own power and objects it has specifically indicated we should gather. All of that points to more than mindless evil. It points to an intelligence attempting to make contact deliberately. With forethought.'

'You seem to be contradicting your earlier words, Mister Grim,' Runar said quietly.

Tiberius spread his hands. 'Merely examining all angles. The strength and power of such a being cannot be overstated. It is contacting us – it is affecting and killing us – from another realm or dimension. The effort needed to do so, as well as the strength of will, is almost beyond comprehension. And yet it needs our help. Think what that might mean, what we might be required to do. We will already be far in over our heads just with the summoning. But what happens if we succeed? Contacting the entity is the first – not the last – step in what we are about to attempt. And so I ask again, are the four of us really doing this?'

'We could learn where Mother is,' Edrea whispered.

Tiberius nodded, but Runar interrupted before he could say anything. 'We could. We could learn truly terrible things about her, and that we are powerless to help her, in the instant before we're all torn apart. We could learn she's been completely enslaved by this messenger, turned into a ravening monster that we're duty bound to track and slaughter.' The three of them were staring at him with expressions ranging from distress to fury. 'Is knowing your mother's fate fair recompense for summoning a creature from another world, or dimension – a creature so powerful it can send splinters of itself across the realms and which might annihilate us and then every still-living creature in Shyish?'

'Runar,' Edrea breathed, and he felt sick at the betrayal in her face, but he pushed on.

'If we do this, it must be for the right reasons. Emotion has no place in this decision.'

'Skoldofr's right,' Aaric said heavily. 'Edrea, you've only just learnt that Hephzibah may still be alive, even if in some tormented place, and that knowledge could colour your decisions.'

Edrea began to gather up the books, slapping them one on top of the other with unnecessary violence, before raking the group with a glare that could melt stone. 'If you remember, it is I who has been pushing to communicate with the entity since the start, before I knew anything about Mother's fate. It was

I who contacted the beast, who faced it down without weapons and sought to understand it. It is I who begged the spirit to speak while you hunted it or fled from it. My intentions have always been clear.'

She opened her mouth to say more, closed it, and then exhaled hard through her nose. 'Before tonight, I would have shouted and told you all I'd conduct the ritual alone. I know now that I can't do that. I need all three of you. But no one should be coerced into something so perilous. So I am going to go to your study, Father, and begin the task of unpicking Mother's final journal to confirm what she did and what went wrong. If you could bring me the books relating to the locket? If you choose to help me, I will be pleased, but I won't seek to influence that choice.'

The three men were still and silent for a long pause after she'd left.

'Lord Gothghul,' Runar said eventually. 'Your daughter is very impressive and more than a little terrifying. You should be extremely proud of her.'

Tiberius snorted, but the stare Aaric levelled on the sharp-shooter sent a cold shiver down his spine. 'I am. And I'll thank you to keep your eyes, hands and intentions away from her.' The old scholar strode away to the shelves, and Tiberius put a quelling hand on Runar's wrist as he began to fumble for a reply. They waited in silence until he'd found the books Edrea wanted and left the library with them in hand.

'I... I didn't mean...' Runar began.

Tiberius snorted again and then laughed quietly before raising a sceptical eyebrow. 'Didn't you? Ah, don't mind me, Skoldofr. For all the affectation of it, I'm not really her uncle. I suppose it doesn't matter what I think. Though if it was up to me, I'd say she could do much worse and you could never do better.'

Runar began to stammer through a response, but Tiberius squeezed his wrist and cut him off. 'It does matter what Aaric thinks, though, so if you do have any, ah, *intentions*, at least wait until after all this, yes?'

Runar could feel the heat in his face as he blushed furiously, the memory of Edrea bandaging his wounds, the memory of her in her nightclothes, surfacing in his treacherous mind. 'I do admire her,' he protested weakly, 'and she's far more likely to keep us all alive through this than I am.'

'Aaric is… old-fashioned about these things, despite marrying Hephzibah, who was even wilder and more ungovernable than Edrea.'

Runar leant a hip against the table and folded his arms across his chest. 'Maybe the problem is him trying to *govern them* in the first place,' he said sourly. 'They're people, not dogs.'

'Enough,' Tiberius snapped, and Runar flushed again and stood up. 'You are in your employer's home and will abide by his rules. The last thing we need is Edrea's wildness rubbing off on you. I need to know we can rely on you, Skoldofr.'

The sharpshooter nodded once. 'You can. Absolutely, Mister Grim. My sincere apologies. It won't happen again.'

'I should hope not,' Aaric growled from the doorway, and Runar grimaced. How much had he heard? He came back in and gestured them to seats around the table. 'Edrea was right, though. We do need to face this practically. We hired you to kill a beast, not confront an unknown creature of unknown abilities and temperament, Skoldofr. There's no shame in leaving if you want no further part in this.'

'I'll stay,' Runar said immediately. 'I was hired to end a threat to the Hollow, and I'll not shirk that contract or break my word. It would sit ill with me to know there was a creature terrorising a town and do nothing about it because I thought it would be someone else's problem twenty-five years from now. So no, I will stay, and I will protect her – and you – with my life if necessary. As my squad did.

'Ever since that shade called my name, I've been in this until the end, my lords,' he added into the thoughtful silence. 'I have no grand illusions about my education or my abilities, but I know you don't suffer fools. And I know you know that I am very good at what it is I do – you wouldn't have hired me otherwise. Miss Gothghul has said we each need to make our own choice, and mine is made. I'm staying.'

'We're all in, of course,' Aaric said, though Tiberius hadn't actually said so. 'Of course we are. We won't leave Edrea to face this alone. All right, then as my unruly *and impressive* daughter suggested, let us discuss tactics. Your thoughts, Skoldofr?'

He was glad the castle's lord could put Runar's words behind them and focus on what came next. Despite both Tiberius' and Aaric's historic experience in the field and the fact that they still fought and had defeated some of the lesser horrors that the Necroquake had woken, neither were particularly young and both had suffered mental and physical setbacks that had stolen some of their strength.

Which meant it was time to prove that his claims to expertise were not simply boasts. 'Location first. The way I see it, we've got two options – the Blood-Rock Peaks, as that was clearly tied somehow to the beast, almost like there was a door of some kind between its master or home or whatever, or here, where the shade appeared. Both have advantages and drawbacks, but I lean more towards bringing it here.'

Tiberius cocked an eyebrow. 'Here?'

'This castle has been cleansed, and while it might not keep out something of the power you're describing, it might at least slow it. Either way, it's secure and contained, and while we need it to manifest in Edrea's circle, every layer of wall and door between it and the Hollow is a blessing in my book. Also, the castle has the added advantage of being home ground. If there's anywhere you should all feel the most comfortable, in the centre of your power, it's here. My suggestion is that we gather everything we

need and congregate somewhere defensible – barricade ourselves in and then send all the staff away. No point putting
anyone else in danger, especially if they're unaware of what
we're attempting. I won't risk innocents.'

'Yes,' Aaric said. 'Here.'

Runar's foot tapped on the carpet, the need to move growing
in him. He swallowed it down. 'At least then, if it does slip out
of your daughter's control, my lord, it's still trapped, at least
partially. It will give us time to try and deal with it. I know Edrea
wants the message, but my occupation is death, and I'm good
at it. If the risks become too great, or the situation demands it,
you should know that I will move to eradicate the entity any
way I can.'

Runar put his hands on the table and fixed them both with
a look. 'I will do so without waiting for permission, my lords.
My concern is keeping all of us alive, and that is not meant as
a detriment to your own prowess, sirs, but the four of us living
through this is far more important to me than whatever message
this creature has for us. I would also recommend you, Mister
Grim, prepare an exorcism and keep it to hand. If we can't kill
it, if we're at risk, we need to send it back where it came from.'

Aaric looked thoughtful and then approving. He gave a short
nod, and Runar breathed a little easier. 'I will ensure Edrea
knows that is the plan. I will impress upon her the importance
that Tiberius dismisses the entity if it becomes necessary. As
you say, no matter how close we are to understanding its message or its presence.'

'And you, Aaric. You need not confront it at all if it will be
too much. And especially if, well, it may not even remember
Hephzibah, let alone show any remorse for whatever happened
to her.' Tiberius was gentle, and Runar looked away, unwilling
to intrude further into their shared grief and memories.

'I will be there,' Aaric barked, and Tiberius wisely said no more.

Runar sought to change the subject. 'My lord, if I may, do either of you have any intelligence from a combat perspective on dealing with this thing? You shot at it on the night, Mister Grim? What about blessings or rituals?'

'Ordinary bullets, ordinary pistol. It did nothing but blast a hole in the wall. As for the cleansing, I didn't get the chance to finish it before it manifested, and I couldn't even begin a banishment before things turned to shit.'

The sharpshooter blinked at the profanity, but he couldn't exactly argue.

'And barely anything my hunters and I did to the beast had an effect. Oh, we hit it all right, multiple times, so many times it should have died there in the town without even reaching the Blood-Rock Peaks, but everything seemed... robbed of its power. As if it caused only superficial damage, and what we did was more likely due to the cumulative effect than any single injury. Moll's arrows were no better than our bullets. I suppose if it was, how did you put it, only a splinter of itself that it has sent across dimensions, then despite the very real wounds we inflicted, perhaps it wasn't *here* enough to be seriously hurt. So, while I'll keep all of my usual ammunition to hand, we're going to need something else – for all our weapons. Mister Grim, if I make some bullets, would you be able to distil some of that cleansing potion for me to quench them in? It might increase their stopping power.'

'Of course,' Tiberius said. 'And I can brew a decent quantity of it and set it in a kettle over a fire or brazier. The steam will permeate the air and might rob the entity of some of its strength.'

The sharpshooter nodded. 'Excellent. And then any prayers or blessings you can speak over the weapons and ourselves. It's asking a lot, sir, I know, but otherwise, it's going to be down to quantity of ammunition and, probably, close quarters and edged weapons.' He shuddered.

Tiberius grinned and topped up his glass from the wine bottle at his elbow. 'I've missed you, Runar,' he said, surprising him. 'Only you would apologise for asking a priest to bless weapons before a fight such as this.' His smile was strained, though, and once again Runar wished he knew exactly what had happened at the Battle of Blood Meridian that had so damaged the priest that he had left the Blackshore Guard.

'As for what happens next,' Runar said, 'even though logic indicates it should be weakened – further from the Blood-Rock Peaks, on its third manifestation in two days and arriving into a room infused with cleansing magic and a trap created by your daughter – we'll still plan for it to overwhelm us. We'll plan for it to be Nagash himself in a towering rage, because we don't know what we're facing, not really. I don't want us going in there thinking we know the outcome. I'd rather be over-prepared and overcautious than possessed or scrabbling around looking for my own head.'

'As you say. In this we are yours to command,' Aaric agreed. Runar sighed silently, relieved. He'd half expected the hero of the Bonesplinter War to insist he was in command, but instead he seemed to sense that it was Runar's input they needed here. 'What else?'

'Edged weapons, as I said. As much as I *do not* want to be close enough to need them, an axe to the face does a lot of damage that isn't – theoretically – as easily absorbed as a bullet. Again, any blessings that can be prayed over the weapons will be critical. Magical weapons you might have picked up during your travels for preference. But I think, based on what little we know, that at least you and I, my lord, are going to be here in nothing more than a support capacity for Edrea. She's the only one I'm convinced can do it real, lasting damage. And I know she's got that locket, but is there anything else we can do to supplement her energy? She takes from her body, breath and blood to channel death magic, yes? Can she take from ours instead?'

Aaric pursed his lips, watching Runar with surprise and new-found respect. 'You'd offer?'

Runar shrugged. 'If there's no other way I can help, then of course. This barrier she's going to erect, if nothing can get out, then nothing can get in, either, and that will include bullets and axes. So if it's all I can do, then I'll do it. If it's a choice between pricking my finger and us all dying?'

'I can bless the locket,' Tiberius mused. 'It might increase the efficacy of what power she does deposit into it. Wouldn't be a lot extra, but it's better than nothing.'

Aaric frowned at the many shelves lining the walls. 'You've stirred a memory, Skoldofr,' he muttered as Runar gave in to restlessness and stood to pace back and forth before the fireplace.

The wind screamed in the chimney, kicking an ember onto the rug; he trod heavily on it before it could begin to smoke.

'A ritual to store someone else's energy, even if they are not learned in magic... Yes, that might be possible. Edrea would need to craft the energy to channel the magic, but at least she wouldn't be using her own constantly. Thank you,' he added, and Runar shrugged.

'There's a good chance this won't really be my type of battle,' he said apologetically. 'But like I said, if I can help, I will. I'd prefer not to lose all my energy, just in case it does somehow break the trap. I still need to be able to defend her in that situation. Other than that, she can take as much as she needs. And now the location,' he finished, returning to the table. 'You know the castle best, my lord. Where do you suggest?'

'The old dungeon. It's still in good repair – we've been obliged to hold the odd malefactor over the years. It's also underground and entirely made of stone, one level up from the cold room, and it's not easy to get out of. Edrea could cast her circle inside a cell. Then we've automatically got a locked door between us and it, plus the weight of a cleansed castle with dozens more locked doors and windows between it and the outside world.'

Runar tapped his forefinger against his lower lip as he thought. A dungeon was made for a very specific reason, after all. 'Sounds good. Let's have a look, shall we?'

'I'll start brewing up the holy water and then head to the armoury to bless the weapons,' Tiberius said. 'I'll do your own when you get back – I know you won't part with them until you must,' he added, and the sharpshooter had to consciously relax his grip on his revolver. He managed a nonchalant grin the priest didn't believe for a second.

They had just reached the stairs leading down to the dungeons when the pounding on the castle door began. Runar and Aaric exchanged alarmed looks and hurried to answer. The thick, heavy bog oak was almost torn from their grasp by the wind as they hauled it open. Rain blew in at them, cold enough to feel like needles.

'My lord! Sir! It's back,' panted a bedraggled, terrified woman with mud up to the knees of her skirt. She was soaked and whiter than a corpse shroud. 'The beast is back, and it's killing us. All of us. *You have to help.*'

CHAPTER TWELVE

The bone-deep weariness from draining her energy was still with her, but Edrea pushed on, deep into the night, reading her mother's final journal with feverish haste and, increasingly, a distress it became harder and harder to conceal.

It had obviously been kept for the express purpose of discovering more about the Fourfold Herald, but even without any other details of her mother's life, the brightness and fierce intelligence and lust for living that she exhibited at the beginning of the journal declined as time went by. Not only her thoughts but her handwriting began to curdle and dim, losing coherence and flair, until words were scratched and stabbed and smeared across the page, feverish and uncontrolled.

Hephzibah's insights were scalpel sharp, as precise and even as the best duardin-made tools – to begin with. Her educated guesses about the Fourfold Herald, the leaps of imagination to bring in threads concerning the Path of the Fallen Four and then the Mhurghast were audacious but logical. Edrea could find no fault in them and, indeed, marvelled at her mother's methodical cleverness. She wasn't sure she'd have made those connections if this had been her own research, but reading them over, she had to agree with her mother's assessment. These disparate events were related.

And yet the entries became more tenuous as the weeks of Hephzibah's pregnancy and preoccupation passed. Musings on the nature of the apparition were to be expected, but Hephzibah's speculations were wild and not based on any of the evidence she'd gathered. She began to write, quite openly, about actively seeking the entity, of sinking into meditation or sending her sight or senses out on a blast of magic, calling to it. Mentions of the bloody-eyed hound of portent began to crop up, even though that particular manifestation had never visited Gothghul Hollow during Hephzibah's time. But she wrote as if she and the beast were old acquaintances.

There were notes in the margins that meant nothing, strings of letters and numbers that had Edrea not been so exhausted and upset, she would have realised hours before were references to book titles and page numbers. When she did make the leap, she scrambled back to the library and snatched down the first few she could find, only sparing the briefest instant to wonder where the others were.

Swallowing her excitement, Edrea checked the page references. The first related to the magical absorption properties of the dead-root plant; the second referenced an ancient practice said to have come out of the wilderness around Necros that was alleged to increase concentration; and the third was a list of ingredients for the very magical remedy she'd spent so long trying to make a couple of days previously. She stared at that last one and then barked a laugh. 'Oh, Mother,' she murmured. 'I wonder if I'll ever match your effortless ability.'

She stuck a bookmark in it for later, but she was thoughtful as she shuffled back to the study. On the surface, the references bore no relation to the mystery or the entity. Were they, perhaps, just symptoms of Hephzibah's wandering focus? Perhaps they were nothing more than notes for herself for other work, and unrelated?

Edrea did what she could to suppress the tangled knot of grief and anger and confusion that was slowly growing at the base of her throat, threatening to choke her, and continued to read. She made careful notes on separate sheets of paper: one for those observations about the entity's identity that were clear and sensible, and a second for hints about the ritual and summoning itself. She listed the first three references she'd checked as well, just in case they became relevant later on. At some point she'd need to check the others, but for now, there was more than enough information in the journal itself. Best to understand that first. It quickly became very clear that Hephzibah had begun to formulate her own ritual for bringing the entity to her startlingly early in her research.

'As if she always knew she'd summon it,' Edrea said, her voice low and scratchy with weariness. Its roughness pulled at her consciousness, and she became aware that the study's fire had burnt down and she was squinting in the light of a single surviving lamp placed on the edge of the desk.

The sorceress sat back, groaning as her spine popped and her joints protested. She needed more food, a lot of hot tea and several hours in bed before she'd be anywhere near her full strength and ready to enact the summoning. Tomorrow night at the earliest. The following dawn for preference.

Edrea tapped the feather of her quill idly on the paper covered in her hasty handwriting, wondering whether the unholy intelligence that was coming would give her the time she needed. She could push through if she had to, but the idea of draining herself again was... uncomfortable. Still, she'd do what she must.

With that in mind, she removed her mother's locket and inspected it again. It sat skin-warm on her palm, and she indulged in a momentary fantasy that it was Hephzibah's body heat she cradled, not her own. Her lips curled slightly. 'Foolish child,' she murmured in a decent parody of her father's voice. Then she sobered. 'Best get this over with now so I've got time to replenish.'

The journal didn't contain any instructions on activating the repository, but she knew the spots to touch to cast magic from it and carefully reversed them, contorting her hand to form the opposite shape. Instantly, the metal heated under her skin as it began to draw her strength and she gasped – she hadn't thought it would work without so much as an incantation. No wonder it had been her mother's most prized possession – it was powerful beyond measure. And just as dangerous.

The drain was steady but not so fast that it left her dizzy. Edrea could monitor her levels, feeling her weariness grow, her limbs become slack and heavy as the flow of energy from her core drained into the locket. She could almost see it slide from beneath her skin and into the repository, the heavy gold of the jewellery taking on a new lustre, a sheen of pure essence. Pure Edrea.

When her head was drooping, too heavy to hold up, she managed to prise her fingers free of the locket, and the thread snapped back into her with a little jolt. Edrea heard ragged gasps echoing in the study, drowning out the dying crackle from the fireplace. She was sweating, a cold and unpleasant film against her skin. Dazedly, she wondered whether there was in fact something dangerous inside the repository. Where were the safeguards to prevent draining due to careless handling? The placement of fingertips was awkward, but not impossible to replicate accidentally. Had Hephzibah disabled the safeguards? She made a note to check through the other journals when she had time. *Assuming we're all alive to check such things.* She let out an exhausted sigh.

Edrea stared at the locket lying on the table, gleaming buttery and malevolent in the low light. The urge to reverse the flow and drag all the strength back into herself was almost overwhelming, but she resisted, sliding the necklace behind the stack of books where she couldn't see it. Then she rang for Young Aethelwych, who'd stayed up in bleary-eyed acceptance that none of them were apparently going to bed, and asked for tea, bread and jam and a few pieces of fruit. Aethelwych, whose mother had been killed by Edrea's mother. She wondered how much of the truth of that night the housekeeper knew. Her stomach cared nothing for inherited guilt and growled its delight, but not even the anticipation of a meal could stop her hands from trembling. By the dead, she was tired.

When the food arrived, she fell on it ravenously and then laboriously continued to make her way through the journal. She had to reach the end before she slept. She didn't. The soporific effect of the food and tea pulled her into sleep within moments.

Edrea stirred and mumbled something, squinting at the line of brightness spearing into her face as she turned over and pulled the blanket up. She nestled back into the warm darkness for a few long, drowsy moments, and then shot upright.

'Morning,' a voice said, and she blinked desperately.

'Uncle Tiberius?'

'With tea and an extremely large breakfast,' he confirmed. 'It's nearly noon.'

'*What?*' Edrea tore at the blankets tangling her legs and discovered she was still in her trousers and shirt, at least. 'How did I get here? What happened? What about the–'

'We found you unconscious and covered in ink at about three this morning and brought you up here. You were snoring.'

Edrea blushed. 'I do not snore,' she snapped.

Tiberius laughed. 'Believe me, lass, you sounded like a hog in a trough.'

She did her best to scowl, but a smile was teasing the edge of her mouth. 'Pass me the tea and leave me to eat in peace,' she growled in mock outrage, and he did so, giving her a quaint little bow as he presented the cup. His smile didn't reach his eyes.

'What?'

'What?' he tried, but he'd never been able to lie to her – not about anything other than her mother, anyway.

'I know that look. Is it Father? Runar?' Edrea made to get up again and he pushed her back into the mattress.

'Eat and drink and I will tell you.' Her stomach was suddenly in knots, but not even that could stop the insistent gnawing of her hunger. 'The beast came back.'

Tiberius' hand shot out impressively fast and he caught the teacup as it wobbled in her grip. 'Twenty-seven dead. Runar spent most of the night in town, doing what he could. We tried to stop him – the beast spared him last time and we didn't want it getting the wrong idea, if beasts can have ideas. He went anyway. Saved more than a dozen lives.'

Edrea's mouth twisted. Those people would have died were it not for his presence, but he'd put the entire summoning in jeopardy. 'I should find him.'

'You should eat. He's asleep. And he's unhurt, I promise. Physically.'

Edrea winced at the implication. 'I'll eat. Do you have a plan, Uncle?' she asked as he patted her hand and stood.

'We do. But we need you strong and rested for it. More to the point, do you have a plan?'

Edrea grimaced. 'The beginnings of one. But if the beast is back, I suspect our deadline just got a lot shorter. It seems like it's no longer willing to wait.' She quickly outlined the letter-and-number references in the journal and asked whether they could gather the books the cipher referenced while she breakfasted and comb through them for a pattern. 'I need to know whether any of them will be of use in the ritual, and I need to see whether Mother modified a standard summoning or not. I'll be down soon. I can't believe you let me sleep so long.'

'I'm not sure Sigmar himself could have woken you,' Tiberius said, and slid out through the door before she could reply.

Edrea sat on the edge of the bed and breathed in the steam from the tea, then took a too-hot mouthful and swallowed hurriedly, cursing. She finally slithered out of the bed when the cup was empty, wincing at the sting of the cold flagstones under her bare feet. She poured herself another cup and stuffed toast in her mouth as she stripped out of her clothes and washed, her thoughts beginning to speed up.

In truth, she'd probably fallen asleep at exactly the right moment, because it had allowed her mind to absorb everything she'd read and sort through it. She did have the beginnings of a plan, one inspired by her mother's but not necessarily a strict copy of it. Irrespective of the success or failure of Hephzibah's summoning, Edrea wasn't her and their strengths were not the same. If she tried to replicate her ritual, with the exception of remaining on the outside of the circle, she knew instinctively it would fail.

Everything she'd gleaned from the story and then the journal told her that Hephzibah was driven by her instincts, that her abilities were as much intuition as they were learnt. Edrea could be similar, but in this they needed to take the opposite approach. She needed the proven efficacy of established ritual, established lore. She was going to work out exactly where her mother had deviated and why, and make sure she didn't do the same.

Emboldened by the decision, she dressed and finished breakfast, treating herself to a final few moments of relative peace. Once she reached the library, there'd be no stopping until it was done and they'd lived to tell the tale of the entity's message – or not.

The house was quieter than she expected, and it took some time to find the others. Young Aethelwych pointed her to, of all places, the old dungeon, but as Edrea made her way down there, grateful for the jacket she'd pulled on over her shirt, she realised their purpose and approved.

Strictly speaking, there were two cells in the dungeon, but Aaric had appropriated one years before in which to store wine and spare furniture. The other was being busily inspected by him and Tiberius. The priest had gripped the bars that formed the fourth wall of the cell and was shaking them, checking their strength and the mortar that held them in place.

Edrea wished, for a single mischievous moment, that she didn't need to conserve every drop of energy she had – the urge to snap her fingers and lock them in the cell was almost overpowering. Aaric must have seen it in her face, for he stepped through the cell's low gate towards her, one side of his mouth curving up. 'There's a look I know well,' he said, and to her astonishment, he leant in and smoothed the tangle of curls back from her brow, tucking a thick ringlet behind her ear. 'Wild hair and devilry in her eye. You look more like her with every passing day.'

Edrea ducked her head and then surprised him in turn, stepping in close to brush her lips against his cheek. 'So, a monster in a dungeon, eh? I can see the appeal, and from this side of the bars, I'll definitely be able to direct the ritual. It makes sense.'

'Plus, this is the only space we haven't cleansed,' Tiberius added, giving the last bar a good shake. It didn't budge. 'So we thought it would be easier for it to manifest here, and then once it has, I add the cleansing ingredients to a boiling kettle and let the steam fill the room. Thought it might weaken it once it's trapped here.'

Edrea hummed her approval. 'You have been busy. I doubt it will do much, but we need every advantage we can get, and besides, it could well help prevent it gaining any mental or spiritual control over us. And where's Runar? Is he all right?'

'Still sleeping. He used up almost our entire stock of ammunition last night, but we sent Viktor to the forge-master in town to buy everything he had and spent the morning making more.'

Aaric grimaced. 'Which wasn't easy after what happened there. The town is... It's been gutted. No one wants to sell ammunition when they might need it themselves.'

Edrea's breakfast churned uneasily. 'Then we'd better not fail,' she said, making her voice big and confident so it echoed through the dungeon. 'If the Collegiate ever deigns to send someone here to find out what happened, we'll be ready to teach them a thing or two.'

'Now you really sound like Zib,' Aaric said with a hint of sourness. 'Absolutely unfounded confidence.'

Edrea squeezed his arm. 'It's not unfounded,' she promised. 'I'm good enough. The four of us are good enough.'

'All right, all right,' he grumbled, but he didn't disengage his arm from hers and there was such fierce pride mingled with desperate worry in his face that she caught her breath. She squeezed again. 'How about we try and live through this first, before we start taking on the greatest magical institution in Shyish?'

'How about-' Edrea began, and then snapped her mouth shut. She stared up into the cobwebbed stone vault.

'What-'

'Quiet.'

They stilled, and Edrea tilted her head, barely breathing. There. Yes, she could definitely... Her stomach dropped into her feet. Faint, on the very edge of hearing, a voice was chanting. Low and seductive, twining with hunger and yearning. Distant over the chanting but still audible, the grandfather clock chimed four.

Edrea's fingers dug into Aaric's forearm. 'It's coming.' She gave him a little shake. 'Get Runar. *Right now.*' Aaric was already running for the narrow, slippery stone stairs. 'And be careful,' she added as his shadow vanished up them. She grabbed the priest next. 'You blessed the weapons?'

Tiberius pointed, and she saw a variety of guns and swords and an axe piled on a table. Beneath were long coils of chain.

'The banishment ritual?'

'Almost ready,' he said immediately, and Edrea became aware of the easy crack of command in her voice. She expected the ex-soldier to bristle at the tone, but he simply watched her, waiting for her next instruction.

'Finish it. There're things I need.' She didn't wait for a reply, just ran for the stairs, pounding up flight after flight towards her room and workbench and shelves of jars and potions and books. Poisons and deadsight and restoratives and stimulants, blinding powder and lung-seize and a score of raw ingredients. As much as she could gather in the time they had left. Which suddenly, appallingly, wasn't very long at all. Especially because she hadn't yet finalised the summoning.

Runar sat in the herbary, staring at the statue of Hephzibah with its shattered face. His exhaustion was a deep, sucking greyness at his core. So many dead, so many more injured, clawed and bitten and missing limbs, scarred beyond recognition. Too many dead. Even one was one too many.

The stone bench was wet from the night's rain, soaking through his trousers. He barely noticed. Aldo, Einar, Moll and Karl. Dozens of Hollowers. And all he'd accomplished was… not dying himself. Elbows propped on his knees, he stared at his hands. They were scarred; they were shaking. The lilac sky of early afternoon was darkening as yet more clouds piled up across the horizon and bore down on the castle with malicious intent.

Despite the cold, his eyes were heavy, and he was about to clamber to his feet and head back inside for a few hours' sleep when Aaric shouted his name. His voice was ragged, and adrenaline sent a bolt of energy through Runar. He stood so fast that he staggered, dizzy, but then Aaric called again.

'Over here,' he shouted, making his way towards the gate in the inner wall. Viktor, the castle groom, poked his head into the herbary and then gestured frantically when he saw the sharpshooter.

'My lord, he's here,' he called back as Runar broke into a run towards him.

Viktor squawked as he was dragged out of the gateway and Aaric appeared, his silver hair dishevelled. 'Edrea says it's coming. *Get in here.*'

'How long do we have?' Runar demanded as he pushed Viktor out of the way with a barked instruction to retreat to the town and then followed the lord of the castle.

'I don't know. Move.'

He skidded through the door and towards the stairs.

'Runar!' Edrea called, and he whirled to face her. She was pale, her eyes dark and glittering.

'What?' he snapped. He needed to get into the dungeon and check the preparations. 'Wait. Why are you up here?'

'I needed some things.' She patted the satchel hanging by her hip, but whatever else she'd been about to say was lost when the clock just inside the front door began to chime four, over and over and over. Runar startled and spun to face it, then just as quickly whirled again when from the kitchen came the sound of shattering glass and porcelain. He drew his revolver and beckoned. Edrea crossed to his side, her ritual knife unsheathed in her hand.

'Are you all right? I heard what happened,' she began, and he cut her off when there were more shattering sounds, this time from the library. The sorceress moved instinctively, her need to preserve the books overriding common sense. Runar wrapped his free arm around her waist and dragged her back against his chest.

'Quiet,' he breathed in her ear, upper arm resting on her shoulder as he aimed the gun towards the library door. He nudged her forward, and together they crept closer. 'Got some poison?'

Edrea's free hand dipped into her pocket and came out holding a small twist of paper. 'If I throw this, hold your breath, close your eyes and move at least six feet. Fast.'

'Got it.' They were within a stride of the library door. Runar shifted his grip on Edrea. He took a soft breath in and shoved her sideways into the wall, held her there for a split second until she understood, and then cleared the doorway. He kept moving, but the objects floating in the room converged on him anyway: books, candlesticks, sharpened quills, inkwells and splinters of glass from the broken windows. All flying with lethal intent towards him.

A heavy leather-bound tome smacked into the side of his head and a shard of windowpane laid open his cheek. Runar resisted the urge to open fire and concentrated on deflecting what he could – the thick leather cuffs he wore on each wrist protected his arteries as he batted away razor-sharp glass.

'Don't come in here,' he yelled back towards the door. 'Get downstairs.'

He didn't know if Edrea replied, because the swirling smoke that had been dancing in the centre of the room suddenly coalesced into a figure edged in crimson. It was humanoid and clawed and fanged, its eyes chips of ember when they bent their burning intensity upon him. If it was the same shade as before, its appearance had degenerated markedly.

'Sigmar,' he started, and then it was on him, a whirling vortex of screeching, clawing, biting motes of molten ash and frozen ice. Edrea was peering in through the door, her mouth a perfect 'O' of horror. Her knife was brandished in front of her and he noted, with that hyper-focus that only came with combat, that she held it the way a fighter would – in a reverse grip. It reassured him even as he bellowed at her again to get downstairs, and then the spirit was anchored to his back by stringy limbs and piercing claws. Runar slapped his hand against the first of many paper talismans stitched to the centre of his bandolier and tore it free. Cupping it in his palm, he reached back past his own head and curved it around the Nighthaunt's barely there skull. The talisman solidified the connection, and he got a firm grip, tore the spirit off his back and flung it to the ground in front of him.

As he hurled it away, the spirit curled a hand or an arm or... something, around the revolver, and the barrel froze in an instant, thick blue-white frost racing along the metal towards the wooden handle faster than Runar could follow it. He pulled, but the ice hit the wood and split it and then spread into his fingers and the bones of his hand.

The sharpshooter yelled in pain but didn't let go, instead slapping his other hand – still cupping the talisman paper – against the barrel. It was enough to break the spirit's grip and send it screeching away, tearing around the library and shredding books and smashing shelves. It scooped up the glass littering the rug before the windows and hurled each piece towards Runar, who threw himself to the side. Slivers of glass dug into his calf-high boot, the tough leather pierced with ease. A second later, spectral fists came down on the big table and the solid corpse-birch wood shattered into kindling.

Runar crabbed sideways. 'Edrea? Edrea, are you still here?' He prayed he wouldn't be answered, that the sorceress had vanished into the dungeon where she would craft a ritual that would save them all, though now he didn't expect to live to see it. If his only remaining task was to distract the spirit until she was ready to lure it – and its full essence – into her circle, then so be it.

There was no answer, and the sharpshooter's smile was grim and utterly without mercy as he swung the library door shut and faced back into the room. 'It's just you and me then, messenger. I suggest you calm down if you want us to understand–'

The spirit latched on to his chest with taloned hands and feet, a gaping, needle-toothed maw screaming in his face with breath that stank of the grave. Claws broke through his shirt – he hadn't been wearing full kit – and anchored themselves in his flesh. Runar grinned into its face – the closer it came to him, the closer he was to it. And he had weapons at his disposal.

He pressed a second talisman against the gheist's flank. It shrieked, its teeth lengthening impossibly until they resembled the beast's fangs, and they lunged down to his throat. Runar got a leather-clad wrist between the spirit's jaws just long enough to press it backwards, choking, until he could bring his revolver to bear. He pressed the barrel beneath its chin and squeezed off a shot.

The bullets weren't blessed, and all it did was puff apart the spirit like a death-clock weed, blowing away into ember and ash. Within a second it was coalescing again. But a second was all Runar needed – the sharpshooter was sprinting for the library door and dragging it closed behind him.

He didn't worry whether anyone might still be here – the spirit had decided he was its next victim. All he had to do was lead it down to the dungeon and pray Edrea was there to spell it into her circle.

Or I could lead it away. Take it out to the moors and trap it within talismans and stab it to death. Save them. Save Edrea.

The temptation was almost overwhelming as Runar raced along the hall, past portraits that leered and reached for him with painted claws, statues that groaned, stone on stone, as they extended limbs to clutch him tight. The sharpshooter skidded beneath a grasping stone claw, sliding on polished flagstone until he was beyond its reach and then coming back onto his feet. He almost missed the turning into the spiralling stone stairway down to the dungeon, losing his balance at the last moment and throwing himself headlong into the entrance.

'Edrea? *You have ten seconds!*'

Runar didn't slow, taking the narrow stone steps three at a time, one ankle twisting and then four steps later the other until he crashed into the walls and stumbled the last dozen steps down into the dungeon.

Someone dragged him clear, and then his world exploded with chanting and magic and power.

CHAPTER THIRTEEN

When Runar burst into the dungeon, the spirit was clinging to his back by claws and teeth, its mouth fastened on the nape of his neck. There was enough blood running down between his shoulders that he'd need stitches. It wasn't Edrea but Tiberius who greeted him at the bottom of the stairs, the words of the banishment prayer tearing the spirit off him. He grunted as its claws and teeth exited his flesh and then gasped when Tiberius doused him in holy water. It was bitterly cold.

'That should buy us some time,' the priest said, panting, 'but not a lot. It's going to be even angrier when it comes back.'

'Just hold it off,' Edrea muttered as she strode into the empty cell and picked up a broom. Methodically, she swept the flagstones, and then carefully drew a circle with chalk while speaking in a language Runar didn't recognise. It was four paces across, and he watched her in between examining his revolver. The handle had split under the intense cold and, he noted now, the palm of his hand was blistered and weeping where it had frozen.

He slipped on a supple leather glove and then bound the grip in strips of fabric to hold the pieces together.

Edrea took a pace out and began again, this second, larger circle being drawn with a stick of beeswax. The language was different too, sharper, its consonants clipped and angry sounding. The hairs on his arms began to rise.

He glanced over as she stepped outwards again and began another line, this one – he peered – in ink? Looked like ink. Again a different language, guttural and grating on the ear. Runar had a vision of it echoing through the skeletal courts of the ancient dead. The magic this time caused a sudden pressure at his temples and behind his eyeballs. Tiberius groaned, a sharp sound he quickly muffled.

'How many more?' Runar whispered, jerking his head towards the cell. The priest held up two fingers and Runar puffed out his cheeks. It was going to get very uncomfortable in here very quickly. He tried to distract himself by checking the rest of the weapons. There was a table facing the cell covered in books and equipment: jars and vials, a pestle and mortar, buckets of water, oil and soil, perhaps, lined up underneath. Edrea's preparations. Her satchel stood next to the table and the sharpshooter gave it all plenty of room as he prowled the edges of the dungeon and looked up the dim stairwell again. They were doing it here in order to trap the entity, but Runar felt like he was the one in a cage. Awaiting his execution.

Edrea began her fourth circle, this one of metal filings tapped very gently in an unbroken line. It was a laborious process, the sorceress on her knees and shuffling very slowly around the circle, this chant profoundly unrecognisable. Beneath it, the clock struck four. Runar chafed his palms against his upper arms, chilled. Aaric was watching his daughter with the sort of focus a snake used to freeze a rodent into immobility. Tiberius was walking around the edge of the dungeon, praying quietly. Edrea's chant came to a stop and Runar glanced over yet again, as if she was magnetic. Seeing her like this, so different to her normal persona – prickly or otherwise – was a revelation. He'd always known of the power coiled inside her, but seeing it was a very different experience. She seemed taller, her shadow blacker in the unsteady light of a dozen lamps and lanterns. She seemed... otherworldly.

In the silence, Edrea was breathing in harsh, rasping pants. She left the cell and crossed to the table, Aaric gesturing behind her that none of them were to interrupt her focus. She dipped into her satchel and took out the beast's claw, the perfume bottle, the locket and the journal, and re-entered the cell, moving as if in a trance. She put the book down in the middle of the inner-most circle with something akin to reverence, and then placed the unstoppered bottle and the claw on top of it. The necklace she hung around her throat, before moving to the outside of the fourth circle and removing her boots and socks. She rolled up the legs of her trousers and the sleeves of her shirt, apparently oblivious to the cold of the flagstones.

Lord Gothghul turned his face deliberately away from his daughter. A second later Edrea began the fifth and final circle, and this time she was using her own blood. Her ritual knife was beautiful and ornate, slender-bladed but large enough to serve as an effective weapon if she needed it to. Without any sort of hesitation, she dragged it across the back of her right forearm. Runar was impressed – and a little nervous – at the equanimity with which she opened up the scar on her arm.

The chanting and drawing of this circle wound the energy in the room so tight that the air seemed to vibrate. There was a tiny window high up on the wall opposite the cells, the meagre light through the glass cut by thick, ugly bars set before it. A faint crackling noise drew his attention and he stared at it, confused, and then swore. Frost was growing across the glass with visible speed, and only his proximity to the small brazier kept the increasing cold at bay. 'Mister Grim?'

'I see it,' the priest murmured. He added a few final ingredients to the kettle of cleansing potion that stood next to the brazier.

In the cell, Edrea's voice emerged on clouds of breath, and the bloody circle she was drawing steamed in the frigid air. Still, she didn't seem to notice as she chanted and the magic drew closer and tighter with every sweep of her bloody finger across the wound and onto the floor. She kept her arm out to her side to keep any stray droplets on the outside of the final circle. Her chanting got louder and the taste at the back of Runar's throat was almost enough to choke him.

'Brace,' Tiberius murmured.

Edrea closed the circle with a string of shouted syllables and the room seemed to bow outwards, the walls themselves almost flexing at the explosion of power in the cell. Instantly, the frost that was now creeping along the walls flashed into steam and a roll of heat poured through the room, ruffling hair and clothes and causing the brazier's coals to blaze white-hot before settling back

In the stillness and the silence after the completion of the circle, they heard, very faintly, an answering voice. An answering chant. At the very limits of hearing, it still sent a ripple of unease through them all.

Runar met Aaric's eyes, and as one, the three men turned to Edrea. 'You can hear that?' was all she asked, and when they nodded, she licked at the cut in her arm, carefully collecting up any more blood before it could run and drip and ruin all she'd accomplished so far. She licked the blood off the ritual knife, too, and the sharpshooter felt his lip curl in an instinctive grimace. He reminded himself that this was Edrea the sorceress, mistress of a hundred languages and unimaginable power, not the woman who'd followed him to the Blood-Rock Peaks and tended his wounds. Not the vulnerable, big-eyed woman who'd asked him to help her run away from home. It did little to still the super-stitious dread whispering in the back of his mind.

'Chains,' she said.

'Where, Edrea?' Runar asked quietly, and had to fight the urge to flinch when her head swivelled, smooth as a snake's, to face him. Her eyes were blacker than before, he was sure of it, glit-tering in a way that didn't quite match with the lanterns placed around the room.

'Bring them in here. Do not so much as set one toe on the circles.'

He inclined his head, thinking there was absolutely no chance of that happening. That ritual space was pulsing with so much energy even he could feel it.

The chains grated horribly as he dragged them across the stone and up into his arms, juggling the heavy, almost slippery links as he crossed to the cell and stepped inside. He slid past the gate and turned to Edrea, the end of one chain flaring wide with the movement.

The sorceress gasped and leapt forward, her feet skipping between the lines of the circles as if she was a dancer, and she caught the trailing end of the chain before it could sweep through the line of blood. Runar froze, clutching the links tight, as she came to a stop close enough to kiss, the end of the chain only a hand's width above the floor, the length pulled taut in her hands.

The world crashed to a halt around them, and in the stillness, as of a bird poised, impossibly, mid-flight, the distant chanting seemed to strengthen for a moment, become a little clearer. A single voice, as Edrea's had been, but tinged with something not present in her tone, something he couldn't quite identify but which made his fingers itch for weapons.

'I'm so sorry,' he stammered as Edrea's breath ghosted across his cheek and her strange, glittering eyes glared at him with such weight and smouldering anger that his knees trembled.

And then she blinked and stepped back, her gaze losing a little of its intensity. 'Fortunately, no harm done, but please be careful.'

Runar nodded rapidly and shuffled sideways, putting the chains on the ground with exaggerated care. Between them, they fixed the end of each of the three chains to the bars of the wall, leaving them coiled in separate piles ready to throw around any entity that looked to be effecting an escape from the five circles. This close, the sharpshooter's skin felt hot and tight, almost blistered, as if he'd been beneath a punishing sun for hours on end. He didn't know how Edrea could stand it, but she appeared unaffected.

Together, they exited the cell, and Runar returned to prowling the edges of the dungeon, knife on one hip, revolver on the other and rifle in his hands. He felt unsafe despite the comforting weight of weaponry.

Edrea was muttering over the table, running one hand over a piece of paper covered in dense handwriting while the other sorted through a dozen small jars and bottles, some of clay, some clear glass and containing pastes, herbs, liquids or... *things*. Parts of things, in some cases.

Runar had managed one more circuit of the room when Edrea dropped the bottle she was holding; she stopped it from rolling off the edge, but automatically. Her face was tense, cords standing out in her pale throat and muscles bunching in her jaw as she ground her teeth. 'Get ready,' she grated, and crossed to Tiberius. She took his hand in hers. 'I need to put the locket in the circles, so hold this,' she said fiercely. '*Do not* release it without my say so.'

Her free hand gripped the locket, and a golden glow blazed forth and slid across their joined hands into the priest. He gave a great, whooping inhalation and seemed to grow three inches.

'It's too much, too much,' he panted, and Edrea severed the connection between them with a frown.

'Already? But I can't take... Never mind. I can.' She started channelling magic into herself in a flood far faster and brighter than the slow trickle she'd sent into Tiberius.

'I'll hold it,' Runar blurted, breaking her concentration. 'If there's some left and if... if it will help – if you can, I don't know, get it back out of me when you need it – then I'll hold it.'

Her skin was almost glowing with the energy she was holding – all her own that she'd stored during the day, and all that she'd poured into the repository the previous night. It was obvious it had replenished everything she'd expended to cast the circles of protection, and equally obvious that there was still more sitting in the heavy gold locket.

Edrea jerked her chin, beckoning him closer. 'It's going to have to sit directly in your body. It's... How can I put this... It's going to sit under your skin and it's going to feel odd. Unpleasant when it goes in, and probably unpleasant for as long as it's in you. You're not trained for this. You don't have to–'

Runar stuck out his hand. 'Do it. As long as I can still shoot and swing an axe while I hold it, it doesn't matter.' She reached for him and his hand faltered, just a little. 'And you can get it back out when you need it?'

Edrea licked her lips. 'That will also be unpleasant, but yes.'

'Good enough. Get on with it.'

It was like touching a lightning bolt. Some torn-off sound burst from his throat and every hair on his body felt like it was standing up. Unpleasant? Runar's back teeth buzzed and he was half convinced his eyeballs were either going to boil dry or burst. He was breathing liquid light, liquid fire, and his nerves were screaming to run even as his bones fused, locking him in place.

And then it was done, the contact severed, and the sharpshooter found himself kneeling on the flagstones, the echo of pain through his legs where he'd fallen. Edrea had already backed away and Tiberius was crouching in front of him. Runar sucked in

another lungful of fire – the priest was *glowing*, a faint shimmer
in his skin and a brighter, glossier one in his eyes.

'Keep breathing, that's it,' Tiberius said, and his voice was bells
chiming. There were hands under his armpits and he forced himself to stand, caught sight of Edrea and nearly collapsed again.
Where Tiberius had a golden shimmer, the sorceress was *incan-
descent*, a human torch filled with so much raw power that she
pulsed with it.

'Take some more breaths and adjust to it. It'll settle, and when
it does, don't poke at it. Focus now. She's about to start the
summoning.'

Aaric had a hand under his elbow, and he guided him around
to face the cell and the circles. The blinding outline that was
Edrea seemed to float over the five circles of protection – and
those, too, Runar could see glowing, writhing softly in different
colours – and placed the now dull locket in the centre. She
muttered something, moved her hands in a series of elegant
gestures, clapped them together once and then held them palm
down over the objects, as if warming her hands at a fire. Faint,
soft light began to rise from them, a delicate lilac at the edges,
deepening to a rich, roiling indigo at the centre.

Edrea continued her chant for another long minute, each
passing second allowing Runar to regain some equilibrium. He
had to remind himself, forcefully, that this was borrowed, alien
strength. He couldn't use it, no matter how much it felt as if
he could punch through a solid brick wall or strangle a daemon
with his bare hands.

'Weapons,' Aaric said quietly.

As well as his usual weapons, Runar took up a well-used, wickedly sharp wood axe. The older men had swords, but Runar had
never had any great skill with a long blade. An axe, though, oh
yes, the sharpshooter knew his way around an axe.

Edrea's voice faded into silence and she turned to face them, still within the innermost circle. She raised her arms and stared at them in turn. The energy was settling now, as she'd promised, and he could make out her features behind the brightness surrounding her. 'Hold fire unless there is absolutely no other choice,' she said, and her voice still had the harmonics from her chanting. Sonorous and liquid. 'We are here to communicate. It is coming to deliver its message. Whatever its appearance, allow it time to speak. Do not be the first to attack.'

She shivered all over, a head-to-toe ripple as sinuous as a dancer's. 'It comes.' It was more breath than voice, and now her face was slack, almost dreamy. Almost worshipful.

'Get out of the cell,' Aaric barked, and his daughter jerked and blinked rapidly. Her mouth fell open and she stepped across the five lines, carefully, her bare feet skipping and her hands moving as she carved a door for herself to pass through each. She stepped over the last line – the blood line – and took one more step.

The cell door swung shut, trapping her inside.

Edrea felt slow and disconnected, so deep in the magic, so close to the presence growing with every passing second, that when the door swung shut she didn't think anything of it. Her mouth pulled up in a small smile, and she was only distantly aware of her father rushing towards her, hands outstretched.

You'll be here soon, won't you? Edrea asked the owner of the dark, haunting chanting, and then she was at the cell door, Aaric on the other side. She pushed, but it remained shut. 'Father? Why are you–'

'It isn't me,' he said, his knuckles showing yellow through the skin where he gripped the barred gate and yanked on it. 'It won't open!'

There was so much power in Edrea that this dull, mundane world was almost hard to focus on, but she made herself concentrate until she understood his words. 'Step back.' She curled her right hand around the bars forming the wall of the cell, not the door, as a precaution, and then touched her fingers to the lock and muttered, drawing on the realm's death magic to decay the mechanism. The gate shuddered in its frame and the squeal of tortured metal was loud, the sudden stink of hot iron permeating the air. The rebound tried to throw her back across the circles, and if not for her grip on the bars it would have succeeded and she would have destroyed the barrier formed by each carefully drawn line.

The quiet contentment that had been sinking over her was abruptly gone, and she recognised that that, too, was the entity's design. Make her not care, make her scuff the circles.

Edrea kept her grip on the bars and slapped herself across the cheek with her other hand, as hard as she could. The pain was bright and shocking, dragging her mind out of the haze that had fallen over it. Her gasp was ragged, but she used her restored focus to blast the cell door again. Another rebound, her right arm jolting painfully in the socket, but nothing more.

'All right,' she said to herself. 'All right, if you want to play, then we'll play. Father, third jar from the left on the table, the ceramic one with the green label. Now, please.'

'You have to get out,' Aaric said as he pressed the jar into her hand.

'I will,' Edrea replied with more confidence than she felt. 'But for now, I'm being tested, will and skill. I cannot fail.' She tilted her head to one side for a moment. 'It's not... malevolent, I think. The test, I mean. It feels more curious than anything. But it wants control, and I'm not giving it that.'

'Don't show your full strength too early,' Tiberius yelled from his place by the brazier.

Edrea snorted. 'Yes, Uncle,' she said, and rolled her eyes for her father. 'Don't worry,' she added, quiet and just for him. 'Not over this. Not so soon. Promise me.' He opened his mouth to protest, and she snaked her arm through the bars and grabbed his jacket. 'I need you to believe in me now.'

Aaric's hand cupped hers and pressed it tight against his chest. 'I believe in you with all my heart,' he said steadily. 'Show it who Edrea Gothghul is. Teach it to respect you. And if it won't, then make it *fear you.*'

Heat rushed into her chest and into her cheeks at his words, at the steady fierceness of his gaze, one warrior to another. He'd never looked at her like that – *no one* had ever looked at her like that. Like she was dangerous and capable and utterly trusted to be both without needing anyone else's help.

I won't let you down, she wanted to say, but didn't. Instead, she patted his chest once and slid her hand free, then put her back to the bars and approached the circle again. She hadn't wanted to do this, but already she could feel a sweet lethargy building in her muscles again. Whatever this entity was, it recognised her power and was trying to counter it. Not violently – not yet.

Edrea entered the circles again, all the way into the centre, and plucked the beast's claw off the journal and set it on the stone. Drawing her ritual knife – *really shouldn't be used for this* – she hacked at the nub of bone where it became claw until she'd sawn her way through. Placing the claw back on the journal, she took the toe joint and retreated to the farthest corner of the cell.

There, she knelt and opened the green-labelled jar, her nose wrinkling at the stench. She dropped the bone in and stoppered it hurriedly. The jar began fizzing, almost vibrating under her fingertips, and the chanting in her head got louder. It was so close. The sorceress waited until the bubbling had subsided and then stood.

The air was beginning to smell like lightning. Edrea rolled her shoulders and walked back to the circle, took one pace out from the blood line and began to draw a final layer of protection, dribbling the contents of the jar onto the stone. As she did, she chanted – and the language this time was that of the Kato-phranes of Shadespire from before the fall.

It tore at her throat as she spoke it, jagged vowels, consonants spat raw and bleeding, the taste of metal on her tongue and tangling down into her chest, thick and viscous and choking. She moved slow and stately, dripping beast bone and spirit-leaf onto the stone, all mixed with her own blood and water from a skypool high in the Blood-Rock Peaks that had reflected only sun and cloud, moon and stars, for five days and nights.

Edrea was over halfway around the circle when the taste of metal became an unexpected mouthful of blood, coughed up and then swallowed down before it hampered her words. The blood came more regularly after that, every few steps until she had to spit it out or risk choking. Or, worse, risk garbling the words. Even a mistimed hiss or wrongly articulated guttural would undo everything she'd woven so far.

She knew her father and uncle would be watching, panick-ing at the crimson spatters on her chin, sliding hot and sticky down her throat to soak into her shirt, but they didn't raise their voices or rush from their places.

And then, finally, after an eternity, it was done. The last words spoken, the last drops from the jar dripped. A sixth circle of pro-tection, the strongest yet, and one likely to enrage the entity as soon as it sensed it.

Edrea crawled a few paces from the circle and coughed up a little more blood. Her chest was burning, but she was still carrying a ridiculous amount of extra energy and life essence. Carefully, she tapped a little of it from the hot golden ball in her core, let its warmth and energy slide through her body, healing whatever was bleeding in her throat and chest.

Light again, energised again, Edrea stood and cracked her neck, sent a bright grin towards the men peering over the barri-cade they'd erected at the foot of the stairwell. She held out the now empty jar and Runar scurried forward to take it, rifle held down by his side. 'Are you all right?'

'Never better,' she croaked. 'Pass me some water though, would you?'

The sharpshooter began to retreat, then paused to cock his head. 'The voice,' he said, and Edrea realised it was louder now, clearer. No longer an inner music that vibrated through her bones and was swept along with her blood.

'Water. Quickly, please.'

He grabbed a waterskin and brought it back to her. Edrea sipped just enough to wash away the taste of blood, only for it to be replaced with the tang of an unfamiliar magic. She grabbed at the cell door and yanked; it still wouldn't open.

Runar backed up until he could aim the rifle at the door's lock. 'Everyone down,' he ordered, and Edrea scrambled to the far corner and huddled, hands over her ears. The shot was deafening, so loud the whining ricochet was almost lost in the echoes, and when she looked, the metal was twisted and ripped and smoking. He pulled at the gate and then scowled. 'Jammed.'

'On three,' Edrea said, and at the count she threw her shoulder at the door as Runar yanked. There was a squeal of metal and it gave under her; she stumbled through and into the sharp-shooter's arms. Runar caught her and she couldn't help the shaky exhalation of relief that stirred the brown hair hanging in his eyes. When she was steady, he let go and together they forced the door shut again.

She was still thrumming with energy and magic and adren-aline, the combination so heady that she might burst – into laughter, or tears, or just shatters of light. She could barely contain it all, and she shouldn't feel so alive, so joyous, but for the first time she was using her skills in front of others, she was being completely, unabashedly herself, and it was glorious.

And dangerous, she reminded herself sternly. *Very, very dangerous.*

Edrea crossed to the table of scrolls, ingredients and jars that made up her own particular arsenal. In the centre was the ritual she'd taken from the blue journal, stripped back to its basic elements and examined from every angle. She could see where her mother had increased summoning energy at the expense of lowering barriers, where she'd made the very specific decision to use her own body – *and therefore mine* – as the vessel through which to summon the entity. The clinical, detached part of her, the part that was pure intellect, could almost understand why she'd done it. The rest of her had skimmed over that section, unwilling to examine her mother's motives too closely.

But that was then, and this was now, and this ritual was Edrea's. She wouldn't repeat Hephzibah's mistakes. The wound in her arm throbbed, but it was a familiar hurt. She dug her nails into it and coaxed a fresh ooze of blood past the soft scabs, then touched a bloody fingerprint to the brows of the three men. 'Don't wipe it away,' she said as Runar automatically recoiled, his hand coming up. She did the same to herself and then recited a variation on the comprehension spell she'd used to communicate with the beast on the moors.

'Though our worlds are different and we share no land, by magic's grace, may we understand. Though our paths not cross, we have words to send, within this spell, may we comprehend. As above, so below, be it fire or be it snow. Within our minds, where knowledge dwells, may our understanding swell.'

The sorcery pulsed through her, the fingerprint suddenly hot against her skin. The mutters and gasps confirmed that the spell was activating on them all, and a faint luminescence haloed around all their heads. 'There,' she said. 'Now we should be able to understand it when it arrives.'

A violent hissing rose from the cell and Edrea jumped, then hurried forward to press against the bars. Smoke was curling up from the edges of her mother's journal and the perfume in the bottle was beginning to bubble. 'Here we go,' she breathed, and stepped back a pace.

'World of living, world of dead, give me written, give me said,' she chanted, arms upraised. 'Across the realms, without the spheres, speed your message for us to hear.' Edrea's long dark curls began to stir, the loose fabric of her shirtsleeves rippling.

Wind from another dimension, with the entity riding its currents towards us.

'Within the living, beyond the death, I call the voiceless and give it breath. In this world, so painful small, reveal your shape, answer the call. Breath for voice and earth for skin, we welcome you – invite you in.'

The wind increased, whipping around the sorceress so that her hair streamed behind her. The lanterns flickered wildly and the light from the small, high window darkened as if storm clouds had gathered in an instant.

'We welcome you – invite you in,' she repeated, straining to open herself, to be a conduit as much as the items in the circle were. 'We welcome you,' she shouted. *'Invite you in!'*

Her father muttered something, but she couldn't pay attention, because she could feel the entity pushing through into Shyish, all its energy and essence and emotion pressing on her, into her, through her and into the world. Responding to her call, her invitation, with vicious laughter and a red-edged hunger that gripped her so hard her lungs were tight with the need of it.

Runar appeared at her shoulder, rifle aimed into the cell, where the journal at the centre of the circle abruptly burst into flames. Tiberius and Aaric were on her other side, similarly armed.

The fabric of the realm was distorting as something clawed its way through. The bubbling of the perfume increased until the bottle shattered and the room was drenched in the scent of Hephzibah Gothghul. Around Edrea, the three men jerked and swore as glass cut into hands or arms. They swore again, and Edrea with them, as the blood from the cuts didn't drip but instead was pulled into the circle, the amount far more than a simple small cut should bleed. The ritual wound on Edrea's own arm reopened, and her blood, too, was drawn through the air into the circle. A cloud of crimson began to spin and whirl into a vortex, and at its centre a shape started to manifest. Dark and hunched and small, a flicker in the air there and then gone, stuttering into existence and winking back out. With each momentary appearance, Edrea felt the connection between her and it grow stronger, dragging at her magic and control.

'It needs our essence, something living in this realm, to complete the manifestation,' Edrea said as Runar tried to clamp his hand over the cut on his wrist and stem the flow of blood. 'My summoning can only draw it so far. It needs life itself to bring it the rest of the way. That's why Mother... That's why she was in the circle instead of outside.'

'Daughter, no!' Aaric snapped, and grabbed for her. She twisted free and darted in through the gate, a snapped command slicing a door through the outermost circle of protection, and hopped over the line. The claw on top of the burning journal was beginning to char, though not from the flames. And then Runar's hand closed around her upper arm in a vice-like grip.

'You are not going in there,' he ordered, jerking her to a halt. Jerking her backwards, so that her bare heel scuffed through the outermost circle of protection. Its magic shattered, earthing through Edrea's skin and body. It tore Runar's grasp free and hurled him out through the gate, while the sorceress was rooted in place by the raw magic crackling through her like lightning. Doing to her what it would do to the entity if it tried to cross the line.

Only she was of Shyish, so while the pain was bright and all-consuming – while distantly, in some far part of her mind

that wasn't occupied with agony, she knew she was screaming –
she focused her breath and will and channelled her power into
a rushed, choking stream of syllables that deactivated the sixth
circle. The one attuned to the prevention of the entity's specific
breed of mind control, a control that had already seduced Edrea
once. She had sacrificed a part of its own body in the creation
of that barrier, and while the claw was still just about intact,
there wasn't enough of it, or enough time, to cast another circle
to prevent further psychic attacks.

The magic dropped, the howling in Edrea's ears faded, and she
found herself on her knees, shuddering through the aftermath
of pain, her throat raw. The magic from the barrier had coiled
back inside her until she was almost bursting with it, sending
flickers of agony teasing along her nerves.

'Edrea? Edrea, can you hear me?' Her father's voice was hesitant. Somewhere behind her, Runar was groaning an apology.

She concentrated and raised one hand in acknowledgement,
then pushed herself back onto her feet before she could think
better of it. A spark jumped from the end of her fingers and
she flinched, wrestling the magic back under control again. She
needed to give it back to the realm, but she couldn't without
disrupting the last flickers of the ritual. So she swallowed it down
and tried not to explode into a million fragments.

This close, the bloody vortex was hissing as it spun, centred
over the relics. Even together, they weren't enough to draw it
all the way through, but Edrea's own life force would be. She
would fill the locket with her essence and the entity could use
that to complete its journey. She would only be in the centre
for seconds.

Delicately, she stepped between the lines, opening and closing
a door in each barrier without conscious input, the motions practised and familiar, until she reached the centre. The presence
was so strong here, so all-consuming, that she felt the hairs on

her arms stand up. She lunged forward, blood misting across her skin, and snatched up the locket from on top of the burning journal, too fast for the flames to do more than warm her fingers.

Edrea straightened and took one step back, and then gasped and stared at the long-fingered, slender hand crushing bruises into the flesh of her forearm, squeezing blood out of the cut. Between one heartbeat and the next, the shadow, the entity, the softly chanting creature of slaughter, had stepped into Shyish. She hadn't even felt it take any of her life force.

The hand was small and pale, delicately boned, but the strength in it was terrifying. Its little finger was missing. The whirling column of blood vanished as if it had never been.

Against every instinct, Edrea froze, and her gaze travelled up the arm to a shoulder, barely clothed in the tattered remnants of a blouse, and on to a face that was painfully young and beautiful – and wildly, savagely unhinged. The girl's mouth opened impossibly wide and she screamed, her eyes glowing red. *Bloody-eyed.* The meat of the girl's shoulder exploded into a welter of blood, a hot splash against Edrea's face, and the report of a gunshot reached her as she blinked the wetness out of her eyes.

The girl screamed again, her mouth opening even wider than before. Her teeth were very long and very sharp, and Edrea realised the enormity of her error even as she tried to twist out of the creature's grasp.

Vampire.

More gunshots, but the girl – *not a girl. Vampire. Vampire!* – was using her as a shield, and though he was a sharpshooter, not even Runar could fire around Edrea and into her captor.

'Mhur!' the vampire screamed. 'Mhur, Mhur, *Mhur!*' She shook Edrea like a dog with a rat, her hand around her throat now, and the wound in her shoulder didn't seem to be bothering her in the slightest. Her feet were bare and filthy, and what might have once been a pair of knee-breeches hung tattered from her hips, ragged and worn thin.

'Her-herald,' Edrea stuttered. 'You're... Fourfold... Herald.' She could barely get any air in past the grip on her throat. Instead of straining against it, Edrea grabbed the crazed vampire by the shoulders, planted her feet and twisted, spinning them around. Runar didn't miss. The bullet took her in the chest, not far from the wound in her shoulder, and the vampire bellowed in pain, her teeth visibly lengthening.

The wounds in her shoulder and chest began to close, the bullets inching their way back out of her flesh. Her eyes were rubies, mindless, empty of everything but madness and hunger. She went for Edrea's throat.

The sorceress focused every scrap of magic she had into the palms of her hands, still clamped around the vampire's shoulders, and blasted all of it into her in one unstoppable, blinding torrent.

The vampire screeched and staggered backwards. Edrea scrambled away, backing through the circles of protection and slamming them behind her while Runar emptied his rifle into the raging creature and kept her from following. The circles were going to be useless, at least for their intended purpose. Edrea might be able to use them for something else, though. Dizziness crashed over her in a wave so intense that she staggered as she exited the last circle, and then Aaric was there, steadying her and dragging her away.

'Vampire,' she wheezed. '*Vampire...*' as they tumbled through the cell door and slammed it behind them.

'You won't kill her,' Tiberius shouted, as Runar squeezed off another shot.

'No, but I'll keep her attention while you find a way to stop her,' he snarled back.

The vampire laughed at his words and his bravado, and it

was mad and tangled, equal parts rage and mockery. She leapt straight up, into the stone vault of the dungeon, and clung there upside down. Runar's rifle followed the motion and he fired, but there was just the click of the hammer on an empty breech. The creature spun away again, on instinct, as easily as if she was standing on the ground.

'Energy,' Edrea gasped, and her father dragged Runar towards them, Tiberius covering the vampire with his own rifle. The sorceress slapped her hand against the bare skin of Runar's neck and sucked the stored power out of him, fast and brutal. His knees buckled and the bullets he was feeding into the breech tumbled from his hand as he staggered, a torn-off gasp of pain bursting from him. Aaric transferred his supporting hands to him.

'More,' gasped Edrea. Aaric swapped places with Tiberius and she drained him too. The magic and the energy were a small, softly glowing ball in her chest, tiny and dim compared with the maelstrom that had been within her before.

Tiberius and Runar were both stumbling, waxy and pale, and Edrea felt barely any better. The vampire still clung to the vault high above, her voice alternating between laughter and sobbing screams. She seemed quite mad.

Aaric was shaking, confronted with the entity that had possessed Hephzibah and driven her away. 'You turned her, didn't you? Zib, my wife? You turned her into one of you!' He was bellowing, tears on his cheeks. 'We thought you took her, but you didn't. You turned her, and she fled so that we wouldn't be the first victims of her thirst!' He snatched up his rifle and shot; the vampire dodged.

Thirst. The people killed by the beast were drained of all fluid until they were shrivelled husks.

Edrea wrestled the rifle out of his hands. 'Help Runar and Uncle Tiberius. Feed them, give them some water. Now, Father.' She was pleading, and her tone broke the spell the vampire had cast over him. A shudder rippled through him and he turned away.

Edrea crossed back to the cell and entered, forcing the door shut behind her. She stood outside the sixth circle. 'Come here,' she called, and dug the tip of her knife into her arm again, reopening the scabbing cut. Pain flared and burnt, familiar and deeply unpleasant. 'You want this?'

The vampire stilled, upside down, her cloud of dark hair swaying as she cocked her head at Edrea. The circles' power stretched up to the roof of the castle itself – she was still bound by them whether or not she stood on the floor. She dropped back down and ran at Edrea, but was thrown back by the first circle.

'Thirsty?' the sorceress demanded, holding up her arm. Blood dripped from her elbow onto the flagstones. The vampire screeched and clawed at the innermost circle before forcing herself through, the magic ripping into her. The second, the third. Each more difficult than the last, each tearing at her will and bones, urging her to stop, give up, remain in the centre where it was safe, where it didn't hurt. The pain warred against the vampire's thirst, each bolt of agony only increasing her rage. Each bolt of magic stealing a little of her strength. Someone had remembered to put the kettle on the brazier, and steam, fragrant and permeated with cleansing magic, was beginning to puff from the spout.

Edrea was taking a terrible risk, but she knew a little about the vampire clans of Necros. About their strengths and weaknesses, their habits and hungers.

'Edrea!' Aaric bellowed, and she held up her hand towards them, not breaking gazes with the vampire.

'The fifth barrier is made from my blood,' she said, and the vampire stilled and then tensed. 'And after that, there's me.' Slender limbs suddenly corded with muscle as the monstrous girl forced herself through the fourth circle, keening as she did, the magic flaring bright and then shattering. Each circle earthed its magic through her body as the sixth had done to Edrea, but the vampire was incapable of absorbing it. *Not native to Shyish, then.*

The vampire fell to her knees and pressed her face to the line of Edrea's blood, licking and making desperate sounds part pleasure, part pain.

'I know what she's doing,' Tiberius muttered, and Edrea flapped her hand, silencing him.

'That's it,' she murmured, soothing despite the frantic beating of her heart. Would it be enough? What if it wasn't enough? 'You haven't fed in a while, have you?' The vampire was snarling as she licked at the thin line of blood, her movements jerky and uncoordinated, pained as the magic in the blood pulled and twisted at her before it shattered. The vampire twitched and screamed, curling in on herself until the blast faded. As soon as it did, she snarled up at Edrea in triumph and began licking at the blood again. As she *ingested* Edrea's will and intent and command. *Bind*, the magic insisted. *Subdue. Constrain.* If the vampire was aware of the magical residue in the blood, she was too far lost in hunger and madness to pay attention.

'But the sixth circle is ineffective,' Aaric hissed. 'It's already shattered. Edrea, you–'

'Quiet.' Edrea snapped the word, not wanting to distract the vampire before she had enough of the blood and will inside her to be sated and suggestible.

The vampire rocked back onto her heels, yowling. Her mouth and chin were streaked crimson, her eyes a darker, more malevolent red. Strands of long dark hair were stuck to her cheeks with blood. There were too many teeth, too much madness, a surfeit of violence. She was a horror, even more so because, under different circumstances, she would have appeared quite innocent. Beautiful.

'Mhur... Mhurghast,' the vampire said now, smearing her long fingers in the blood and then licking them clean.

'Yes, Mhurghast,' Edrea said, her mouth dry. She'd felt safer confronting the beast on the moors than she did standing two paces away from this slender young woman who shone with dark cruelty. 'Tell us your message. You *are* the Fourfold Herald, aren't you? You've been seeking to impart your message for more than a hundred years, and now you can. Tell us of the Mhurghast and the Path of the Fallen Four. Tell me. Speak.' The last word was imbued with command, carried on a wisp of magic.

The vampire moved, so fast that Edrea didn't see it happen. One second she was on her knees in the cell, and the next Edrea herself was on her back, her skull ringing with pain from where she'd smacked it into the stone, and the girl was sitting on her stomach, Edrea's cut arm pressed to her mouth. There was the bright, tearing sting of teeth entering her flesh, and then a hot rush of dizzying pleasure and surrender as the vampire began to feed.

Bind. Subdue. Constrain.

The magic is in the blood.

Edrea fought against the overwhelming bliss and channelled authority and command into her blood as she let the girl drink, focusing her will and magic into a suggestion of docility, of acceptance. She was rushing headlong towards unconsciousness, not sure whether it was blood loss or the spellcraft taking its toll, or maybe the vampire's own glamour as their eyes locked.

Surrender, the vampire said.

Surrender, Edrea said back.

She raised her hand, unsure whether she was going to push the creature away or drag her closer, bare her throat for her, offer her everything, when the vampire pulled her teeth out of Edrea's arm and let it fall. She rocked back where she sat on the sorceress' stomach, a long, low growl of pleasure easing from her mouth. She made another noise, this time small and sleepy, her features going slack and contented, and then she curled up on Edrea's chest as if for a nap, her thin limbs spidering around the other woman.

This close, she seemed very young, barely into womanhood when the Dark Kiss had taken her. With her dark hair, pale skin and slender form, it was easy to see why they'd all mistaken her for Hephzibah. For Edrea herself.

Edrea stared over the tangle of the vampire's hair towards the cell door, where Runar was pushing through, gun up. Aaric and Tiberius flanked him, also armed. Tentatively, Edrea put her arms around the girl lying on her, murmuring soothing nonsense, and delicately brushed her mind against the magic she'd sent into the vampire's body along with her blood.

Bind. Subdue. Constrain.

She met her father's eyes and nodded, a tiny little dip of her chin. Everything she'd expected, everything she'd tried to plan for, was useless, because whatever else this girl was besides vampiric and mad and the killer – or transformer – of her mother, she was also a girl mumbling gently to herself and heaving out pleased little sighs, her fingers tracing aimless circles on Edrea's shoulder as if they were the best of friends.

She was no daemon, but she was very, very dangerous, and they were going to have to deal with that soon. Edrea's grip on the last dregs of her magic was loosening, the magic-debt beginning to loom, but she couldn't afford the crash that would come if she took another stimulant to keep going. There was a definite chance she'd wake up dead if she did that.

She had been prepared to hate whatever she summoned, to take its message, question it and then destroy it the way it had destroyed Hephzibah and her family. She couldn't do that now, and not just because her will rode the vampire's system or, perhaps, the vampire's rode hers. It was an uncomfortable thought, that maybe she was the one who'd been subdued. Maybe this was all the hallucination of her dying brain as the vampire drank her dry. Edrea pressed her sore head back into the stone, hard, and let the burst of pain provide a little clarity.

Still alive. Probably not hallucinating. Definitely not as in control as it appears. And yet... And yet there was a connection between them, a strange kinship that she couldn't explain or justify. She'd felt it with the beast, not just hearing its howls but standing face to face with it, and again with the shade she'd been convinced was her mother. Now, with the girl in her arms, that sense of knowing, of recognition, was undeniable.

This *thing* had tortured and broken her mother, turned her into a monster herself, most likely, and in so doing destroyed her father. But Edrea... Edrea wanted to *know her*. Not just the message that she hopefully still carried, and not just an explanation of all she'd done, but the girl herself. The desire sat uneasily in her heart, mingled with hate and vengeance and the need to punish.

She took a calming breath. 'My name is Edrea Gothghul,' she murmured, stroking the girl's hair and trying not to fidget beneath the weight pressing her into the icy stones. 'You had a message for my mother, Hephzibah Gothghul, twenty-five years ago. You have a message for me now. About the Mhurghast. Can you speak?'

The vampire tensed, fingers suddenly digging into the sorceress' flesh. Three rifles cocked in unison, and Edrea glared at the men looming over them.

The vampire lifted her head, and her red eyes were normal now, a lovely deep grey. She licked her lips and shifted to look up at the rifles pointed at her. She stretched like a cat and then sprang off Edrea's body and hit Aaric full in the chest. Three rifles spat flame and bullets but all of them missed. Aaric went down hard, and the vampire's teeth were already tearing through the meat of the arm he'd managed to throw up between them in defence.

Her father screamed. Blood sprayed. And Edrea lost control.

A bullet tore through the vampire's back, another through her thigh, but the pair were thrashing too hard to risk any more.

Runar stepped up and clubbed the vampire around the head
with the stock of his rifle. The blow ripped her mouth away from
Aaric's arm, tearing the flesh further, and he screamed again,
and then Edrea was scrabbling over the stones. She threw herself onto the girl's back, looping her arm around her throat and
getting it bitten again for her efforts. The locket was in her other
hand, and she had no idea if this would work, but she activated
it and pressed it to the side of the vampire's neck.

The repository sucked at Edrea's magic as hungrily as the vampire had at her blood, and she used the last of the link between
them to access any innate magic the vampire herself possessed.
It was there, unfamiliar and red, a pool of ability and intention
and will, and Edrea pushed herself into it and fed it to the locket.

The vampire thrashed in her grip, Aaric grunting and glassy-
eyed and spattered in his own blood beneath them. Runar
slammed into Edrea's back, wrapping his arms around her and
the monster both and dragging them clear. Tiberius looped one
of the chains around the girl's legs and lower body, all he could
reach among the tangle of people and limbs.

And Edrea was... inside her. The vampire was ancient, the
stretch of her life incomprehensible to Edrea, and she'd been
in that place-that-wasn't-a-place for an unknown period of time
that the sorceress suspected might have been centuries. Might
have been longer.

Stop, she commanded her. *Stop fighting and we will feed you.
We won't hurt you. Stop.*

Edrea's body was burning, unfamiliar magic passing through
her into the repository, sparking through her senses and filling
her with a terrible, burning need. The vampire was more than
just hungry; she was ravenous, and not just for blood and more
palatable fare. For contact. Touch. Understanding.

'I've got you,' she whispered right into her ear. 'I'm here.
You're safe now.' It was ridiculous to tell something of such vast

and ancient power that she was safe, but slowly the girl's strug-
gles lessened until she was limp, though she did flick out her
tongue to swipe across the bite marks she'd left in Edrea's arm.
The chain was tight around her ankles and wrapped up to her
waist, enough to at least limit her movement. Tiberius locked it
to the bars of the cell wall, panting.

'See to Father,' Edrea told him. Tiberius nodded and backed away,
and the sorceress spared Aaric a single look. If the vampire had
killed him... but he was breathing, at least. 'Runar, you can let us
go now as well. Fetch the goat from the yard. Our guest is hungry.'

Runar made a faint noise of protest but obeyed. The vampire
didn't make any further attempts to attack, and carefully Edrea
moved her fingers off the locket so it no longer drew magic. This
time the vampire sighed, and the hands that had been pinned
to her sides by Runar's grip came up to rest on Edrea's arm,
still looped around her throat. They were gentle; they were cold.

When the sharpshooter came back leading the goat, he'd
switched his rifle for the axe. He shrugged slightly, unrepentant.

The echo of the vampire's magic was still in Edrea's system,
an echo of her hunger, and her mouth watered as he shoved
the goat into the cell. The vampire pushed away from her and
beckoned. The goat approached, docile, and she knelt among her
chains and buried her face in its soft throat. The animal bleated
once and collapsed.

Edrea wobbled and Runar put his arm around her. 'You need
to rest. The ritual... the blood loss.'

She nodded tiredly. 'Soon. When we've spoken to her.' Tiberius
had dragged Aaric out of the cell and now they followed, pulling
the wrecked door shut behind them. Runar helped her kneel by
her father's side. He was conscious but very pale.

Tiberius was bandaging his arm. 'He needs stitches,' he said
without preamble. 'They're tears, not punctures.' He glanced at
Edrea's own forearm. 'You might need a few yourself.'

The number of throbbing pains through her body was great enough that she hadn't really examined her arm until now. The initial bite was clean, punctures either side of her spellcraft cut. The second was messier. Edrea shrugged. She could deal with it later.

'I still have one dose of your remedy,' Runar said.

'Give it to Father,' Edrea said just as Aaric insisted he give it to her.

'You're the only one equipped to deal with her in any meaningful capacity,' Aaric insisted, though his lips were pale with pain and blood loss. 'Do as you're told for once, you stubborn woman,' he grumbled before she could protest further, and she couldn't suppress a startled laugh. Runar handed her the little vial and she drank the last of the thick liquid.

'Mhurghast.'

Tiberius' low reassurances came to a halt and Runar's hands tightened on the axe. Edrea looked at the vampire.

'Mhurghast is coming. The Four are coming. Four.' The goat was scraps of bloody skin and a collection of bones broken open to get at the marrow. The vampire stood, her chin and throat and chest and hands sticky with blood, and snapped the iron chain binding her legs as if it was paper. Her voice was rusty with the echo of screams.

Runar shouted and hefted the axe; Edrea wrenched on his arm, holding him back. 'Don't,' she said, but let him pull her another step away from the cell. As if that would make any difference. Edrea had no more control, no further tricks.

The vampire still looked wild and a little lost, but the jerky, unfocused gaze and the manic laughter had both settled. She stared at them and licked her lips. Her nostrils flared, and Edrea felt a trickle of panic slide through her.

'The Mhurghast?' she prompted, and the vampire twitched and then, very deliberately, took a step deeper into the cell. Her fists were clenched as she fought for control.

'The blight from Mhurghast builds, little ones, and the Fallen Four are its unholy emissaries. First one to carve a bloody path, and then the others will follow in time. They will sweep across the Mortal Realms, bringing destruction of a kind thou canst not begin to comprehend. O my beautiful, brief little candle-flickers – thinkest thou know horror? Thinkest thou understand death?' The vampire spread her bloody hands and then thoughtfully licked them clean.

'Thou art but flames soon quenched, and, my children, Mhurghast is the flood. The Heralds come not just to destroy but to obliterate. Imagine it, mortals – people shredded and flayed, their souls enslaved and bodies twisted into forms of perpetual torment and horror. They will eat their own children, murder their own parents – and it will be a delight to them.'

The dungeon was utterly silent when the vampire stopped speaking. Edrea was holding her breath; she suspected they all were. She hadn't thought much about the message itself, pre-occupied with ensuring the messenger arrived and its century-long reign of terror on Shyish was stopped. A reign that suddenly seemed to be nothing but a minor inconvenience in comparison with this dire prediction. Edrea felt sick, barely able to comprehend the vampire's words.

'What are these... Heralds?' Aaric croaked.

'Beings of unimaginable power,' the girl said, suddenly restless. Runar tensed at Edrea's side, fingers tightening on the axe. 'It was they who trapped me. Mortals were beginning to heed my warning – the candle-flickers burnt bright with determination. I had hope then. I thought that...' She laughed, bitter and bleak. 'And so, when they tired of tormenting me, they locked me up in madness and left me to suffer.'

Edrea winced and exchanged a glance with Runar. Neither of them wanted any elaboration on what would constitute tor-ment or suffering for an immortal of such obvious power. The vampire's magic, now that Edrea had tasted it, called to her. Such strength...

'You turned my wife into a vampire,' Aaric hissed suddenly, as if nothing else was important.

The vampire shifted slightly so she could see him where he lay on the stone. 'Is that so?' She didn't sound very interested. 'Why?'

The girl shrugged. 'I have lost count of the number of Dark Kisses I've bestowed in my life. My children are everywhere, little one. What is another to me?'

Aaric struggled to get up, but Tiberius restrained him.

'You killed my hunters. When you were the... the beast.'

The vampire looked at Runar and a small smile quirked the corner of her mouth. She advanced to the cell door but didn't push through it. 'Thy scent, yes, it has a familiar tang. An edge of fear I recognise.' Edrea grabbed the back of his shirt and held him still. The girl held up her hand. 'You cut off my finger,' she said, waggling the stump. 'While it will grow back, thou art impressive to have managed such a feat. The deaths of thy companions are a fitting payment for such.'

Runar sucked in an outraged breath. 'How–' he began, and Edrea tugged sharply on his shirt.

'We mustn't provoke her,' she murmured.

The vampire smiled, exposing far too many teeth. She swept her gaze across them. 'We do not have time for childish grudges, my candle-flickers. Mhurghast will soon unleash its atrocities across all the realms. The fate of all sentient life lies within our hands, and time is a luxury you, at least, do not have. Thy wish might be to live quiet lives, but that is a luxury none of us have.'

Edrea felt her mouth drop open. 'Us?'

'I have tasted each of you,' the vampire said. 'I know thy strengths and abilities, thy weaknesses and preoccupations' – her gaze flickered to Aaric – 'and I know also that Mhurghast will be aware of my escape. It will come – and with it will come the apocalypse. Together, we will stand against Mhurghast's hordes and the horrors it portends. We will find a way to end its evil.'

She pointed to them each in turn. 'Sorceress. Killer. Scholar. Priest.' She tapped the centre of her own chest and arched an eyebrow. 'Ancient immortal hell-bent on vengeance.'

She proved her point by flashing out of the cell and across the space between them to snatch the locket from Edrea's throat. She flickered back out of range before Runar could even flinch, let alone swing his axe. The vampire showed her teeth again and activated the repository. Edrea felt the tingle of unfamiliar magic flooding out of the locket. 'Much better,' the girl breathed, her features seeming to brighten beneath their gory crimson mask.

When it was empty, the vampire walked slowly back towards them and held it out. Edrea pushed Runar's axe down and held out her palm, accepting it. 'One day, we will talk about your actions here this last month, and those twenty-five years ago,' Edrea promised in a quiet, level voice.

The girl put her head on one side and ran a finger down Edrea's cheek. 'Why do I feel as if I knowest thou?' she murmured, the shock of the words – of the acknowledgement that the connection went both ways – stealing the sorceress' breath. 'It shall be as thou wish, Miss Gothghul. Once we have saved all sentient life, perhaps?'

There was a long silence, heavy with unanswered questions and a million fears.

'We do not know you, vampire,' Tiberius said. He held up a talisman, a twin-tailed comet, in his left hand and a vial of holy water in his right. 'Why should we trust you?'

The vampire's hand fell from Edrea's cheek and she stepped back, flinging her arms out wide. 'You think you can kill me now? Dusk is falling, candle-flickers, and I only grow stronger when it does. But in truth, yes, you can trust me. The Fallen Four will extinguish all life in all realms, and they are only the harbingers of what will come afterwards. Mhurghast will eat the stars themselves. I may have done things thou findest unimaginable over the centuries of my life, I may be crueller and more indifferent than anyone thou hast ever met, but the Heralds are as far above me as I am above you. And after all, children, if they kill all life, who will I eat?'

She smirked and folded her arms across her chest even as Tiberius brandished his talisman and Aaric made a noise of disgust. 'Thou hast summoned me here. Thy course is set and annihilation is coming. Wilt thou fight it with me?'

'Yes,' Edrea said. Without hesitation, without regret.

And slowly, with varying degrees of reluctance, Runar, Tiberius and Aaric agreed. Because the vampire was right – she *was* cruel, and she *was* indifferent, but sometimes it took a monster to fight a monster. Edrea had a feeling they'd all be monsters by the time this war was done. She wondered if she'd be able to live with the consequences of her actions, or whether they'd turn her cold and cruel like the beautiful girl before her. She wondered if it mattered.

It's a small price to pay to stop the apocalypse.

'There is one thing we should know before we commit to this,' she said slowly. 'Will you tell us your name?'

This smile was alluring, and it was deadly. The vampire took a pace away and dropped into a curtsey that was beautifully elegant despite her ragged clothes and bare feet. She brushed back her clouds of dark hair and met their eyes one by one.

'Genevieve,' she said slowly. 'My name is Genevieve Dieudonné'

ACKNOWLEDGEMENTS

Huge thanks to my editor Hannah Hughes for thinking of me to bring this first story of Mhurghast to life and the resurrection of a particular character with an avid following. I look forward to more adventures with Edrea, Runar and the rest.

Thanks also to Rich Stokes, desk editor, and Toby Selwyn, copy editor, for their sterling work in picking up inconsistencies and helping me not look too much of a fool.

Grateful thanks also go to Svetlana Kostina for the glorious cover art.

Finally, huge thanks as ever to my family, friends and fellow authors (particularly the Bunker Buddies) for their support throughout the writing of this novel, and to the late, great Peter Cushing and Christopher Lee, who I always had in mind for Tiberius and Aaric respectively.

ABOUT THE AUTHOR

Anna Stephens is a UK-based writer of epic, gritty, grimdark fantasy. She is the author of the Warhammer Horror novel *Gothghul Hollow*, as well as the co-author of the Age of Sigmar portmanteau novel *Covens of Blood*. Her story 'The Siege of Greenspire' features in the Age of Sigmar anthology *Oaths and Conquests*, and her other works for Black Library include the short stories 'Ghastlight' and 'River of Death'.

YOUR
NEXT READ

THE BOOKKEEPER'S SKULL
by Justin D Hill

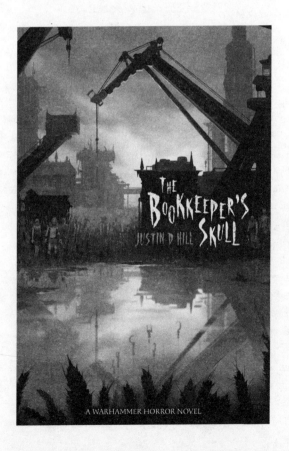

An extract from
The Bookkeeper's Skull
by Justin D Hill

The solemn bells of the Cathedral Ignatzio tolled over the Evercity that morning, as I stood in the baroque stone doorway of my attic room and took a last look at my childhood. This lofty chamber had been a refuge from the madness of my home world, but I could not stay here. Not now that I'd been summoned by the responsibility of my birth. I took in a deep breath, telling myself I was ready.

On my shelves were ranks of metal Guardsmen, boxes overflowing with long-discarded playthings, and the few books that had helped shape me: *Wain's Illustrated Lex Imperialis*, *Thorn's Book of Martyrs* and *101 Devotions for the Young*. But there were older companions, too.

I saw the stiff poses of my most treasured toys, lying in the shadows. They had wooden arms, legs and heads, uniforms of embroidered cloth, bodies of fur and flesh. Time and play had ruined most of them. Staring back at me were empty eye sockets and black, glassy optics. Tufts of stuffing peeked through worn torsos. Only one of them moved: Gambol, my clown. He stood out with his red hair, whitened skin, blue diamonds stitched over his eyes, and a broad, red smile tattooed upon his face. He rocked back and forth on his sutured haunches, the bells on his harlequin's uniform ringing gently as he scratched at the brass flesh-plug behind his ear. His voice was boyish, despite his adult size. 'Ruddie go?'

'Ruddie go,' I said in our childlike pidgin.

He sniffed ostentatiously as a tear rolled down his pockmarked cheek.

'Who Gambol play with?' He pulled an exaggerated sad face and started to sob theatrically. 'Gambol sad.'

I could see that. When I was young, I had thought of him as my closest friend. Now, I was unmoved by these cheap displays of fake emotion. In truth, he was once some criminal or heretic that had been turned into a wealthy kid's plaything – his legs amputated, his brain hacked into and his neural pathways slaved to a simple spectrum of emotions. Growing up, I had occasionally wondered what crime he had committed to deserve such punishment, and whether something lurked still beneath his neural circuitry. Was there a malevolence in his bloodshot eyes?

Gambol scratched behind his ear again. His fingers came away bloody.

'Itches,' he said, but his flesh-plugs had always festered.

'Gambol must not scratch,' I told him.

'Itches,' he said again, and fresh blood covered his nails in a red glaze. He held them up for me to see.

I didn't know what he wanted me to do about it.

'Pain is a sign of life,' I told him.

I dragged that parting out, but I've since learnt that it is kinder to leave people behind without fuss. There's no point in prolonging torment, or apologising, or asking for forgiveness. It's better just to rip off the plaster, as they say. Pull the trigger. Put the shot right between the eyeballs – or even better, in the back of the head. A brutal kiss, where skull and spine meet.

But I didn't know any of that back then, as I stood in the doorway of my refuge, trying to be kind to an old friend.

'I'll be back,' I lied.

Gambol wiped his hand on his quartered livery. Suddenly he was bright and cheery. 'Back? Gambol wait! When you back?'

'I don't know.'

'Today?'

'No.'

'Tomorrow?'

'No.'

He flinched at my tone and opened his mouth in an exaggerated wail, his blue-diamond eyes squeezing another torrent of tears down his face. I should have shot him there and then to put him out of his fake misery. But I was in a hurry, and through the ancient walls of my ancestral home, I could hear the cathedral bells tolling solemnly, reminding me of my duty that morning. It was the hallowday of Saint Helena Richstar, and I had been summoned.

'Gambol sad!' he called as I turned my back on him. They were his last ever words to me. I didn't bother answering, but shut the door, the click of the lock sealing my childhood firmly in the past.

Some say that partings are hard, but the truth was I felt lighter after I left Gambol behind and made my way down the grand staircase, one hand on the ironwood banister to guide my steps in the darkness.

This stairway descended through the heart of the ancient palace that my mother had bought lock, stock, and with all the paraphernalia of a noble household when she had arrived on the planet. The walls were lined with antique portraits of complete strangers: men and women in gilded Militarum uniforms with high shakos and gold braids, like shrines to ancient battles. The unknown faces were severe, their eyes haunted by illustrious careers, fighting and dying for the God-Emperor across the wide Imperium of Mankind. And there were their mementos as well: crossed lances with musty tassels, venerable powerblades, and hunting trophies from across the Gallows Cluster – a mix of heads and fangs and horns and antlers, mouldering pelts exposing white skulls, glassy eyes dulled by veils of ancient cobwebs, and the stink of naphthalene preservatives.

Halfway down I smelt the musky reek of the greenskin head. The monstrous creature had always terrified me with its broken tusks and beaded, blankly staring eyes. The mount bore the name of the Battle of Cinnabar's Folly and that of the man who had killed the beast: a General Everard Richstar. I had learnt about him in my histories. He'd been a reputable Guardsman until he had fallen in the bloody rout at Oukk.

At the bottom of the stairs was a wide landing with thick carpets and ten-foot doors opening off into various rooms of further pomp and grandeur, home to more historical figures I would never live up to. One set of doors, leading to my mother's apartment, was ajar. I heard her voice calling my name. 'Ruddie?'

She sounded as if she had just noticed my approach, but I knew she had been watching me ever since I left my chamber. The whole palace was covered by her surveillance picters. Their crystal eyes had been silently following my progress.

I used to joke that nothing was ever hidden from my mother, but I've since learnt that there are two ways of keeping confidences: not telling anyone anything or, if you must, killing them once you do.

Death is a true friend. It keeps all secrets.

My mother's boudoir had the musty air of a museum, dedicated to my childhood. On the wall hung my old tasselled caps, stiff jackets and embroidered shoes, while a chosen assortment of my toys cluttered the black-lacquered shelves.

Mother had never been a happy woman, but she cherished

the past in the misapprehension that she had been happier then. Her discontent was like a weight upon all who knew her, and I looked forward to leaving it all behind as I entered her room.

She was sitting in her high-backed leather throne, facing away from me. The throne swung soundlessly round, revealing its occupant.

'Mother,' I said, and bowed.

She wore a black lace dress with a ruff of furs about her neck, and an ornate black headdress lit with fairy lights, dark against her silver hair.

My mother was a curious sight, even for the Evercity. Sub-dermal implants had turned her eyes to gold, and her skin silver. In the half-light of candle flames, she shimmered, but it was hard to read emotion in her metallic visage. She let out a long breath of smoke and took me in, from boots to head.

From her long ivory pipe came the sweet scent of narcotics. They left me feeling nauseous, but they were one of her only joys. 'Ruddie,' she said, exhaling smoke along with my name.

An augmetic monocle covered one eye. In its light I could see the flicker of a pict-image against her skin. The miniature screen went dark as she moved the monocle aside and I looked into her gilded eyes. They gave nothing away as she regarded me.

'I wanted to look good for father,' I told her. Over my black bodyglove, I wore a suit of combat armour made by the finest artisans in the Evercity. She beckoned me forward, her silver skin catching the flickering light, and nodded silently.

'You look like him.' When she said that, it was not a compliment. Father was an ugly man and I had inherited his craggy looks. 'Be careful, Ruddie,' she said. 'Or you will end up like him in other ways.'

Her words stung me.

Now, of course, I know better. I have known handsome men and beautiful women who were not much served by their good looks, and I have got used to being an ugly man. I've learnt to not let other people hurt me. Feelings are like tripwires. A blank conscience is the difference between wakeful and dreamless sleep.

Something in my mother's lap moved. It was one of her pet simians, squatting amongst the drapes of her skirt, dressed in a hat of velvet and a jacket of silk brocade. About its neck was clasped an electro control-leash, the neuro circuits buried in the scruff of its neck. I think it was called Imp, though I made a point of not keeping track of any of her pets' names. I had never liked any of them: they had always been rivals to my mother's affection. When she lifted it up and pressed it to her chest I refused to be baited, but then it reached down and dragged my clock-work Titan, *Rhadameor*, from the folds in her gown.

The winding mechanism had long since broken, the blue-and-flame paintwork was chipped and worn, the inferno cannon re-welded onto the arm more times than I could remember, but it was dear to me. 'That's mine,' I said.

'You don't play with it any more. You're all grown up.' The words held an edge of spite.

'No,' I said, 'but it's still mine.'

A montage flashed through my head of sitting with Gambol and the other playmates my mother had bought – human and augmented. We had filled my bedroom floor with metal Militarum. My bed was the gates of the Imperial Palace on Holy Terra, and *Rhadameor* had smashed its way through the legions of traitors.

She was trying to hurt me, and I refused to show any emotion.

She saw that her ploy had failed, or maybe, in her narcotic stupor, she felt a pang of guilt. 'It seems that only yesterday you were just a boy. And now look at you...'

My mother's eyes blinked and I saw a golden tear make its way down her silver cheek. Beneath all the frippery and glittering façade, she loved me. It was a stifling, choking love, but it was well meant. And she knew that she was losing me.

'He's a hard man,' she warned. 'He will brook no weakness.'

She spoke from experience, of course. She was the last of my father's three concubines and had spent most of my childhood lamenting her luck at being brought to this planet, but as she spoke, my eyes must have taken on that glazed, hard exterior because she stopped herself and took a deep breath.

'I bought this for you,' she said at last, and took something out of the voluminous folds of her midnight lace skirts. Her silver arm shimmered as she held it out to me.

For once I was lost for words.

The autopistol was priceless, with a carved ivory handle and an exquisitely patterned barrel, acid-etched with entwined vines and the Imperial aquila etched on either side. But it was the Tronsvasse symbol stamped into the barrel that struck me dumb.

It was the mark par excellence, of beauty and craftsmanship, and expense. And, even for my mother, it must have cost a fortune.

'Mother!' I breathed. I felt a genuine wave of humility. It was so unfamiliar that it stuck in my throat. I had to cough to clear away the emotion. 'Thank you,' I said at last.

'I asked the Cardinal Archbishop to bless it. And he blessed these as well.' She handed me a heavy package of hard rounds. 'They fragment upon impact,' she told me. I held them up. Each one of the snub-nosed bullets had been hand-ground by artisans into the shape of a flower. 'Manstoppers,' she said.

I knew, of course. Xenos-hunters used them to stop the foes of humanity in their tracks. There was an image in one of my books that showed how the shards ripped through the flesh of the target.

I thanked her many times and she nodded stiffly.

'You had better go. Arcad is waiting for you downstairs.'

'I don't need him,' I said. She started to argue but I was adamant. 'What will father think if you send one of your lifewards with me?' My logic was clear. If I was to prove myself his successor, I had to set myself high standards.

She fell silent. The simian nudged her finger to encourage her to scratch again.

'I will be fine, I promise.' I patted the Tronsvasse at my side.

Her fingers curled protectively about the creature in her lap. Its blank eyes blinked slowly at me as it clutched my Titan in both hands.

'Remember,' she said, 'you were mine first.'

'You're right. I was,' I said.

The past tense stung her and there was ice in her voice as she answered, 'Well, go to him then.'

I nodded curtly and stepped forward to embrace her. She did not stand. The smell of narcotics had worked its way into her clothes. She was stiff in my arms. We were silent for a moment, mother and son, till at last I started to pull away. Her fingers clutched my arm, and her hoarse whisper spat into my ear. 'They *will* try to kill you,' she said. 'You must be ready. And when they come for you, do not hesitate.'

She slapped my cheek to make me remember. The blow smarted and her nails left scratches across my face. I blinked and nodded. I had known this for years. It was burned into my soul. I did not need to be struck again.

'Go, if you must,' she said.

I walked to her doorway, took a deep breath, and closed the double doors.

Those were her final words to me. A month later she was dead. But I did not know that then, and if I had, I do not know that I would have done anything differently. Each life runs its own course, and it was the Emperor's will that hers should end.